DIARY OF A BURNED OUT PASTOR

DIARY OF A BURNED OUT PASTOR:

A novel by James C Blocker

JAMES C BLOCKER

XULON PRESS

Xulon Press
2301 Lucien Way #415
Maitland, FL 32751
407.339.4217
www.xulonpress.com

Paperback ISBN-13: 978-1-6628-2866-9
Hard Cover ISBN-13: 978-1-6628-2867-6
Ebook ISBN-13: 978-1-6628-2868-3

AUTHOR'S NOTES

"Shepherd the flock of God, which is among you, serving as overseers ... And when the Chief Shepherd appears, you will receive a Crown of Glory"
(1 Peter 5:2,4).

The above scripture speaks specifically to the *faithful* under-shepherds. Though not flawless, they have a heart toward God. This novel was written with the intent to *encourage* and *inform* those under-shepherds. Encourage them not to give up and inform them that they are not alone in their struggles.

Before writing this novel, one of the questions I asked the pastors that I interviewed was: "What would you like this book to say?" I received many responses. One, in my view, summed up all the other responses. This pastor requested, "Whatever you do, please make it *real*."

"Real" is defined as: *Occurring as a fact, true, genuine, factual.*

In the context of this work the word "real" becomes synonymous with "raw." While I will attempt to be raw, my purpose is *not* to be vulgar.

Still, some readers may find the contents *too* raw. If you, the reader, fall into this category and are offended by some of the depictions and language that are portrayed in this work, it is not my intention to shock or offend just an attempt at being real.

Pastors Are People Too

More than laity, pastors, attempting to live up to impossible expectations, forget they are mere humans.

For whatever reason, be it pride, zeal, envy of others, fear of failure, competitiveness etc., many have pushed themselves beyond the breaking point, unable to meet the self-imposed demands placed on them.

Ministry is sometimes romanticized by the accolades arising from a congregation and the status symbols of driving a late model car, living in an upscale neighborhood, or the occasional banquet in their honor. Many pastors enter the pastorate idealistic. In time, however, the reality of ministry intrudes, rousing the novice pastor from his/her naivety, resulting in disillusionment and feelings of dejection.

To the "Church of the Firstborn"

To the "Church of the Firstborn" I write and pray by the mercies of God this work helps you assist the man or woman of God whom God has chosen to watch over your souls as you become more sensitive and understanding. And if you are not already engaged in doing so, pray for your pastor; he/she needs it more than you realize. Encourage them, stand with them, and hold up their hands, as Aaron and Hur held up Moses's hands during a battle which resulted in Israel's victory over the Amalekites (Exod. 17:10-13).

Pastor burnout: a leader of a Christian congregation who has mentally or physically collapsed due to overwork or stress.

IN THE DARKNESS OF MY MIND

In the darkness of my mind
I could not find
Release from my grief
So, the pain remains
In the darkness of my mind
Rev. Elaine Ivory Lee

This book is dedicated to Elaine Ivory Lee, my sister in Christ, longtime friend, and extraordinary editor. You left us too soon.

Elaine Ivory Lee
March 16, 1949–May 31, 2020

ACKNOWLEDGEMENTS

Special thanks to the pastors, both male and female, for allowing me into their confidence. Additional thanks to the pastor's spouses and to the PK's (Preacher's Kids) for their candid interviews.

To my beta readers: Dorothy Brown D. Min, Myrna Hallenbeck, Dana Holmes, Elaine Lee*, Beryl New, Mark Turner, and Annette Wilson, who took time from their busy schedules to read this material prior to publication and share their thoughts on this project.

To Markita Roberson, thank you my sister in Christ, for your superb editing skills.

Not to be forgotten is my family: My wife, the lovely Wandra C Blocker Ph.D. (Thank you for your input sweetheart). Our offspring: Tamara Blocker-Walker, Tanya Blocker Esq., and James C Blocker 2nd. To our daughter in love, Kayla Blocker. To our son in love, Savage Walker (pronounced Sa-Varg) and our grandchildren: Jamar Blocker, Denir Walker, and Kayla Walker.

And last but not least, the Maranatha Tabernacle family, whom I've had the privilege of serving as pastor for more than thirty years.

*Deceased

DIARY OF A BURNED OUT PASTOR:

A novel by James C Blocker

PROLOGUE

Reverend Carl Boston sat at the funeral of his best friend and colleague, the Right Reverend Dr. Morgan L. Kendal. Morgan was forty-five years old. He left to cherish his memory, his wife Lorraine and their son Lester, who was sitting on the front pew with other relatives, numb and bewildered, staring straight ahead and focused on Morgan's bronze casket. Morgan was donned in full regalia, a bishop's cross around his neck and a bishop's ring on his right hand, although it had been a posthumous elevation.

Carl ached inside, wondering what was so terrible that the only way out for his best friend was to put a gun in his mouth and pull the trigger.

Carl and Morgan met thirty years earlier when they were in their teens. At that time, they were known as "boy preachers" along with other teen preachers. It was a title they wore proudly. From that time on, they remained close friends.

As the years passed, they went into full-time ministry as pastors. The last time Carl and Morgan were together was a week before his death. Morgan was in a jovial mood; there was not even a hint something was amiss.

While sitting at the funeral, Carl grieved and thought, "Was there some small clue I missed? Did he attempt to say something I didn't catch?"

Carl shared with the audience a funny anecdote Morgan told the last time they were together.

The audience laughed at the story, which was a welcome breath of fresh air amid the smoldering pressure of the question that haunted Carl, Morgan's family, church members, and friends.

"Why?"

None of those that gave remarks at the funeral, including Carl, addressed the "why." Instead, they attempted to console themselves with platitudes such as: "He's resting in Jesus's arms. Even if he could, he wouldn't return to this evil and perverse world," and "We'll surely see him again someday."

Bishop J. I. Howard was the eulogist and Morgan's mentor. He was an astute seventy-five-year-old minister and biblical scholar who was well versed in rhetoric, imagery, and storytelling. Living up to his reputation, he preached Morgan through the Pearly Gates and straight up to the Throne, never mentioning the circumstances surrounding Morgan's untimely demise. Closing his sermon, he regaled the audience with a story.

Bishop Howard, with his distinctive deep tone, began leisurely. "When I was a boy, my father played with me and my two brothers on Saturday nights. My brothers and I fell asleep while playing with my dad. As each of us fell asleep, one-by-one he'd take us upstairs, change our clothes, and put us to bed.

"When Sunday morning came and it was time to go to church, he'd wake us up at the same time. When we fell asleep, we wore our blue jeans. But when we woke the next morning, we were clad in our pajamas."

At that juncture, he began to crescendo into a "hum." "Rev. Dr. Kendal just went to sleep before the rest of us. When he went to sleep, our heavenly Father took him upstairs. He fell asleep wearing mortal attire but will wake dressed in immortality. We may fall asleep at different times, but in that great 'gittin'-up' mornin'..."

Then in full voice, he said, "Hey, glory! We're gonna rise together. When that trumpet sounds, while we fall asleep wearing mortality, we're gonna wake dressed in immortality. Can I get a witness?!"

The entire church was on their feet, clapping and shouting, "Amen." However, moving it was to the audience, Morgan's wife Lorraine remained seated, somber-faced and still, her eyes fixed on Morgan's casket.

CHAPTER ONE

T wo weeks had passed since Morgan's funeral. Neither Carl's theology, personal philosophy, nor life experience could make sense of why his best friend and colleague, who appeared to have it all, had taken his own life. On this afternoon, Morgan's wife Lorraine called Carl and asked if he would come to the house because there were a few things she wanted to discuss with him.

Morgan lived in a three-bedroom high-ranch brick house on a tree-lined street in a quiet neighborhood. When Carl arrived, he saw Lorraine staring out of her front door window and biting her bottom lip. She opened the door before he reached the front steps.

Carl smiled when he saw her and, without saying a word, greeted Lorraine with an embrace and a kiss on her cheek. After a moment or two, Carl released her trembling body and noticed her eyes were puffy and red. Cuddling her hands, he asked, "How are you doing, Lorraine?"

She cleared her throat and responded, "It's hard, Carl. It's real hard. I know you're busy, and I'm sorry to disturb you..."

"Please don't apologize. If you need me for anything, just call."

"Thank you, Carl. Actually, I do need you to do something for me."

"Sure, what is it?"

"Follow me downstairs."

As she escorted him through the living quarters, he recalled from prior visits to the house, Morgan's basement office, which was dedicated to his vast library. His file cabinets were filled with his sermons and articles. The bookshelves were stacked with books and other reading materials of various genres; a collection that had taken Morgan years to amass.

Now, however, the once-packed bookcases were bare. All that was left in the library were empty shelves and boxes filled with Morgan's books and other reading materials. As they descended the stairs to the basement, Lorraine said, "Carl, I know Morgan would want you to have his collection of books."

Surprised at her generous offer, Carl said, "Are you sure you want to give away his entire collection?"

"Carl, take it... take it all, please. I can't stand to look at it. There're too many memories. Whatever you can't use, give it away to someone."

Carl needed a small moving truck to cart away the collection. He felt guilty accepting her generous gift because for years he'd admired and envied Morgan's vast library of scholarly and out-of-print books.

The next day, Carl rented a U-Haul and had the books delivered to his church. While sifting through the trove of Morgan's materials, one black hardcover book stood out. What drew his attention was that it was the only book in the box with no inscription on the cover identifying its contents.

Carl was curious and opened the book, unaware of the secrets it divulged. On the first page, in Morgan's handwriting, it read: "The

Me Nobody Knows." It was Morgan's diary. Exaggerating the find, Carl equated the discovery of the diary to the unearthing of the *Dead Sea Scrolls*.

He debated within himself, "I wonder if I should read it, discard it, or give it back to Lorraine." Then he thought again and concluded, "Discarding the book is not an option. However, if I give it to Lorraine, it might reveal something that would cause her even more anguish." He was left with one option. "Perhaps I should read it first, and if it contains anything incriminating, I'll guard the reputation of my best friend and dispose of it."

Carl read a few pages and paused. Then he got further into the reading. The diary started out benign, but later the passage took a notable turn. Carl slammed the book shut as tears filled his eyes.

He wiped his eyes, read a few more pages, then got into his car, threw the book into the backseat, and left for the restaurant to meet his colleagues for their monthly breakfast gathering.

———

Arthur Wright, Peter Austin, Carl and Morgan had made a commitment five years before to get together at least once a month because they needed the fellowship. All their churches were in New York City.

Arthur was the eldest at fifty years old and the pastor of Calvary Church in Brooklyn. Peter, forty-eight years old, was the pastor of Resurrection Temple in the Bronx. Carl Boston was forty-five years old and the pastor of Ephesians Church in Harlem. Morgan Kendal, also forty-five before his death, pastored The Green Avenue Church in Brooklyn. Each had been pastoring for at least fifteen years.

Their breakfast meetings followed a similar pattern: One of them would open with a church joke. Sometimes they boasted to the others about their church's attendance and how many joined on a given Sunday. On occasion, they complained regarding one or more of the members that were acting contrary along with demeaning other ministers whom they believed to be dishonest. Other times they commented on how things in the church had changed so drastically from previous years.

Carl, reminiscing one time, said, "I remember when I conducted revivals out of town. I didn't stay in some fancy hotel. One of the members of the church would put me up in their home for the duration of the revival.

"Preachers, let me tell you, I've had some strange experiences staying in several of these folk's homes. I'll never do that again.

"One time, I was staying in this pastor's house; I was single at the time and in my early twenties. That night the pastor's daughter came into my bedroom as I slept and climbed in the bed with me.

"Now check this out, y'all. Her parents were in the next room."

Arthur, with a snicker, said, "C'mon preacher, fess up—what happened after that?"

"Believe it or not, nothing happened. I told her to get back to her room. I was young, devoted, and serious about ministry."

Even if something had happened, Carl didn't feel comfortable enough with them to admit it. Besides, if something had happened, it occurred years before and served no purpose for him to confess.

Arthur, with a raised eyebrow, sighed but said nothing else.

Then Morgan said, "Actually, I believe you, Carl. If you'd notice, those men in the Old Testament didn't start messing up until they got older."

Arthur chuckled and asked Carl, "Hey Doc, now that you're older, are you messin' up?"

As Arthur spoke, Carl thought about a pastor that was guilt ridden about an extramarital affair and confessed it to another minister in confidence. The minister betrayed the pastor and made the affair known to the presidium of their denomination, resulting in the pastor being defrocked. Carl knew to have a moral failing was anathema among his colleagues.

Peter, interrupting, said, "Stop it, Arthur. I know where you're comin' from, Carl. I wouldn't trade a million dollars for the experiences I've had in ministry. But you couldn't pay me a million dollars to go through them again."

"These guys nowadays have charisma, but no calling," grumbled Morgan. "They insist upon staying in the best hotel suites, flying first class, being picked up from the airport in a limousine, and then they require a huge amount for an honorarium."

Arthur sniggered and said, "Like Pastor Jason Easterly from D.C. He needs the money to support all of those illegitimate kids and his girlfriends."

"You don't know if that's true," said Peter.

"Well, I was told by a pastor that lives in D.C. that it's true, and according to him the whole town knows about it."

That is the way many of their conversations went. If the question of a moral failing or problems in their marriages arose, the discussion would be diverted before something was revealed.

Carl often left the meetings feeling empty and that nothing was accomplished. He loved meeting with these pastors and enjoyed the fellowship, however after meeting with them, he wanted to take away more from their time than how things used to be, a good church joke, or gossip about corrupt preachers.

When together, they laughed a great deal, which released much of the stress they had as pastors. This time, however, the breakfast meeting would take on a different tone. They would not be focused on preacher gossip, church attendance, or how things used to be.

Carl was reading an article from a magazine while waiting for the others to arrive entitled, "Dying to Preach: Pastors Committing Suicide." Carl and his colleagues had no idea this breakfast gathering would lead to a series of revelations that would bring them to a defining moment in their lives.

CHAPTER TWO

Arthur and Peter arrived at the restaurant together. Carl greeted them with a half-hearted smile, then said, "Hey Reverends, how're you doing?"

Peter gripped Carl by his shoulders, gave him a pat on the back, and asked, "How're you, preacher?" Arthur gave him a loose hug, patted him on the back, and then sighed, but said nothing.

As they sat, Carl responded, "Well, I'm making it."

"C'mon preacher how're you really doing?" asked Peter

"I'm okay."

Then Carl said, "Hey preachers, I was just reading this article while waiting on you. This is gonna blow your minds."

"Let's hear it, preacher," said Arthur as he perused the menu, deciding what he was going to order.

"Can you hold up a minute?" asked Peter "I have to call my office."

Carl, eager to read the article, said, "The article is titled, 'Dying to Preach: Pastors Committing Suicide.' From what I've read so far, suicide among pastors is more prevalent than one would think."

Peter placed his phone on the table. Arthur continued looking at the menu; however, his breathing was erratic as he stared at the same item on the list.

The server came to the table, brandishing a full toothed smile, a pen in one hand and an order pad in the other. With cheeriness, the server said, "Good morning pastors. How're you all today? Are you going to order right now, or are you waiting for Reverend Kendal?"

They all became still and looked at each other, thinking, "Who's going to break the news to the server?"

Then Carl said, "Reverend Kendal died more than two weeks ago."

Her mouth and eyes stretched open. "Oh no, what happened?!"

They were not about to reveal to her the circumstances surrounding Morgan's death.

Carl said, "Just one of those things you don't expect."

Arthur smiled at her and asked, "Can you please give us another minute or so?"   .

"Sure, take your time. I'm so sorry to hear of Reverend Kendal."

As she left to tend to another table, Peter tapped the table with the tips of his fingers and said, "What does the article say?"

Carl began reading. "Pastor Isaac Hunter has reportedly taken his own life according to an undated suicide note found last year, but his death is far from the only pastoral suicide in recent months.

"Reverend Ed Montgomery, pastor at the Full Gospel Assemblies International Church in Hazel Crest, Illinois, shot himself in front of his mother and son.

"In November, a Georgia pastor killed himself in between Sunday services. Larrinecia Sims Parker, the wife of the Rev. Teddy Parker Jr., found the minister in the driveway of their home with a self-inflicted gunshot wound, Houston County coroner's office reports. Also—"

"Does it mention Morgan?" asked Arthur

"Yeah, man, let me finish."

"Let me see it," said Peter

Carl handed Peter the magazine. He read to himself, shook his head, and with a disbelieving look, as though it was his first-time hearing of Morgan's death, exclaimed, "I can't believe this."

Then he read the article to the others: "Pastor Morgan Kendal of New York, who served as Pastor of The Greene Avenue Church in Brooklyn, was found slumped over the steering wheel of his car by his sixteen-year-old son, Lester Kendal. Pastor Kendal died of an apparent self-inflicted gunshot wound. So far, no suicide note was recovered."

"I wonder if there is a suicide note in the diary," Carl thought. He was tempted to reveal what he had found among Morgan's books. Still in a dilemma, he thought he should read it in its entirety before even considering telling the others about it.

The magazine article was surreal and hit much too close to home. Arthur, Carl, and Peter froze and stared at each other, thinking they might be susceptible to suicide. They were vexed that someone they knew personally had his epitaph reduced to a statistic by a columnist who had never heard of Morgan before this incident.

Then Peter noticed something on the following page that Carl had overlooked. "Wait a minute, y'all. It says here Morgan's mentor, The Right Rev. J. I. Howard, was one of those interviewed for the article."

The article quoted Bishop Howard as saying, "I was Rev. Morgan Kendal's mentor ever since he graduated from Bible College. I am devastated beyond words. He was more than a protégé, he was like a son to me and my wife. We have no children of our own, and my wife is inconsolable at the loss of Rev. Kendal, whom she loved like a son. Rev. Kendal was a scholar and a great preacher with a beautiful family and a great future ahead of him. My wife and I will deeply miss him."

Carl knew from talking with Morgan how much he respected Bishop Howard and how close he and his mentor were. Morgan had many of his mannerisms and had adopted several of his expressions when he preached. There was a definite "ministerial family resemblance."

Carl also knew firsthand how much Bishop Howard loved Morgan. It was said one could not imagine another mentor-mentee bond any closer than that of Bishop Howard and Rev. Kendal.

After Peter completed reading the piece, Arthur sounded-off. "I don't know how these guys could take their own lives. Don't they realize there's no forgiveness for self-murder? They're lost."

"Give me the chapter and verse that says if you commit suicide that you're automatically going to hell," retorted Carl.

"What about the scripture that talks about self-murder?"

"Name me the chapter and verse."

Arthur glanced at Peter, expecting some assistance, but Peter looked at him with no change in expression and not uttering a word.

"Listen, Carl, I know we don't like the idea our friend is lost, but..."

"So, are you conceding that you have no scripture to support the view that those that kill themselves are hell-bound?"

"Look, Carl, it is what it is, and neither you nor I can change it!"

"Arthur, you don't know what people are going through who take their own lives, and you should keep your mouth off those you know nothing about-!"

Peter interrupted the exchange. "Okay, preachers, keep your voices and tempers in check. Protect the collar."

Neither of them said anything else until the server came to take their orders. Carl's brows were drawn together, his veins protruding on his forehead. Arthur, who always smiled and was courteous to the server, gave his order without looking in her direction. It was evident, even to the server, there was tension at the table.

After the exchange with Arthur, Carl was convinced if he shared the diary with Arthur, he would use the diary as fodder to furnish gossip about Morgan.

Reviewing in his mind the article and what Bishop Howard was reported to have said, Carl decided he was going to inform the Bishop of the diary. Carl's heart ached for the aging preacher. He reasoned, "Perhaps if I let Bishop Howard read the diary, it will give him closure."

During breakfast, there were no words exchanged between the three. Carl's mind was focused on a portion of the diary he'd read.

They finished their meals and decided not to remain and talk afterward, as was their routine. Before leaving, Carl extended his hand to Arthur and said, "Listen, Reverend, no hard feelings. Okay?"

Carl shook Arthur's hand and stared at the wall and repeated, "No hard feelings, brother."

Arthur glanced at Carl and said, "I'm good, Preacher."

Then Carl turned to Peter and asked, "Hey Doc, did you drive?"

"No, I rode in with Arthur."

"Peter, I want to talk with you about somethin'. I'll take you home if you don't mind."

"Fine, no problem."

Peter looked at Arthur and said, "You don't mind do you, Arthur?"

Arthur quipped, "Nah, I didn't want you in my car anyway."

Once in the car, Carl said to Peter. "Listen, man, I'm faced with a dilemma, and I need some advice."

From the look on Carl's face, Peter knew that it was serious. "Sure, what is it?"

Carl reached in the back seat of his car and handed him the diary.

"What's this?"

"Open it and read it."

Peter opened the diary but did not read beyond the first paragraph. His eyes widened, and he asked, "Where did you get this?"

"Lorraine gave me Morgan's entire book collection. The diary was nestled among the books; she probably didn't realize it was there."

"What're you going to do with it?"

"I'm gonna let Bishop Howard see it. You read the magazine article; he's devastated. Morgan was like a son to him."

"What good will that do?"

"I was thinking it may give him a sense of closure. I really feel for the old man. What do you think?"

Carl had already made up his mind to let Bishop Howard see the diary. He just wanted Peter to agree with his decision and share the onus of revealing Morgan's memoirs.

Peter did not respond right away, but contemplated awhile, then said, "Okay, maybe you should."

"I thought I'd call him right now and see if he's available to see me. I'd like you to come too if you have the time."

Peter sighed, "All right, call him."

Carl called Bishop Howard and said, "I have a matter of great importance to discuss with you. I've come across something I think that you should see."

Bishop Howard cleared his throat and said, "It'll have to wait, son."

Carl was caught off guard by what he perceived as a curt response from Bishop Howard.

"Oh, um, sorry Bishop."

"That's okay, son. I'm about to take my wife out of town for our fiftieth wedding anniversary. I'll be gone for a couple of weeks. I can meet with you when we return."

"Oh, okay. Congratulations, Bishop. Um, sorry to bother you. I guess I'll have to wait. I'll see you in a couple of weeks or so. Please excuse the intrusion."

"No problem. Looking forward to it."

Carl ended the call and said to Peter, "The Bishop said he's leaving town today."

Peter checked his phone and said, "My wife just texted me. I must go, anyway. Why don't you and I get together tomorrow?"

"I'll give you a call," said Carl.

After driving Peter home, Carl thought, "If I make available to Bishop Howard the personal and perhaps incriminating thoughts and actions of Morgan, some might consider that a betrayal."

Despite that, he reasoned, "Since there is no malice intended and Bishop Howard was Morgan's spiritual father, it should be all right if I share its contents with the Bishop."

CHAPTER THREE

After running a few errands, Carl went home that evening and placed the diary in a place he figured his wife Trisha would not look. He and his wife had dinner, then retired to his study to watch television. Trisha laid her head on his lap with her legs curled up on the couch. She kept commenting on the program they were watching with Carl responding, "Yeah, uh-huh. You're right, babe."

"Where's your mind, Carl? You're not paying attention to a word I'm saying."

"Yes, I am," he said defensively.

"You promised me that we were going to spend time together alone tonight without any interference from your *mistress*."

Trisha often referred to the church as Carl's mistress.

"My *mistress*, as you refer to it, is not even on my mind. It's just you and me tonight, babe." Then Carl bent down, and his lips brushed her cheek with a light smacking kiss.

Carl never shared church scandals or church gossip with Trisha, in the name of protecting her innocence. He knew he could not share Morgan's diary with her. Trisha and Lorraine were the closest of friends, and he was not sure what damaging information might be in the diary.

Trisha took a deep breath and said, "Carl, I'm going to bed. Are you coming?"

"I'm coming. I have to do something first; I'll only take a minute."

Carl knew when Trisha asked if he was coming to bed, it was her code for bedroom romance.

When Trisha went upstairs, Carl rushed to retrieve the diary from its hiding place, thinking, "Let me read as much as I can before Trisha calls me."

In the diary, Morgan recounted a prayer meeting:

> *Wednesday night prayer service and the faithful are praying and petitioning their needs. However, as they are entreating God, my mind is preoccupied with the pressures of the ministry.*
>
> *Much of the congregation—and even my own wife and son, who rarely attend church—have forged themselves against me. I'm all alone, with no one to help me bear this heavy load.*
>
> *My assistant minister up and left with no explanation given, taking at least twenty key members with him. I found out after he left that he was undermining me, all while claiming to be standing by my side. Also, the church organist was accused of molesting one of the children in the choir. The parents are not just suing the church; I am also named in the suit.*
>
> *To make matters worse, the Dark Lady was in church tonight, sashaying herself up to the front pew and sitting down as though she owns the building. Clad in her usual dull brown*

dress which hugs her shape, accentuating her curves. She is a composite of every infamous seducer I've ever read about.

Dear God, help me! Every time she enters the sanctuary, she becomes the center of my attention. Even when I attempt to read the Bible, pray, or preach a sermon, I'm inundated with thoughts of her.

I know I shouldn't have, but I've engaged her in conversation on several occasions. Even so, I was able to resist her obvious advances and kept control of myself. Now, however, I am overwhelmed, my defenses are decimated, and I can't fight.

The ushers are on the job, their eyes peeled, looking out for those that come to the sanctuary with evil intentions. Making sure a stranger does not pillage the belongings of the congregants while their eyes are shut when they pray.

The church's equipment is secure under the watchful eyes of the security team, and when the sanctuary is vacated, the alarms are set and only those that can be trusted know the alarm code. Everything is safe and secure.

Yet there's nothing in place safeguarding the vulnerabilities of the shepherd. Everyone is so engaged with what they are doing that no one seemed to notice this enticer invading the sanctuary.

"We're not worried about our Pastor," testified Brother Williams at a banquet in my honor. "God's got him." Obviously, my smiles and public persona has convinced him,

along with other members of the congregation, that I'm always on top of my game.

But what does one do when they feel no one, not even God, has got them and one's faith is replaced with trepidation? I know I shouldn't feel this way, but the problem is I do.

The challenges of ministry that once fed my passions are now beginning to wear me down. In the past, I welcomed the battle, believing God was with me and there was no way I could be defeated. However, with the steady barrage of attacks, I am exhausted.

I returned home and pleaded with the night, "Please grant me a restful sleep, so I may face the challenges that will ensue at daybreak." My plea is ignored, and at the crack of dawn, I found myself deprived of rest and devoid of resolution. Sleep brought no reprieve from the continuous pressures brought to bear against me.

Carl pondered, "How come he's never shared any of this with me? Especially the lawsuit. And who *is* this Dark Lady?"

"Carl, come to bed!" called Trisha.

Carl grumbled under his breath, "She would call me now." Then he said, "I'm comin', Trish!"

———

Seven o'clock the next morning, Peter called. Carl was still in bed but was about to get up and head to his study to continue reading the diary before Trisha awakened.

"Hey, preacher, are we going to get together today? I've cleared my calendar."

Carl whispered, not wanting to wake Trisha, "Yeah, hold on a second, Peter." Carl got out of bed and walked to another room to continue the conversation.

"Do you, uh... mind if... Arthur comes too?" asked Peter

"Yes, I do mind. I hope you didn't tell him about the diary."

Peter's silence confirmed Carl's suspicion.

"Why did you tell him?! You know how he is! If I'd wanted him to know, I would've told him!"

"Listen, Carl, Arthur is a part of our group. He's just as concerned about Morgan as we are."

"Arthur's only concerned with spreading gossip and—!"

"C'mon, Carl, he's not like that."

"Yes, he is, and you know it!"

"I know him, Carl—*this* he will keep to himself. You should've seen him when I told him about the diary. He was hurt that you chose not to tell him. He said, 'I thought we all were like brothers.' He was almost in tears."

Carl did not respond right away but thought about the time he was in a financial bind, and Arthur gave him the money and would not accept repayment. Also, the time his wife was out of town, and he became ill. Arthur got out of his bed and drove him to the hospital in the middle of the night.

Carl sighed and said, "Okay, bring him along."

———————

They arranged to meet that afternoon at their usual restaurant. Carl requested the private dining area which seated about fifteen people. The manager of the restaurant accommodated Carl as he had done on prior occasions. In the past, Carl used the private dining area for closed meetings with politicians and other special guests.

When Arthur and Peter arrived at the restaurant, Carl was already in the room and seated. Arthur and Carl greeted each other as though they were strangers passing late at night in a dark alley, neither knowing what to expect.

"How're you, Carl?" said Arthur

"I'm good."

Arthur was thinking Carl did not want him there. Carl was wondering if he made the right decision by allowing Arthur to be a part of the meeting.

Peter noticed the tension between the two and said, "Let's clear the air, brothers. Arthur, Carl's afraid that you're going to spread the information to someone outside of this group. Carl, Arthur feels bad that you don't trust him."

Arthur spoke up first, "Carl, I assure you, what is said here will remain here. All I can give you is my word."

"Arthur, I'm sorry you thought I was leaving you out of the loop. Morgan was my closest friend; I must protect his reputation. I figured the fewer people who knew about this, the better. I hope you understand."

"Yeah, I understand, preacher."

Arthur still felt alienated but pretended to accept Carl's explanation because he was anxious to get to the reading of the diary.

Arthur and Peter stared at Carl as he removed the diary from his brown attaché case. The scene was reminiscent of the reading of a will in which each heir anticipates a sizable portion of the estate.

Carl read the part he had read the night before regarding the Wednesday night prayer meeting and the Dark Lady. His throat was parched afterwards. Raising his glass to his mouth, he sipped the water that he ordered before their arrival. Then, before venturing into the unknown, he said to himself, "I should've read the whole diary before sharing it."

As Carl was about to continue, the server entered the room. With her distinctive smile and cheeriness, she asked, "How're you, Reverends? Please excuse the interruption, but I need your drink orders."

They gave their drink orders and said nothing else. Being an experienced server, she knew that this was not the time for polite chit-chat, so she dispelled with any small talk and exited the room.

As with Carl, Peter and Arthur could not help but speculate on the identity of the nameless woman Morgan referred to, and how involved he was with her.

Except for the muffled murmuring of the customers outside of the closed door of the private dining area, the room was so still a whisper could be heard at its lowest decibel.

Carl took deep breaths, and his heartrate accelerated. Peter's eyebrows drew together; the veins in his forehead bulged. The corners of Arthur's mouth drooped, his eyes peering straight at Carl's face.

Carl continued reading the diary:

> *I'm not sure if I should fight—hang in there and continue to contend with the challenges of ministry—or flight—say 'the hell with it' and quit. Then again, what does one do when one is too weak to fight and too weary for flight? Still, my congregation and colleagues look up to me. I know the congregation will not understand if I choose to quit. I know what they will say. "All of those sermons you've preached about holding on to God, from whom your help comes. Why don't you take your own advice, Pastor?" They have no idea how many nights I've cried out in desperation, "God, where is my help?!"*
>
> *My colleagues will damn me with the unfaithful and the unbelieving, saying: "God has given you so much. I thought*

you really had it. If you really have faith, you will hang in there!"

Carl Boston, who's like a brother to me, will not condemn me. He would, though, be disappointed, as would my mentor Bishop Howard whom, like a father, has invested so much of his time and energy into my life.

God bless Lorraine who has suffered in silence these many years because I was so committed. She will most likely blame herself if I leave the ministry. I fear my son, who admires me, will lose the respect he has and no longer esteem me as an example of invincibility.

Carl choked, paused as his thoughts *screamed*, "Morgan why did you do this?! You didn't have to take your life, man. You should've shared your feelings with me." Attempting to disguise his grief, he said, "Sorry, preachers, something got caught in my throat."

Peter's bottom lip quivered as he fought to hold back tears—not as much for Morgan as for himself. For months he also contemplated announcing to the church he was stepping down as pastor.

Arthur, faring no better, was forced by the revelations in the diary to face his own moral shortcomings, which he had struggled for years to conquer without success.

CHAPTER FOUR

S uddenly, there was a knock at the door. Carl, annoyed by the disturbance, grumbled, "Who is it?"

It was Milton Smith, one of Peter's parishioners. Milton walked in, smiling and waving, and said, "Hello, Pastors. Pastor Austin, I saw your car in the parking lot, so I figured you were here."

Peter, with a scowl on his face, said, "What is it, Milton?"

"Pastor, I hope I'm not disturbing you, but I would like to speak with you."

Peter's nostrils flared and he said, "Look... ah, look—see me during office hours!"

Milton bowed his head and said, "Sorry, Pastor." Then he left the room with his chin buried in his chest.

Carl and Arthur glanced at each other, then stared at Peter. Peter, with the corners of his mouth turned down, shook his head and said, "The people made me this way, brothers."

"I hear you, Reverend," said Arthur. "I have a hundred Miltons in my church. They act as though they're the only members in the church."

Then Peter said, "It's just that Milton's always so needy, calling me at some ungodly hour of the night to say little to nothin'. When I give him advice, he either doesn't do anything or does the very opposite of what I advise him to do."

"Doc, my folks don't have my number," said Carl. "A few of the members used to call me regularly and insist on speaking to me right then. When I told them to call me at church during office hours, some of them said, 'I want to speak with you when I feel like talking. I can't wait for your office hours', like I don't have family and other things to attend to.

"My wife gave me all sorts of flak for being on the phone with the members so much. Man, you need to do like I did—un-list your number and give it out only on a need-to-know basis, like to church officers and people like that."

"You're probably right, Carl," said Peter. "I just wanted to be available to the people and not be one of those Ivory Tower Preachers. You know the kind I mean; the aloof shepherds that don't want to smell like the sheep."

"I'll bet he doesn't give a dime in the offering," said Carl.

"Not one red cent," said Peter. "Check this out, y'all. One of the other members said they saw him at another church, standing in line to give a large offering because the evangelist told them if they gave, they would get a big blessing.

"Even when I have guests visiting the church, he tries to monopolize my time with his nonsense. Y'all, I'm sick and tired of being taken for granted."

Then Arthur said, "You think that's something, listen to this. I'll do you one better. One of my members I supported financially—I mean buying her food and paying her rent on a consistent basis, sometimes with money I couldn't afford to give—received a settlement from an accident. After receiving her settlement, she gave the bulk of the money to the 'miracle man' preacher who came to town in a crusade for a week, claiming God instructed her to give it. Then, after squandering the rest of the settlement, she had the audacity to ask me to pay her rent when the expected windfall promised by the *miracle man* didn't materialize."

"Let me tell y'all something. All this drama from some of the members is affecting my health," said Peter. "My doctor even warned me to get rid of the stress, or he'll have to hospitalize me. My wife heard that and went berserk, and I quote, 'This doesn't make any *damn* sense. Why do you put up with this stuff? Now your health is threatened because of these ingrates. Let *me* call them. I have a few choice words for them!'

"I had to wrestle the phone away from her to stop her from calling the members. I was shocked when I heard her talk and act that way. Before that, she never used that kind of language or performed like that."

Arthur made an audible sigh then said, "Okay, enough of that for now. Let's get back to the diary."

Carl continued reading:

> *I'm supposed to teach a Bible class tomorrow night. My head is overwhelmed with thoughts of everything except the Bible lesson. To make matters worse, I haven't read my Bible in months.*

I also should be preparing myself for an important church business meeting. I just do not have the desire or the energy to prepare or even attend the meeting. God help me! I feel like some lazy jack-leg preacher. How did I get myself into this predicament? It's not supposed to be this way. I should've gone into law, or teaching, or anything else. But now it's too late. There is no way out of this mess I've created. There is no way out of this.

Some have claimed they were helped by my ministry, but I know they didn't mean it. I even have some ministerial awards that I am sure were given to me because they had no one else to give them to. I've done nothing all these years, just wasting my time preaching and preaching for nothing.

When alone, I sob uncontrollably at times. I did not realize until now that one could cry until there are no more tears yet continue to weep.

I used to love pastoring. It was the reason I got up in the morning. Now it's like the albatross in Samuel Taylor Coleridge's poem, "The Rime of the Ancient Mariner"—a psychological burden that feels like a curse. God, I have not slept in days. I can't go on like this. Perhaps it would be better if I was not present anywhere."

It was the end of the page and although there were numerous pages left in the diary, Carl thought, "I guess Morgan is about to get to the suicide note." Carl paused and took a deep breath. Then he said to his colleagues, "What say you, brethren? Do you want me to continue reading?"

Peter and Arthur stared at Carl for a moment, then Arthur said, "Yeah, keep reading."

Carl froze for five seconds, staring at the diary before touching the upper corner of the page with his index finger. Then he turned the page a little at a time.

The server came in with their drinks and asked, "Are you ready to order now?"

Carl snatched his finger from the page, slammed the book shut, took his handkerchief out of his pocket, and dabbed his brow, then said, "Yes, we're ready."

After they ordered their food, Carl said, "I was just thinking brothers, maybe we should hold off reading any more for now."

"Why, what's the matter?" asked Arthur.

"Nothing, I just feel that we've heard enough for today."

"I don't see why we can't read at least a few more pages. What do you think, Peter?"

"Arthur, it's obvious why Carl is having reservations. Morgan was his best friend."

"Is that it, Carl?" asked Arthur. "Listen, man, if you can't handle it, I understand. Let's table it until tomorrow."

Carl gazed at the wall for a few seconds, exhaled then said, "I'm good. Let's do it."

"Are you sure?" asked Peter.

"Yeah, let's do it."

Carl clapped his hands, rubbed them together, then in the same motion, opened the book and continued where he'd left off:

> *Today was an extraordinary day. I feel wonderful. Sunday morning service was one of the best services we've had in a long time. The Spirit of God was present in an exceptional way. Although I hadn't studied, or even read my Bible in months, the message bore abundant fruit. God gave me clarity of thought, and the revelations flowed like rivers of living water. I could not keep up with the spiritual insights I was receiving. Many came to the altar and repented. To God be the glory!*

> *Although I was pleased with the message, I was not totally satisfied. It could have gone a lot better if I had studied. I know there is so much more the Spirit wanted to say. I'm going to preach that message again, only next time I'm going to be better prepared.*

> *Even the Dark Lady, who was sitting in the back row, could not distract me. I haven't felt this good in a long while. To quote a verse from an old spiritual: "Sometimes I feel discouraged and think my work's in vain, but then the Holy Spirit revives my soul again."*

Carl smiled and said, "Gentlemen, our food should be here soon. Let's eat and leave the reading on a positive note. I'll call you tomorrow, and we'll get together then."

"Sure," said Peter.

Arthur sighed. "Okay. If you say so, Doc."

CHAPTER FIVE

O n the same afternoon the pastors were meeting, Carl's wife Trisha had arranged to spend the day with Lorraine, along with Peter's wife Yolanda, Debra Porter, widow of Pastor Joseph Porter, and Mae Jones, wife of Pastor Clyde Jones. Trisha was the first one to arrive at the house.

"Hey, my sister, I'm here," she said, giving Lorraine an embrace. "Have any of the others arrived yet?"

"No. As usual, you're right on time and the first one to arrive. I'm glad you're here before the others. I have somethin' I want to tell you. Somethin' I can't share with anyone else."

Trisha's brow furrowed, and she stared at Lorraine. Lorraine's eyes teared as she cleared her throat. Then she said, "Trish do you want something to drink?"

Lorraine's voice cracked as she cried, "Oh, Trish!" Then she wept.

"What's wrong?"

At that moment, the doorbell rang. Lorraine wiped her eyes with her hands, then went to answer the door. As she walked to the door, Trisha whispered, "We'll talk later." Lorraine nodded her head.

Yolanda and Debra had arrived. Both walked in with their arms out-stretched toward Lorraine, cuddling her with a group embrace and a kiss on her cheek.

As they walked to the living room, Trisha raised an eyebrow and asked, "Where's Mae?"

"You know her, late as usual," said Yolanda, "She's probably waiting for the gates to open to let her out of that exclusive community she lives in."

Trisha said with a chuckle, "Yolanda, you're just jealous that your man ain't got it like that."

Then Lorraine said, "Having things is good, but I'd trade it all just to have my Morgan back."

Debra nodded her head and said, "I feel you, sister. I watched Joe work himself to death. Even after his first heart attack, he missed his checkups at the doctors, and when he did go, he didn't always do what the doctors told him to do.

"Just before he died, the doctor warned him, 'Reverend Porter, take a vacation and get away from the stress. I'm telling you this is not good.' Joe thought the church couldn't get along without him.

"Instead of taking a vacation, he started a few new ministries, ignoring the fact that those ministries needed maintenance to keep going.

"Even when we went on a so-called vacation, it wasn't really a vacation because he'd end up preaching somewhere."

"How long has he been gone?" Trisha asked.

"A year next month."

"It's been a year already? It doesn't seem that long."

"Why didn't he assign someone to take those extra ministries over?" asked Yolanda.

Debra raised her voiced. "He did!"

"Sorry, Debra, I didn't mean to upset you."

"Forgive me for shouting, Yolanda, but it just gets me so mad. Those he assigned to do the job promised to do it, then ended up not doing it, or not to Joe's standards. Joe was like, 'If you ain't gonna do it right, I mean with excellence, then I'll do it myself.' I used to tell Joe, 'Excellence does not necessitate perfection.'"

"My husband's the same way," said Trisha. "Totally fixated with doing things perfectly. It's his obsession. I understand that you want things done right, but when the smallest mistake is made, he goes into a tirade. Mumbling to himself and tossing in bed all night. I don't think God wants us to be fanatical; after all, no one's perfect."

"That's just what I used to tell Joe. He'd say, 'Debbie, you don't under-stand my drive or what God told me. God gave me the vision.' As though God expected him to carry out the vision alone. He had no idea how I was willing to be his helpmate, so he left me out of a lot of things where I could've helped."

"I know what you mean, Debbie," said Yolanda. "Sometimes I'd give Peter advice, and he would not accept it. Then when someone else told him the very same thing, he'd give them all sorts of accolades for their so-called spiritual insights.

"I remember when Peter used to travel on out-of-town trips with just his personal secretary. My husband's so blind, he can't see that his secretary wants him. When I made him aware of it, he told me, 'Baby, you're just imagining things.' But when Mother Carey told him the same thing, he said to me, 'Mother Carey is a spiritual woman. I'm glad she's a member of our church. The church needs people like her who can discern spirits.'"

Then Trisha said, "Don't get me started. One of those church heifers who is always in need of *counseling* from Carl, smiles in my face, bringing presents and even buying things for the house. She must think that I'm a fool. I know she wants him."

"Beware, heifers bearing gifts," said Yolanda.

Trisha giggled and said, "Amen, sister."

Yolanda remarked, "Why do you think our men can't see or refuse to see what these women are up to?"

"Let me ask you all a question," said Debra. "What does your husband love more than his church?"

Before anyone had a chance to respond she blurted, "Nothing! And these church hussies know it. That's why they work so hard at what your man loves."

Lorraine was sitting in her chair, staring at a picture on the wall of herself and Morgan on their wedding day and thinking, "I thought this gathering was about me. They're just complaining about their husbands."

Then there was the blaring of a car horn. "Excuse me y'all," said Lorraine. She walked to the door to see who was causing such a ruckus in what was usually a quiet neighborhood.

With her head hanging out of the car window, she yelled, "Hey girl, check this out!" It was Mae in her brand new metallic-blue Mercedes.

She got out of her car, shut the door, and walked to the house. She greeted Lorraine with a hug, then pointed at the car and said, "Look what my king got his queen. Do you like it?"

Lorraine twisted her mouth and responded, "It's nice, Mae."

"My man wants me riding in style," Mae boasted.

Lorraine and Mae walked into the living room, and Mae said. "Sorry I'm late girls, but I had to pick up my new baby. She's parked outside. I tell you, I didn't sleep all night I was so excited about my new car."

"Is that why your eyes are so red?"

"Well, actually, I was showing my appreciation to my hubby last night before he left town to preach today."

Trisha chuckled and said, "Girl, you're a mess."

"There ain't nothin' wrong with a little bump and..."

"Don't say it, Mae," said Trisha.

Lorraine sat in her chair texting with her eyes glued to her phone.

Debra asked, "Are you okay, Lorraine?"

"Yeah, I'm just thinkin'."

"Join the conversation, Lorraine," Mae urged with her arms waving.

"I'm just listening," Lorraine said. She then caught Trish's eye. "Come join me in the kitchen and help me fix lunch."

The women chatted while in the kitchen. Afterward, Trisha returned to the others with sandwiches. She was breathing heavily and biting her bottom lip.

"Is everything all right, Trish?" asked Debra.

"Yeah. Why?"

"Well, when you went into the kitchen you were fine; now you look as though you're bothered."

"Yeah, whatever."

Debra did not inquire further.

Soon after, Lorraine walked out of the kitchen wiping her nose with a tissue and dabbing her eyes. No one questioned her; they assumed she was mourning over Morgan.

"We're here for you, baby," Yolanda said.

They continued to exchange experiences they'd had as pastors' wives. Lorraine was reacting to the conversation with an occasional smile and a chuckle. Trisha, however, remained still and stared at the wall.

As they were all about to leave, Trisha hugged Lorraine and whispered in her ear, "I don't care what they say, they can't do that."

They left Lorraine's house at six-thirty. Once outside, Mae said to the others, "Hey, girls, where're y'all going? Why don't we take a ride in my new car?"

"I've got to go," said Trisha. "Carl will be home soon, and I have to fix dinner."

"What about you, Yolanda? Debra? Let's hang a little while."

Yolanda said, "I wish I could, but I have to go."

Debra shook her head but didn't say anything.

"Don't tell me y'all got old on me. Ah, c'mon, let's have dinner at Ida Kae's. Y'all love Ida Kae's. It's my treat."

"Maybe some other time, Mae," said Yolanda.

They got into their cars and went their separate ways.

———

Mae sped off. Spinning her tires, she drove to the corner and slammed on the brakes, her tires shrieking to a halt. She called her husband.

"Hey, lover-boy, when're you coming home? I miss you."

"Mae, I told you before I left this morning that I would be gone for seven days. You already know that. Why are you asking me that?"

"Baby, why do you have to be there so long?"

"Mae, please don't start. You know—

"All I know is that you were home for only two weeks last month."

"Mae—"

"Only two weeks, Clyde!"

"Mae, I don't understand you. You have everything, and yet you complain. How do you think I pay for all those things you have? None of your friends have what you have. I don't understand you."

"Clyde, what's her name?"

"What?"

"You heard me…"

"What are you trying to say?"

"I'm not *trying* to say anything. I said it."

"Mae, I have to go. They're calling me."

"Are *they* calling you, or is *she* calling you?"

"I'll call you later tonight when you've calmed down."

"Don't bother!"

After they hung up, Mae thought about the time before he started pastoring, before he was in such demand as a preacher. He was popular, and many of the other women wanted him. Clyde was six-foot-four, muscular, and always a meticulous dresser. Whatever he did he put his all into it.

Then she cried and shouted to the empty air, "He gives everything else attention but me! All I wanted was someone who'll love me!"

Mae opened the glove compartment and reached for what she called her calm-me-down pills. Then she said, "Looks as though I'll be sleeping with Prince Valium again tonight. Not yet though—I need a pick-me-up first."

Under her front seat was an almost empty half-pint bottle of what she labeled her *pain juice.*

"Lord, if the people of the church only knew my agony. If they only knew."

Mae turned the bottle up to her mouth, unburdening the decanter entirely of its contents. Then, driving as though attempting to shatter the sound barrier, she raced through stop signs and traffic lights until she noticed the blinking red and blue lights in her rearview mirror and heard the dreaded sound of a police siren. Mae pulled her car over to the right, praying the squad car would pass her by and go after a *real* lawbreaker. The car pulled up behind her and stopped. Stepping out of the car in uniform and sporting high-strapped boots was a police officer. Mae's hands shook, and her heart pounded. As he approached her car, she said to herself, "Jesus help me."

"Miss, may I see your license, registration, and insurance card, please?" said the officer.

Mae was thinking, "Oh, dear God, my husband's known in this town. If I'm arrested, it's going to get into the papers, and we'll have to move away from this place."

Mae, fumbling in her pocketbook for her credentials said, "What's the uh, prob-problem officer?"

The officer, holding the flashlight from his shoulder and shining it into her face, said, "Ma'am, you ran through the traffic light a couple of blocks back, and you were speeding." Then he stared into her face, his eyes bulged, and he said, "Mae Benton, is that you?"

She recognized his voice after he called her name and she said, "Maurice?" Mae sighed in relief, then said, "Wow, how have you been?"

Maurice Thompson was a former boyfriend from high school with whom she was in love back in the day.

"Mae, what have you been up to? Are you married?"

"Well, uh... yeah. And you?"

"Divorced."

Mae smiled then, unconsciously twirling her hair between two of her fingers. She had not thought about Maurice in years. Even so, she pondered, "He sure looks good in that uniform. I must be careful because I've wondered, even after I was married, what might have been had Maurice and I hooked up."

"It's been years, Maurice."

"Yes, it has."

"You haven't changed a bit. So, you're a law officer now."

"Yeah, Mae. I can't allow you to drive in your condition."

She chuckled and said, "In what condition?"

"I'm not going to give you a ticket, but you have to leave the car. Park the car in this hotel parking lot. It'll be okay. I'll call you a cab and inform the hotel manager."

"Thank you, Officer Thompson." Mae was beaming as she pulled into the hotel parking lot.

Maurice walked to the car and said, "Let me have your address."

He gave her a sheet of paper and a pen. She wrote her information and handed it back to him. After reading it, he said, "Wow! You must be doing quite well; this is the posh part of town."

"It's just a house."

With raised brows he asked, "Is this your cell number?"

"Yeah, I thought you might want to call so we can catch up sometime."

"Are you sure, Mae? I don't want to cause you any problems."

"Sure, it's cool."

Maurice phoned for a cab. As they stood in front of her car and waited, they reminisced about high school, those they had not seen in years, and what had been happening personally for each of them since graduation. When the cab arrived, they hugged and gave each other a kiss on the cheek.

Maurice said as he escorted her to the car, "When's the best time to call you?"

"Can you call me around noon?"

"I can call tomorrow if that's okay."

Mae was thinking, "Say no, say no."

She smiled as she got into the cab and said, "Looking forward to hearing from you." Then she rode off.

CHAPTER SIX

T he next day, Mae's housekeeper knocked on the bedroom door and said, "Ms. Jones, the Reverend is on the phone."

"Thank you."

Mae picked up the phone and said, "What is it, Clyde?"

"I called you last night on your cell and on the home phone. Why didn't you answer?"

"My phone died, and I was out."

"Where were you?"

"If you were here, you would've known."

"Mae don't start with me this morning!"

"Are you coming home today?"

"Look, I'm not going to argue with you nor repeat myself!"

"Bye, Clyde."

Mae hung up the phone. Clyde called back numerous times, but she refused to answer.

At eleven a.m., the guard called and informed Mae of a guest at the gate. "Ms. Jones, Ms. Debra Porter is at the gate. Should I let her in?"

"Yes, by all means."

Mae thought, "Why is Debra here?"

The housekeeper let Debra in and said, "Have a seat. Ms. Jones will be with you in a minute."

"Thank you."

Mae tottered out of her bedroom. "Hey, Debbie, what's up? Is everything okay?"

"Everything's fine."

"What brings you by this morning?"

"Just out of concern for you." Debra was eyeing her friend skeptically.

"Excuse me?"

"You seemed a little out of it yesterday."

"What do you mean?"

"Well, for one thing, your eyes were bloodshot, you were talking louder than usual, and you sped off in your car like you were in the Indianapolis 500."

"Oh yeah, that reminds me. I hafta get my car. Would you drive me downtown?"

"Why is your car downtown? Mae, what's going on with you?"

"I ran into an old boyfriend last night."

"What?!"

"Don't worry. Nothin' happened."

"Then why don't you have your car?"

"It's a long story. I'll tell you about it later."

"Is everything okay with you and Clyde?"

Mae frowned, shook her head and said, "To be honest, no."

"What happened?"

"Ministry happened. I know you won't agree with this, but the pastoral ministry is where many marriages go to die."

"Mae, you can't mean that."

Mae peered into Debra's face. Her eyes were hard and icy.

Debra said, "I guess you do mean it."

"It wasn't always like this," said Mae. "Before Clyde became a pastor, we did a lot of things together. Now he's just too busy to take off even two weeks, claiming 'I can't miss consecutive Sundays. The church needs to see me'.

"As you know, when we started the church, there were only eight members. In three years, the church grew to over a thousand people. He didn't start out trying to build a so-called mega-church. He just wanted to do ministry and help people. I really believed God had put his approval on the ministry.

"After a while, I noticed Clyde began straying from the course and started putting more emphasis on the number of attendees and finances."

"Believe me," said Debra, "I know how easy it is to lose your focus."

Mae continued, "The church became more of a corporate empire than a ministry. Do you know what I mean? If you remember, in our first church's sanctuary, there was a neon sign on the wall above the platform that read, 'Jesus Christ Center of Attraction.'"

"Yeah, what happened to that sign? I liked it," said Debra.

"When we moved to a larger building, Clyde said it didn't go with the décor of the new sanctuary. I should've recognized that as an omen that his focus was deviating from the emphasis on a Christ-centered vision to a corporate-centered business.

"Because of the rapid growth of the church, Clyde was invited to many conferences to speak. At first, I traveled with him, but that kept me away from Geraldine and Mary too often. My mother was raising our daughters. So I told him, 'Clyde, I think I should stay home and be with our girls more often.'

"I thought he was gonna say, 'Yeah, you're right, and perhaps I shouldn't go as often either.' But he didn't."

"Did you tell him how you felt?"

"Yeah! I even suggested we get counseling. At first, he refused, then he relented. So, we got counseling from one of his preacher buddies."

"And how did that turn out?"

Mae scowled then exclaimed, "Are you kidding me! The cards were stacked against me from the start. His friend explained how important Clyde was to the body of Christ and that I should understand his special calling. Not once, did he say anything about Clyde's responsibility as a husband and a father. Nor how I shouldn't be raising our children by myself."

"What happened next?"

"I might as well be honest. After being left alone so much and him not paying attention to me when he was home, I sought out and enjoyed attention from other men." Mae's hands trembled.

"Mae, are you okay?"

"Give me a second, Debbie." As Mae tottered back to her bedroom to take a Valium, the phone rang. Mae checked the caller's ID. It was

Maurice, calling at noon on the dot. She knew if she answered in her current vulnerable state, they were going to get together.

––––––––

Mae was in the bedroom a long time, prompting Debra to call her. "Mae are you okay?"

No answer.

Debra called out again—still no response. She walked to the bedroom, called to Mae once more, then peeked in the door. Mae lay sprawled out on the bed. Her body was quaking and drenched with sweat.

Chapter Seven

Debra rushed to the bed, shook Mae's shoulders, and yelled, "Mae are you okay?! Mae! Mae!"

Mae stared at the ceiling, unresponsive.

Debra summoned the housekeeper and said, "Call 911 now! Do you have Pastor Jones's cell number?"

"Yes, ma'am."

"Call him and let him know Ms. Jones is going to the hospital." Before she could move, Debra shouted, "Hurry up!"

With trembling hands, the housekeeper dialed 911, then Clyde's cell phone and left a message. In a matter of minutes, the ambulance arrived and took Mae to the hospital.

Debra grabbed Mae's cell phone from her bed and brought it with the intent of calling one of Mae's family members. She followed the ambulance in her car to the hospital.

———

Debra's body shivered as she sat in the waiting room, rocking back and forth.

The Doctor came into the waiting room and asked Debra, "Are you related to Ms. Jones?"

"No, Doctor, I'm just a close friend."

"Do you know of any relatives we can call?"

With all the commotion, Debra forgot she had Mae's cell phone in her pocketbook.

"Doctor, I can't think right now, but her husband should be here a little later. He's coming from out of town. What's wrong with her?"

"I'm sorry, I can't divulge that information to a nonfamily member."

Three hours later, Clyde rushed into the hospital, panting and sweating. Barely catching his breath, he said, "Debra, what's going on?"

"She passed out on the bed. The doctor is waiting to see you."

After speaking with the doctor, Clyde came back into the waiting room, blinking back tears.

Debra, assuming the worse, asked, "Clyde, how is she?"

"The doctor said that she'll be all right."

Debra sighed a deep sigh of relief. "Oh, thank God. What's wrong with her?"

Clyde stared at Debra for a few seconds, stumbled over his response, and said, "She-she had a bad reaction from some pills." Then he broke down in tears.

"What pills?"

"She's been taking Valium because she's been restless and couldn't sleep." Then he shook his head and said, "I don't understand it. She has everything anyone could ever ask for."

"Clyde, as you know, my husband died almost a year ago and left me well-off. However, I'd trade it all to have my Joe back with me. Are you hearing me?"

"Debbie, I'm not sure if you've noticed, but I'm not dead yet."

Clyde's sarcastic retort did not go unnoticed by Debra. She was tempted to respond in kind but decided against it. Her brow furrowed, and she said, "Clyde, just because you're alive doesn't mean she has you. Just a question, brother pastor—how often do you leave Mae alone while you travel?"

"Debbie, I have to travel. The work of the Lord must go on. Mae knew that when she married me."

"Isn't being a good husband and father a part of the Lord's work too?" Debra countered. "I'm sure you don't want to lose your family."

"If I don't go to these conferences, I'd be blacklisted and wouldn't receive any more invites."

Debra's eyes widened and she said, "Clyde, I don't believe you just said that."

Just then the doctor approached him and said, "Reverend, you can see your wife now."

Clyde walked toward Mae's room with his shoulders slumped, and his eyes peered at the floor. He walked in the room, went to her bedside, bent over, kissed her on the cheek, and whispered in her ear, "Mae, how are you feeling, sweetheart?"

Mae, lying on her side with her back facing him, did not react.

"Can you hear me?" Still no reply.

Clyde stood over the bed and said, "C'mon, Mae. Let me see that pretty smile."

Mae's chest heaved.

"How are you feeling, Mae? Don't worry, baby, you're going to be just fine. I'm here for you, sweetheart, and I'm going to get you the best care money can buy."

Mae whipped her head around and said, "Clyde, go to hell! It's your fault I'm in this mess. You've ruined my life. Do you even know why I take Valium? It's because I'm trying to beat this addiction to alcohol. If you paid attention to me, you would've known that. It's incredible how you know what's goin' on everywhere else but can't see what's goin' on under your roof. Charity begins at home, Clyde. At home!"

Clyde stood straight up, his body stiffened, and he scowled. "Wha-what Mae? Did you just? Oh, never mind."

Mae turned on her side, her back to Clyde.

As Clyde turned and walked out of the room, he said, "I'll be back."

———

Debra was sitting on the couch in the waiting room. Clyde sat next to her, looked at the floor, shook his head, and said, "Mae blames me for her negative reaction to Valium."

Debra stared at Clyde. His voice cracked, and he said, "Did you know, along with everything else, that she's an alcoholic?"

"Clyde—"

"An alcoholic!"

"Clyde, listen to me. Listen to me."

Clyde was almost shouting as he repeated, "An al-co-*holic*!"

Matching his tone, Debra said, "Listen to me, Clyde!"

With his arms to his sides and his hands rolled into fists, he said, "What're my friends and the church members goin' to say?"

Debra interrupted. "Mae's not an alcoholic. And even if she is, this is between you and her. Clyde, she needs you now more than ever. Do you hear me?"

Clyde shook his head as he turned his gaze from Debra and said, "I don't understand it. I don't understand it."

Debra reached into her purse to get some tissues and felt Mae's cell phone. "Oh yeah, Clyde, I just remembered I have Mae's phone."

She removed the phone from her purse, and as she passed the phone to Clyde, it rang. Clyde's eyes narrowed as he read the name on the caller's ID. He answered the phone and grumbled, "May I help you?"

The voice on the other end said, "I'm sorry, I must have the wrong number."

"Do you want to speak to Mae?"

The person on the other end did not answer, but Clyde could still hear background noise, so he knew he did not hang up.

Before Clyde and Mae were married, they informed each other about all their former relationships, so nothing would arise later that the other was unaware of.

Clyde, knowing of Maurice, said, "Maurice, do you want to speak to my wife?!"

Maurice said, "I'm sorry, sir. I'm a police officer, and I wanted to make sure she recovered her vehicle."

"What about her car?"

"She was too sick to drive, so I suggested she leave her car and retrieve it the next day."

"Where's the car?"

Maurice gave him the address but didn't tell him the car was in the parking lot of a hotel.

"Thank you. Oh, and uh, by the way, Maurice, do not call this number again."

"No problem, sir."

Debra's countenance drooped, and she asked, "What was that about?"

"That was one of Mae's old boyfriends calling. That lying jerk claimed to be a police officer. He said Mae was sick and had to leave her car. Why was she with him? My wife's whoring around. I've never cheated on Mae, not even once."

"She ain't cheating on you, Clyde..."

"It all makes sense now! She accused me of cheating just the other night, trying to deflect onto me her adultery!"

"Clyde, stop it! She wants you and only you. Not just expensive stuff. You! And I know that for a fact!"

Clyde said nothing else and just stared at the wall.

Then Debra said, "I'm going in to see how Mae's doing."

Debra walked into the room, and Mae said, "I guess Clyde told you I'm a drunk, huh?"

"Listen, Mae, Clyde thinks you're messing around."

"What makes him think that?"

"An old boyfriend called your phone. I brought your phone with me to the hospital just in case I needed to reach one of your family members. I gave your phone to Clyde. Just as I handed the phone to him, someone named Maurice called. He claimed to be a cop. Clyde believes he was lying."

"What did Clyde say to him?"

"He told him to never call you again."

Mae sneered and explained the incident with Maurice.

"So then Maurice was telling the truth."

"Yeah, and like I said, nothing happened."

"I think Clyde's jealous," said Debra.

"Good. Maybe now he'll spend more time with me."

———

The doctor came into the waiting room and said, "Reverend, we're going to discharge your wife. When she gets home, she should go straight to bed and get plenty of rest."

"Doctor, is there something else I can do in the meantime?"

"Make sure she rests for now. If there're any complications, give me a call."

"Thank you, Doctor."

Clyde went to Mae's room and said in his most monotone voice, "Mae, you're being discharged."

"Clyde, I'll stay and help Mae get dressed."

"Thank you, Debbie."

Then Clyde, speaking in an insolent tone and with a raised eyebrow, said, "Oh, Debbie, would you mind following me in your car to my house, then afterward take me downtown to pick up Mae's car?"

"Sure, no problem."

He turned and went back to the waiting room.

Clyde sat there, motionless, peering straight ahead. Those in the waiting room observing Clyde's austere expression wondered if he'd received a negative medical diagnosis of a loved one, or if someone he knew just died. After only a glance, however, they looked away, fearing he would notice them staring.

As far as Clyde was concerned, those in the waiting room were insignificant, invisible beings possessing no form. Moreover, the only way they could be of any worth to him is if they could relieve his emotional agony.

Clyde made an audible sigh as he recalled simpler times before he and Mae were married. The carefree days of his youth, before he had a wife nagging him all the time. 'You travel too much, and when are you coming home?' There was no arguing, fussing or fighting every time he had to leave town.

———

In the room, Debra sighed and said to Mae, "You said something at the house just before you went into your bedroom."

Mae, sitting on the side of the bed, said, "What did I say?"

"You said you enjoyed getting attention from other men. What did you mean by that?"

"Oh, nothing. I would just go to a makeup counter at the mall, get made-up and flirt with my eyes a little. Sometimes the men would look at me and throw a wink and a smile my way. Believe me, sis, that's all. Why do you ask?"

"I was just wondering."

Mae giggled and said, "Girl, I ain't about to get involved with anyone— at least not in this town, anyway." She paused, gazed at Debra for a few seconds, her face slowly forming a grin. "Now, Maurice, on the other hand, is a different story."

"Mae, don't even joke like that."

Mae gazed straight ahead and continued to smile.

She finished getting dressed, and they walked into the waiting room. Mae's hair was disheveled and her eyes puffy. She said to Clyde, "I'm ready."

As they walked to the elevator, Clyde reached for Mae's hand, but her hand went limp at his touch. Despite this, Clyde continued holding on.

Debra followed them home, and Clyde escorted Mae inside, helped her into bed, then left, getting into Debra's car. He gave her the address to where Mae's car was located. As Debra drove, she glanced at Clyde, trying to read his expression. Clyde kept his eyes forward and murmured to himself.

He recognized Mae's car in the parking lot as they approached the hotel and shouted, "What's this? Stop the car!"

Debra jerked her head around, looked at Clyde, and asked, "What is what?"

Clyde jumped out of the car before it came to a full stop, then rushed to Mae's car and said, "I have to go. Thanks, Debbie."

Clyde sped off, cutting Debra off in the process. She slammed her brakes to avoid hitting Mae's car.

"Clyde!" Debra shouted, leaning on her horn. He kept driving, not bothering to look back. When he arrived at his front door, he turned the engine off and stared out the windshield. The corners of his mouth were turned down, his brow gathered, and his nostrils flared as he took long, deep breaths. Clyde decided to call a fellow minister on his cell phone.

"Arthur."

"Hey, Preacher. What're you up to?"

"Just sitting here in front of my house in my car, trying to decide whether I'm going inside or not."

"Yeah, it gets like that sometimes."

"I don't think you understand; I mean, I'm trying to decide if I'm *ever* going inside again."

"Clyde, talk to me. What's going on?"

"Mae's having an affair with an old boyfriend."

Skeptical of the claim, Arthur asked, "How do you know that?"

"I had her cell phone when he called. I just came back from retrieving her car from downtown in a hotel parking lot."

"How did you know to look for it there?"

"He told me! I need to get away for a few days before I do something I'll regret."

"Clyde, aren't you supposed to be at a conference this week?"

"Yeah, I was, but Mae got sick, so I came home."

"How is she?"

"The doctor says she'll be fine."

"How much longer will the conference be?"

"For my part, just two more days. I was going to stay for the rest of the conference to hear some of the other presenters but..."

"Then maybe you should go back to the conference for the two days before you do something rash. Where're the girls?"

"They're on a college tour."

"Then you're good to go. Look, Clyde, everyone has problems. Even those you least expect. What I'm about to say may help you, but you must keep this to yourself."

"I will."

"Everyone knows how in love Morgan and Lorraine appeared to be, right? Well, in his diary, he confessed to having an affair with a church member."

"Who told you that?"

"I read it myself."

Clyde was quick to dismiss Arthur's claim. "Doc, I'm going to go inside and get ready to go back to the conference." He added coolly, "Thanks for listening."

"Anytime, Preacher."

Clyde exited the car and stood at the door for two minutes with his hand on the doorknob. Then he took a deep breath before entering and walked to the bedroom, where Mae was asleep.

"Listen, Mae, we have to talk!" he shouted.

Mae woke, startled by Clyde's voice. "Clyde, what... what, do you want?"

"We hafta talk."

"About what?" she asked in a raspy voice.

"I know you and Maurice are having a sexual affair!"

She sucked her teeth and said, "No, we're not."

"Why was your car at the hotel then?"

"Because that's where I left it." Her face twisted and she fumed. "Clyde, you have some nerve coming in here and accusing me of an affair. I know you're scheduled to speak at the conference for three days but were going to stay for seven. Were you going to spend time with your woman? Also, the other week when you were out of town, I didn't tell you, but I called the hotel where you were supposed to be staying, and they said you never checked in."

"I didn't do anything!" Clyde shouted at the top of his lungs.

"And neither did I! So, where were you then?"

Both of their voices echoed throughout the house, in earshot of anyone that happened to be passing by outside.

Clyde, concerned that the live-in housekeeper, who was a member of his church, was in her bedroom and possibly listening, lowered his voice. "Look, look, I have to go. We'll finish this when I return."

Mae's eyes widened. "Where do you think you're going?"

"I'm going back to the conference. I'm scheduled to minister tomorrow. The doctor said you'll be fine, so I don't see any reason for me to stay. Stay at your mother's house until I get back."

"Clyde, I didn't marry my mother. I married you. If you take your ass back to that conference, I'm through with you!"

Clyde knew Mae well and realized this was no idle threat. Her measured tone and the intense look in her eyes convinced him she meant every word.

CHAPTER EIGHT

C lyde walked into the kitchen, his face contorted. He was pacing back and forth, massaging his temples as he mumbled to himself. "Mae has some serious control issues. She's always doing this. If I give in to her, it will make me appear weak."

Clyde got a bottle of water from the refrigerator, sat at the table and continued grumbling. "Mae can be such a pain at times."

He opened the bottle, took a sip, put the bottle on the table, then clutched his head with both hands and said to himself, "I don't want to lose my wife. I just wish she wasn't so controlling. But Lord, you know I love her. If she leaves, what are the people in the church going to say, especially those whose marriages I've saved by the grace of God?"

Just then the phone rang. It was one of the officials of the conference.

"Pastor Jones, are you coming back to the conference? Brother, the half has not been told of the many testimonies we've received from your message yesterday morning. You indeed have a special gift. No one else can do what you do."

As he was talking, Clyde recalled a message he preached a year before entitled: "Obey God, No Matter the Cost."

After the phone call, Clyde said to himself, "I *must* do the will of God, regardless of what it will cost me."

Clyde's mind was made up. He went back into the bedroom. Mae was sitting up in the bed, her eyebrows drawn together and her mouth pouting. Clyde folded his arms, sneered at his wife, and said, "Okay Mae, what do you want from me? Let me know, and I promise I'll listen."

What persuaded Clyde to stay with Mae instead of going back to the conference was, while talking to the official he thought, "The officials of the conference are only interested in knowing when I would be returning. He did not inquire if Mae was better, worse, or—God forbid—if she died.

"Those guys don't care about me; all they want is my gift."

Mae responded, "Clyde do I have to tell you? By now you should've figured it out."

Clyde fumed, "Just tell me, Mae."

"Okay Clyde, we need counseling."

Raising his voice, he said, "For what?! Sorry, Mae I didn't mean to yell. I did promise to listen. Okay, if you think we need counseling, I'll call Pastor—"

"No!" she protested. "I want an unbiased, objective view, from someone who neither of us knows."

"Mae, that's what I'm talking about. Why do you think you always hafta control everything?"

Mae, matching his rant, said, "You chose the last counselor, and all he did was council me, and never once did he give you any advice or suggestions on how you can make this marriage better. And I didn't say a thing. If we're going to go to counseling, this time it's going to be on *my* terms."

In the absence of a rebuttal, he stared at Mae and started getting ready for bed. After five minutes, he said, "Mae, do you have someone in mind?"

"No, I don't. I'll ask around tomorrow."

Clyde got into bed, pulled the cover over his shoulders, and closed his eyes with his back facing Mae.

Mae said, "Clyde, you ain't going to sleep yet. We still have an issue we haven't resolved. Where were you when you didn't check in to the hotel?"

Clyde turned around, faced Mae, and sighed. "Pastor Hayes insisted I stay at his home, being it was my first time in his town. He said he would be insulted if I didn't. So, I stayed with him."

"Why didn't you tell me that?"

"I guess I should've, but if you needed me, I figured you'd call my cell phone. By the way, why did you call the hotel?"

"I thought you were lying to me and were in another town with someone else."

Clyde sat up in the bed, widened his eyes, and asked, "Why would you think that?"

71

"Well, for one thing, you're gone quite often, and when you return you don't reach for me."

"Mae, I was tired, and I have a lot on my mind."

"You used to reach for me all the time and tell me how beautiful I am. I guess I'm not beautiful to you any longer."

"It has nothing to do with you. As I said, I have a lot on my mind. Not to change the subject, but are you ever going to tell me why your car was in a hotel parking lot?"

Mae explained that she was pulled over by the police and that was why her car was at the hotel.

With an incredulous stare, Clyde said, "And the cop just happened to be Maurice."

Mae raised one eyebrow and nodded her head.

Clyde's eyes bulged, then he said, "You were driving drunk!"

"Clyde, I'm not an alcoholic. I apologize; I shouldn't have told you that. I did it to get your attention. I've noticed when others call you with a problem, you give them your undivided attention. So, I figured if I had a problem, you'd give me, if not the same attention, at least a little."

"Then why were you speeding?"

"I'd finished off an energy drink, and you know how hyper and jittery I become after drinking high doses of caffeine."

"If you knew that, why did you drink it?"

"I was lonely and depressed."

"Why didn't you say something to me?"

Mae scowled and said, "Clyde, are you serious?! Don't you remember me beggin' you to come home?"

"Yeah, but you didn't say you were depressed."

"Answer me this, Clyde. Why were you going to stay at the conference after you were finished preaching?"

"I wanted to hear the other speakers."

"But you were only here for two weeks last month. Why wouldn't you just come home?"

"I just wanted to hear the other preachers. What's wrong with that?"

"Damnit, Clyde, you were only home for two weeks last month. What's the matter with you?!"

"Mae, why do you have to curse to make your point?"

Mae sucked her teeth and rolled her eyes.

"I don't understand what the problem is," said Clyde.

Mae sighed and said, "And that's what makes it so pathetic." She turned off the light on the nightstand, yanked the covers over her shoulder, turned her back to him, and said, "Good night."

Clyde mumbled as he turned over. "I don't understand you; I really don't."

As they lay beneath the covers, his foot inadvertently touched her leg. Mae could not imagine anything more cringe-worthy than Clyde touching her. She snatched her leg away and moved her body to the edge of the bed.

Mae tossed around in the bed and made a deep moan.

"What's wrong Mae?"

"Nothing. I'm fine," she said as she sniffled.

"Mae, what's wrong?"

"I said nothing's wrong."

Mae reached over to the night table next to the bed, and without turning on the light, she opened the drawer and grabbed a bottle of pills.

Clyde, hearing the rattling of pills, asked, "What's that?"

"Just something to help me sleep."

Clyde turned on the light from the night table on his side and saw Mae opening a bottle of Valium.

"Mae, you just got out of the hospital. You shouldn't be taking those pills."

"Leave me alone. I need to sleep. Don't act like you're all that concerned about me. The only thing you're concerned about is *your* church."

Clyde reached over her and grabbed the bottle. Mae screamed, "Leave me alone, Clyde, and give me the bottle! I ain't kiddin'!"

Mae tried grabbing the bottle from Clyde, but he kept switching the container from one hand to the other. During the scuffle, the bottle fell on the floor, spilling the pills.

"Look what you've done!" fumed Mae. Then she slapped his face, her head shaking, burst into tears and shouted, *"I hate you!"*

Clyde knew if he reciprocated with a slap she would not soon recover from the blow. So he held her wrists.

Mae struggled and yelled, "Let me go! Let me go, damn you!"

Clyde continued holding her. She squirmed for several more seconds, then realizing she was no match for his strength, she composed herself and said, "Clyde, I see you want to be immature about this. Would you let my wrists go now, please?"

As soon as he let her go, he retrieved the pills from the floor and put them in his night table drawer.

"You happy now?" asked Mae as she stood fixing her nightgown and walked toward the bathroom.

"Mae, I'm sorry. Come back to bed, please."

Mae turned, bowed, and said, "Oh, holy apostle, please grant me passage to relieve myself."

Clyde leered at Mae but did not speak. After she shut the door to the bathroom, he tiptoed to the door and was about to put his ear to it. Just as he approached the door, she opened it.

Clyde stumbled over his words and said, "Ar-are you finished?"

Mae said nothing and went back to bed. Clyde went into the bathroom, closed the door, and searched around. Clyde was not sure what he was looking for or what he might find, but he could not shake his suspicion Mae was hiding something.

He finally gave up and went to bed. He eased into bed and touched Mae on her shoulder. Mae grumbled, "What is it now, Clyde?"

"Mae, we need to talk."

"About what?" she asked indifferently.

"Mae, I want us to work this out."

Mae spun around, stared into Clyde's face, and said, "If we don't, I want out of this farce of a marriage."

Clyde exhaled, turned over, and gazed into the blackness.

CHAPTER NINE

E arly the next morning, Clyde's phone rang. He looked at the caller's ID, then waited for the phone to ring five times before he answered. He took a deep breath, then said, "Hey, Arthur."

"Hi, Clyde. How did things work out last night? Did you go back to the conference?"

"No."

"Why not?"

"I wasn't up to it."

"So, how're things with you and Mae?"

Clyde coolly responded, "Fine."

"See, I told you she wasn't messin' around."

Then Arthur chuckled and said, "I'm glad things worked out. After speaking with you last night, I thought that you might go postal or something."

"No, I'm good. Arthur, I've got to go."

"Okay, just checking up on you. Have a good day."

"Yeah, you too. Bye."

After they hung up, Arthur thought, "Why is Clyde so abrupt with me now after baring his soul last night?"

————

That afternoon, Arthur called Peter. "Preacher, have you heard from Carl? Are we going to get back to the reading of the diary?"

"I haven't heard from him today. I suppose he'll get back to us sometime later."

"Peter, what's your take on what he's read so far?"

"I don't know, Arthur. I..."

"I mean what do you think of Morgan's extracurricular activity?"

"You mean with the Dark Lady?"

"Yeah."

"Well... I think we shouldn't accuse someone before knowing all the facts."

"C'mon Doc, what else could it be?"

"I don't know. Hold on, Arthur, Carl's calling me."

Peter switched over to Carl. "Carl, what's up?"

"Peter, I think I'm going to stop reading the diary."

"How come?"

"I guess I'm having a crisis of conscience."

"Why?"

"I don't feel comfortable reading it at all, let alone to others."

"Wait a second, Carl, I have someone on hold. Don't hang up."

Peter switched over to Arthur. "Listen, Preacher, I have to call you back."

"What's going on?"

"I said, I'll call you back."

Peter switched back to Carl and said, "Okay, I'm back. Carl, be honest with me. Does this have anything to do with me telling Arthur about the diary?"

"Like I said, Peter, I probably shouldn't be reading it myself."

"Are you still going to let Bishop Howard read it?"

"I don't know."

"Didn't you say that it would bring him closure? And besides, Lorraine needs closure too. There may be something in the diary that will help them cope with the suicide."

"Peter, you have a good point but..."

"Carl, I have a feeling you're not being straight with me. What's the real reason you don't want to read the diary?"

Carl paused for a moment before he answered, then said, "Man, I'm pissed! Morgan and I were closer than brothers. Why didn't he tell *me* what was going on?!"

Carl began sobbing profusely. Afterward, he collected himself and said, "I'm sorry, Peter, but I lost an irreplaceable lifelong friend."

"It's okay, Carl, I understand. When you're ready to get back to the diary, let me know."

"I need to think about it."

Carl paused for a few moments, then said, "Peter, how's your schedule tomorrow?"

"I'll make time."

"I'll call you tomorrow and let you know what I've decided."

"Sounds good. Talk with you tomorrow."

"Okay."

Immediately after Peter hung up, Arthur called.

"Peter, what's going on with Carl? What did he say?"

"He's having reservations."

"You mean he *still* feels bad about reading the diary?"

"Arthur, Carl's devastated. When I speak to him tomorrow, I'll get back to you."

"No, I'll call you. You may forget."

Peter chuckled and said, "Okay, Preacher."

———

The next day, Carl called. "Peter, I thought about what you said concerning Lorraine and the Bishop, and it makes sense. There's some work being done at the church tomorrow, and I have to be there. They should be finished by six. I can meet with you then at my church."

"Carl, I noticed you didn't mention Arthur."

"Yeah, I know." Carl took a deep breath and said, "Okay... bring him too."

"I'll see you tomorrow."

———

Late afternoon the next day Arthur had not called. Peter thought, "This is not like Arthur. He would've called by now." Peter called

Arthur several times, but each time the phone went directly to voice mail. Concerned, he called Arthur's home phone. Arthur's wife Angela answered.

"Wright's residence."

"Hi, Angela, this is Peter. Is Arthur around?"

"No, he said he was going to be at the church office all day."

"Thanks, Angela, I'll call him there."

Peter called the church and Arthur's secretary said, "I'm sorry, Reverend. Pastor Wright called and said he will not be in the office today. Perhaps if you call his cell, you might reach him."

"Okay, thank you."

Peter didn't bother calling his cell phone again but left for Carl's church. When he arrived at the church, he was met by a worker and escorted to Carl's office.

He entered the office, greeted Carl with a smile, shook his hand and said, "How are you, Pastor?"

"I'm fine, Reverend. Where's, uh...?"

"He was supposed to call me but, um..."

Carl laughed and said, "Maybe you'd better check the morgue."

"Knowing Arthur, he's probably counseling one of his ministers or something like that."

"Oh well," said Carl, "let's get to it."

Carl reached into his desk drawer, retrieved the diary, and flipped through the pages until he got to where he'd left off. Then he said, "Okay, here it is."

> *Things I took for granted, like the support of the church board, ground into dust when the church was purchasing property across town for a youth center. The board and I omitted to check the zoning laws before putting down a nonrefundable fifty-thousand-dollar deposit. Later, we found out the area was not zoned for a youth center, and we lost our deposit.*
>
> *The board had voted unanimously to purchase the property. Yet in the business meeting with the church, those cowards sat there, not owning up to their involvement with the decision to purchase the property. Deacon Williams, who behind closed doors was my strongest supporter, stood, pointed his finger at me and ranted, "Pastor, it appears you don't know what you're doing!" Following his lead, Mary Stewart—whose entire year's offering amounted to less than one hundred dollars—raged, 'You're too careless with our monies.' Then she mumbled, 'Black folks don't know nothin' 'bout business.'*
>
> *Meanwhile, the board sat quietly as the people took me to task for losing their money.*
>
> *I need to get away from all of this. I have a reserve saved but not enough to retire. Being the church's founder, much of my*

funds are wrapped up in this church. I should have taken the church that was offered to me years ago instead of pioneering a church. If I had, I'd be well vested by now and probably able to retire.

All of the times I've given up my salary to pay the church's bills while everyone else was paid. The church promised to pay me back years ago. No one appreciates all I have done and sacrificed. From now on, I am going to take care of me and mine.

Tonight, I took the long way home and to further delay arriving home, I stopped and got something to eat. I dread going home because I know Lorraine wants to talk to me about not keeping my appointments with the members.

The president of the youth auxiliary has been calling the church office every day, attempting to get an audience with me about a fundraiser they want to do for the church. And I've been avoiding him for three weeks. When I see the president of the youth auxiliary in church, I put him off by telling him, "I'll get back to you." The truth is, I don't want to be bothered. He wants to ask me whether they should have a concert with guest choirs or just our church choirs. I have no idea what to tell him. God help me, I cannot focus.

The last thing I wanted to do was talk about it with Lorraine. When she spoke to me, I made up an excuse to go to another part of the house. She followed me and insisted I speak to her about it. I burst into a rage and said, 'Lorraine, don't you understand that I just want to be left alone?!'

Then she said, 'We need to communicate, Morgan. Let me know what you're feeling. I'm your wife.' She kept talking, and I went into my study and blasted the music on my radio. She could not compete with the commotion and left my study.

Lorraine and I have not been intimate lovers for more than a year. God bless her, she's endured a lot, and I love her and want her to stay, but I don't know how long she's going to put up with this, along with my other issues. I'm imprisoned. God do you hear me?!

I feel trapped and smothering in a six-by-six foot box. My heart beats erratically at times, accompanied by pressure in my chest. My father died of a heart attack at fifty-five years old. I'm a mere ten years away from fifty-five. I am built just like my father and will almost certainly suffer his fate.

Oh, how I yearn to have one tranquil sleep, or perhaps remain poised in the image of death until God calls me in the resurrection and rouses me from my slumber. For me to sleep is much better than this life.

Is my idea of God a false one? Am I deluded into believing in a Higher Power that does not exist? Or am I losing my mind?

Suddenly, there was a knock at the office door. Carl closed the diary and said, "Come in."

The door opened; it was the church's janitor. "Pastor, I'm about to lock up. Do you have your key?"

"No, I don't. I mistakenly left it at home." Carl looked at Peter and said, "Preacher, we're going to have to do this another time. I'll call you."

Peter suggested, "We can go to the restaurant and continue."

"I told Trisha I won't be out late and…"

"No problem, Doc. I hear you."

After Peter got into his car, he called Arthur's cell. When there was no answer, he called Arthur's home.

"Hi Angela, this is Peter. Has Arthur returned yet?"

"Yeah, did you reach him at church?"

Measuring his response, Peter said, "Um, no, he had stepped out of the office."

"He's been upstairs in the bedroom ever since he arrived home. Do you want me to call him to the phone?"

"Yes, please, if you don't mind."

Angela came back to the phone a few moments later and said, "He said he'll call you later tonight."

"Is he okay?"

"I think so. He didn't say he was sick or anything."

"Okay, thanks. Goodnight, Angela."

"Goodnight."

Arthur, secluded in his bedroom with his head in his hands and his eyes overflowing with tears, lamented, "God, I've failed you again. *Please* forgive me! I know that I've promised you over and over that I'd never fail again. You know my heart, Lord. I beg you, *please* don't judge me by my failed promises."

Angela proceeded upstairs and, hearing a faint sound emanating from Arthur's bedroom, knocked on the door and asked, "Arthur, are you okay?"

Through the closed door he said, "Yeah."

"Don't forget to call Peter."

"Yeah, yeah, okay."

She retired to her bedroom.

CHAPTER TEN

Arthur called Peter the next day, and Peter asked, "Hey, Preacher, what happened to you yesterday?"

"I'm sorry, Doc. I got tied up at church in counseling, and it took longer than I expected. You know how it is sometimes."

"Arthur, I called the church, and your secretary said you were not there."

"Oh, oh yeah; she didn't see me come in. I came into my office through the back entrance. She told me you called, but I had to leave in a hurry. I had an appointment and was running late. Then I got so involved that I forgot to get back to you. Sorry, Preacher."

"I was just wondering because you said you were going to call me and…"

"Yeah, I know, but as I said, I got caught up into something and forgot to call. Did you meet with Carl?"

"Yeah."

"Anything new?"

"Just that he felt betrayed by some members within his church."

"What about the Dark Lady? Any mention of her?"

"Arthur, why are you so obsessed with the Dark Lady?"

"I'm not obsessed."

"Then why do you keep bringing her up?"

"I just mentioned her twice. Don't make it seem as though that's all I talk about."

"Uh-huh. To answer your question, no, it didn't mention the Dark Lady."

"Okay, that's all you had to say. When're you and Carl going to meet again?"

"Look... uh, I don't know... I have to go. I promised Yolanda I would take her to breakfast at this fancy restaurant she's been dying to try."

"Call me when you set a time when you and Carl will be meeting."

"Yeah, yeah."

As soon as Peter hung up the phone, it rang. Peter picked up the phone paused for a few moments, then said, "Okay, tell her I'll be there as soon as I can." He hung up, turned to Yolanda, and said, "Babe, can I have a rain check? I must go. There's an emergency."

Yolanda's nostrils flared and she said, "What emergency?"

"The call was from Millie; Sister Emma called the church and said her husband is drunk and becoming violent again. I'm going to their house to see what's going on."

"Didn't he take a swing at you the last time you were there when you tried talking some sense into him? You don't need to go there again."

Peter shook his head, looked Yolanda in the face, and said, "Yolanda, you don't understand the heart of a pastor."

"I may not understand the heart of a pastor, but I do know what makes sense. And I know that it doesn't make sense to go over there and risk harm unnecessarily."

Peter put his right hand on her shoulder, looked her in the eyes, and said, "Yolanda, let me do my job, please."

Yolanda thrust his hand from her shoulder and shouted, "That's not your job! That's your passion, and you need to recognize the difference!"

Peter's brow furrowed. "What do you suggest I tell her then?"

"Tell her to call the police. Maybe if they bop him upside his head a few times with their nightsticks, he'll stop his nonsense. I know Millie's been your secretary for only a month, but she needs to screen your calls better."

"I can't back out now. I've already committed myself."

Yolanda closed her eyes for a moment, exhaled and said, "Peter, help me understand something. You promised to take me to the restaurant two weeks ago and didn't. But when Sister Emma calls, you are more than willing to..."

"Okay, okay, Yolanda, you've made your point." Peter mumbled under his breath, "Now how should I word this?"

Yolanda overheard him, took a deep breath, rolled her eyes upward, and said, "Tell her the truth, that you have a previous engagement. My goodness. I don't understand what's so difficult."

Peter sat on a chair in the kitchen and stared at the clock on the wall as though its digits were a Magic Eight-ball that would reveal to him the correct course of action.

Yolanda stood over Peter, staring down into his face. Then she picked up the phone and handed it to him. Peter hesitated.

"Do you want *me* to make the call?" she asked.

"No... no, I got this."

Peter called and explained, "Sister Emma, I will not be able to come presently because I have a previous appointment."

"Pastor Austin, can you come later today? It doesn't have to be right now."

"I won't be able to do it later, either. I think it's time to find you a safe place to live. It doesn't appear that your husband's going to stop his violent behavior. I'll have my secretary call Brother Hayes. He's in charge of the shelters for battered women."

She sniffled and said, "No... no, that's okay, Pastor. I wanted *you* to come. But if you can't do it, you can't do it."

"Are you sure, sister? I'm concerned that he may hurt you one day."

"Yeah, I'm sure. Have a good day, Pastor."

"If you change your mind, call the church. I'll tell Millie to expect your call."

————

Emma hung up without saying another word. Afterward, she called one of the members of the church.

"Hello, Kimberly."

"Hey, Emma, what's going on?"

"You know what we talked about before?"

"You mean about Pastor Austin not being accessible to the members?"

"Yeah." Then in a gruff voice, she said, "Well, I asked him to come and talk to my husband, and he said that he's too busy to be bothered. But he ain't too busy to count my tithes though. The litmus test of a good pastor, for me, is if he can't be there when I need him, then what good is he? I'm thinking of changing my membership and joining Mount Moriah Church."

"Emma, calm down."

"I'll call you later and let you know what I'm gonna do."

"Okay, I'll speak with you later."

After she hung up, she called Mount Moriah, a church in her neighborhood that she visited on occasion. She made an appointment for that afternoon with the Pastor, Jeremiah Riley.

Emma was led into the office by his secretary, where she smiled and greeted the Pastor.

"Hello, Pastor Riley, my name is Emma Richards."

Pastor Riley was six-foot-three and dark-skinned with salt-and-pepper hair and a thick jet-black mustache. He leaned back in his chair behind his desk with his hands folded in his lap and asked, "How may I help you, Sister Richards?"

"Please, just call me Emma."

"Okay."

Then she broke down in tears and said, "I need help. Frank, my husband, is a drunkard, and I need to talk to a pastor."

"Are you a member of a church?"

"Yes, I am."

"What about your pastor?"

"I called him, but he's always too busy to see me."

His eyes narrowed, and he grumbled, "That doesn't make sense; counseling the parishioners is part of every pastor's job."

"I wouldn't lie to you, Pastor."

"No, it's not that I don't believe you; I'm just amazed. What church do you attend?"

"Resurrection Temple."

"Oh yeah, from the other side of town. Pastor Austin has preached for me a time or two."

"When I first started attending there after leaving my former church, he seemed be available to the members. Now that the church has grown, he no longer has time to minister to his congregation. I've spoken to several members, and many of them are thinking of leaving."

"What about you?"

"I feel the Lord's leading me here. I'll be here next Sunday with a friend who is also thinking of leaving Resurrection Temple."

"Sister, I would like to meet with you and your husband. Do you think he'll come with you on Sunday?"

Emma smiled and said, "If I tell him I'm not going to Resurrection Temple, he just might come with me."

"When you get here on Sunday, tell my secretary you have a special appointment."

Emma exhaled and said, "Pastor Riley, I feel better already. Thank you so much."

Pastor Riley rose from his seat, walked around the desk, hugged Emma, and said, "God bless you, sister."

Emma left the office and called Kimberly as soon as she got in her car.

"Hey, girl."

"Hey, Emma, are you okay?"

"Yeah, I met with the Pastor of Mount Moriah this afternoon, and I'm going to visit on Sunday. I believe the Lord's leading me to join, and besides that, he's one good-looking brother. If I wasn't married..."

"Emma!"

"Girl, I'm just kidding. You should come too."

"I can't. The choir's singing on Sunday, and I have a lead part in the song."

"Kimberly, they're using you, exploiting your gift. I'm in the choir too, but I must obey God. You need to go where you can be free to worship without being harassed. Didn't you tell me that the choir director made a pass at you? If his wife finds out about it, she's going to blame you. You've been at Resurrection Temple since you were very young, and you know better than me that no one's gonna defend your reputation when the feathers hit the fan."

"Emma, I told you he smiles at me a lot; I didn't say he made a pass at me."

"Why do you think you get to lead all those songs?"

"I only lead two songs."

"Uh-huh. Open your eyes, Kimberly. You don't need your name tarnished."

"Emma, like I said—"

"Frank's calling me. I'll call you back later."

"Okay."

————

On Sunday morning, Emma called Kimberly and said, "Are you still coming with me to Mount Moriah?"

"I never said I was going with you."

"Just come this one time with me; I need your support. Frank's in a drunken stupor and is in no condition to go to church."

"I told you I have to sing in the choir."

"By the time the choir performs, Mount Moriah's service will be over, and we'll make it before the choir sings. Come on, Kimberly, I need you. This is a friend emergency."

"Okay, but I *must* get to Resurrection Temple before the choir sings."

"You will; I promise. I'll be there in twenty minutes to pick you up."

Emma arrived at Kimberly's home twenty minutes later. As Kimberly entered the car, Emma said, "Thank you, Kimberly; you're a real friend. Not like others in the church that claim to be a friend." Emma looked her up and down, smiled and remarked, "By the way, you're looking good, girl."

"Thank you." Then Kimberly scowled at Emma and said in a stern voice, "Emma, remember, *I must* get to the church in time to sing!"

"Don't worry. I'll tell you what, if the service goes longer than expected, we'll leave before it's over. Okay?"

When they entered the church, the pastor's secretary recognized Emma from her visit the other day. She approached them and said, "Sister Richards, the pastor asked me to seat you in the reserved area he has for special guests."

Then Emma said, "I have a friend with me."

"Yes, I know, the pastor mentioned you would. There're two seats reserved for you."

An usher escorted Emma and Kimberly to the reserved seating area. The Pastor came to the podium, his face beaming, and said, "We have a couple of special visitors here today. Sister Emma and your guest, stand up please. They're here this morning to become members of the Mount Moriah family. Give them a hand, everyone."

The audience gave a rousing applause.

When they sat, Kimberly looked at Emma, partially covering her mouth with her hand, and whispered, "What is he talking about? I ain't gonna join this church. Did you tell him that I was gonna join?"

Emma whispered back, "No, I didn't tell him that."

"Then why did he say that?"

Emma shrugged her shoulders and said, "I don't know."

After he finished his sermon, he said, "Sister Emma, I want you and your guest to see me in my office after service about your new membership."

Kimberly looked at her watch, gasped and said, "Emma, I have to go. I can't stay to see him."

"Kimberly, it shouldn't take long."

Kimberly's eyes bulged, and she ranted, "I've got to go. Do you see the time?"

Emma kept looking forward and did not respond. When Kimberly stood to leave, the Pastor announced, "The doors of the church are now open. Sister Emma, come up front and bring your guest with you."

Addressing the audience, he said, "I love it when the Lord leads individuals to join Mount Moriah, as with Sister Emma and..." He paused and looked at Kimberly and asked, "What's your name, sister?"

Kimberly was caught off guard and, too nervous to admit in front of one hundred congregants that she was not joining, answered, "Kimberly Townsend."

Then he said, "Sister Richards and Sister Townsend are coming by 'Christian experience.' Let's give them a warm welcome and the right hand of fellowship."

The officials of the church lined up to shake Emma's and Kimberly's hands, their faces beaming. Kimberly, grinding her teeth, curled her lips and thought, "I don't believe Emma did this to me!"

CHAPTER ELEVEN

After the church service ended, Emma and Kimberly stood outside Pastor Riley's study waiting to be called into his office. Kimberly's eyes shifted impatiently between her watch and a clock on the wall. "Emma, this is taking too long. I must go *now*!" she fumed. "I won't be able to get to the church on time unless you drive me."

"You heard what the Pastor said; he wants to see us. I have to be obedient."

Kimberly's eyes bulged and she ranted, "Emma, I told you I had to get to the church! Why are you doing this?"

Emma's brows came together, and matching Kimberly's rage, she said, "How was I supposed to know that he wanted to see us? You act as though I did this on purpose!"

Kimberly sucked her teeth and was turning to walk out the door when Pastor Riley's secretary beckoned them. "Sisters, the Pastor will see you now."

When they walked into his office, he smiled and said, "I'm sorry it took so long, but I had some important business, and it took longer than I expected. So, talk to me, sisters, what made you join Mount Moriah?"

Kimberly's mouth pouted as she took deep breaths and stared at Emma.

Emma said, "Well, Pastor, as I told you before, I feel led by the Lord to join this ministry."

"And you, Sister Kimberly?"

Before she could respond, Emma added, "Pastor Riley, I wasn't totally forthcoming with you the other day. I left Resurrection Temple because I don't feel comfortable there anymore." Then she broke down in tears. Pastor Riley reached for a tissue out of the dispenser on his desk that was there for such occasions. He handed her a tissue and said, "What's wrong, Sister Emma?"

Emma stared at the floor and said, "Kimberly, I know how much you love Pastor Austin and how close you are to him and his wife. I didn't want to tell you this, but one time he came to my house unannounced when Frank wasn't there." She rubbed her finger over her lips and continued. "At first, he talked to me about Frank, then the next thing I knew, he grabbed me and tried kissing me. I had to fight him off."

Kimberly and Reverend Riley stared at her with their mouths parted.

Emma's head remained bowed as she glanced out the corner of her eyes to view their reaction.

———

Meanwhile, at Resurrection Temple, the choir was about to sing the song Kimberly was meant to lead. The director was poised on the stage to direct the song but did not realize Kimberly was missing.

Then the MC announced, "And now a selection from the choir."

The seventy-voiced choir, seated on the choir stand behind the ministers, stood all at once like a well-trained army. The musician played the introduction as they waited for Kimberly to take her place at the microphone. When she did not approach the mic, the director mouthed to the musician, "Where's Kimberly?"

He shrugged his shoulders and shook his head. The director scanned the choir, then the audience, in search of Kimberly.

The musician played the introduction a second time. Then the director signaled the musician to play another song. Grinding his teeth, he pointed at another member of the choir and directed her to the mic.

———————

Back at Mount Moriah, Kimberly's eyes overflowed with tears as she embraced Emma. Then she said, "Emma, why didn't you tell me this before?"

"Like I said, Kimberly, I didn't know how to tell you. I know that you've been a member there since you were a young girl."

"Let me say this, ladies..." said Pastor Riley

Emma, interrupting him, pleaded, "Pastor, please don't mention this to Pastor Austin."

"Don't worry. Your secret's safe with me. I was just going to say these preachers are going to answer to God for their shameful conduct."

Then Emma took Kimberly by her hands, stared her in the face and said, "Kimberly, I feel that God wants you to join Mount Moriah too."

Pastor Riley chimed in, "I feel the anointing. I *know* this is God." Then the pastor summoned his secretary. "Sister Marcy, get me two membership applications please."

The secretary entered the office with the applications and handed them to Emma and Kimberly. Then the pastor said, "I want you to fill in every space that pertains to you."

Emma's pen was cocked and ready to be fired, but Kimberly stood frozen, pen in hand, staring at the membership application. Then she took her pen and tapped the application with its tip. She reminisced about her first visit to Resurrection Temple, and how excited she was to be a part of the church. She thought on the many sermons that had blessed her, along with lifelong friends she had met there. Then she recalled how after her brother died, Pastor Austin came to her aid and sent her away to recuperate, at his expense.

She was invited to his family retreats and was treated like family, by his wife and son, whom she babysat until he was ten years old. And besides, Pastor Austin had never done anything to her and was not known for such behavior, that she was aware of. Kimberly sniffled as she stared at the application.

"What's wrong, Kimberly?" asked Emma.

Her mouth quivered and she wanted to tell Pastor Riley she had a home church already. Before she could mouth the words, he urged, "Kimberly, you *must* obey God! Thank God that you found out how he really is."

"C'mon, Kimberly. Can't you feel it in your spirit?" asked Emma.

Then Pastor Riley said, "Kimberly, if you change your mind later, all you have to do is tell me."

Kimberly knew the only way to get them to stop pressuring her was to fill out the membership application. So she did.

CHAPTER TWELVE

T he next day at Pastor Clyde Jones's house, he and his wife Mae were sitting at breakfast. Clyde was rambling on about the church. Mae, with a raised eyebrow, sighed audibly and interrupting, said, "Clyde, I found a professional marriage counselor, and I made an appointment for us."

"Okay, good," he said, noting that she had not wasted any time.

"Do I know the counselor?" he asked.

"No, you don't. A friend of mine recommended him."

"When's the appointment?"

"I'm waiting for a call back to confirm. It will either be Thursday or Friday at noon. But most likely Thursday."

"Okay, Thursday will work for me. I have a two-day seminar on Friday. I'm going to be flying back on Saturday night though. I was originally scheduled to stay longer, but I called and told them I *must* be back by Saturday." Clyde winked at Mae and blew her a kiss.

Then he said, "If I could get out of it, I would, but I made the commitment a year ago. Do you remember me mentioning it to you, sweetheart?"

Mae rolled her eyes toward the ceiling and said, "No, Clyde, I don't."

"No need for you to answer like that," retorted Clyde.

Mae grunted, then sighed.

On Thursday morning, Clyde woke Mae and said, "Get up, Sleeping Beauty, and get dressed. Let's get to the counselor. You know how I hate being late."

"Clyde, the appointment's for Friday."

"You told me it would most likely be Thursday."

"I *know* what I said!"

Clyde threw his hands in the air, raised his voice and said, "Mae, you led me to believe it would be Thursday! Why didn't you tell me this before now?!"

"Don't yell at me!"

"I didn't yell at you."

Mae paused, then scowled and said, "So, what are you going to do? Are you still going with me to counseling?"

"Mae, I can't back out of the engagement now. I made this appointment a year ago."

Mae turned on her heels and as she strolled away said, "So, I guess you've made your decision then. You're choosing *your* ministry over *our* marriage. I *knew* you didn't want to go to counseling."

"Mae, why don't you just call and reschedule?"

"Never mind, Clyde."

"Are you going to call and make another appointment, or what?"

Mae furrowed her brows and said, "Just forget it, Clyde."

Clyde threw up his hands, shook his head and said, "Whatever."

For the rest of the day, they avoided talking to each other.

When they got up the next morning, Clyde asked Mae, "Are you going to take me to the airport?"

Mae snatched up the keys to the car and said, "C'mon, Clyde."

They rode in silence to the airport and when they arrived, Clyde said, "Mae, pick me up at six p.m. tomorrow."

"Uh huh."

"Love you," said Clyde.

He reached over to Mae to give her a kiss, but she jerked her face away and stared out the driver's side window. Clyde shook his head and left to catch his plane.

The next night, Clyde's return flight landed on time. He stood outside looking for Mae. He waited for a half hour and when she did not come, he called her cell phone, but there was no answer. Then he called their daughter Geraldine's cell and when she answered, he said, "Hi, Baby."

"Hi Daddy, where're you?"

"I'm at the airport. Did you and Mary enjoy the college tour?"

"It was nice, Dad."

"Good. Is your mother there?"

"Yes, she is. Hold on Daddy. Mommy, it's Daddy."

Then he heard Mae's voice. "Thank you, Geraldine."

After that, the phone went dead. He called three more times, but there was no answer. Clyde clenched his jaw and said to himself, "Mae ain't coming."

He flagged down a cab, arrived home, and discovered that the house-keeper was there alone.

Clyde asked, "Mother Sommers, do you know where Ms. Jones has gone?"

"Pastor, she told me that her and the girls will be staying at her mother's house for a while."

"Thank you, Mother."

Then he sauntered to his bedroom, sat on the bed, and rocked back and forth.

———————

Pastor Carl Boston lay in bed on Saturday morning, cuddling with his still sleeping wife. His mind was still engrossed with the diary, and he wondered if he could persuade Trisha to visit with Lorraine today so he could continue reading. He rose from his bed, went to his study, and retrieved the diary from its hiding place with the intention of reading as much as he could before Trisha awakened. He went to the bathroom and left the diary on his desk, thinking Trisha was still asleep. When he returned to his study, Trisha was in his study with the diary in her hand, peering down at the desk as though looking for something. Carl's face tensed up. Trisha, still holding the diary in her hand, furrowed her brow and said, "Carl, have you seen my dress receipt?"

Carl continued staring at Trisha. Then she blushed and said, "Oops, never mind, I just remembered I left it on the dresser."

Carl exhaled and said under his breath, "That was close."

Trisha placed the diary back on the desk.

Then Trisha said, "Carl, I'm going to return a dress and do a little shopping. Do you want to come with me?"

Carl knew from experience she was not going to return until late afternoon or early evening. He thought, "This would be a perfect opportunity for me to pore over the diary."

"No, Trish. I'm going to stay home and do some reading."

"I'll be back soon," said Trisha

Trisha got dressed and as she prepared to leave, Carl walked her to the door and said, "Enjoy yourself."

They gave each other a quick kiss on the lips. He watched as she drove down the block. Then he poured a cup of coffee, went to his study, sat at his desk with his coffee and opened the diary. His hand shook as he flipped the pages. When he reached the page where he left off, he paused, took a deep breath, closed his eyes and turned the page. Then he opened his eyes and read:

> *It's Sunday and I'm not able to perform. But, if I don't, I'm dead in the water. The congregation is expecting me to preach them out of their seats, like the previous Sunday. And they appreciated my sermon which translated into the highest church offering in six months. God knows we needed it. How do I explain to the congregation that I don't have it this morning? How do I preach them to new heights when I am at my lowest point? How do I convince them of God's peace when just last night my violent outbursts drove me and my family to the edges of despair?*
>
> *Nothing that happened last night warranted such an explosive response from me. Lorraine asked me about talking with the young people regarding the fundraiser they were planning. I had been avoiding them for a month.*
>
> *I responded to her by screaming. "Didn't I tell you not to ask me that again!"*

She said, "They keep coming to me and asking me about it. You don't have to get mad."

"Don't tell me that I'm mad! I hate that!"

She asked me, "Morgan, what do you want me to tell them?"

I shouted, "Didn't I just tell you not to talk to me about that again?"

With that, I slapped her face. Surprised by my violent behavior, she let out a scream and clutched her cheek. Less than a second later, Lester rushed into the room. I had finally hit rock bottom. I was a raging madman. I knew where to place the blame, but instead I used my son, whom I pray forgives me, as a scapegoat. Lester stood staring at me with narrowed eyes, his hands by his sides and balled into fists.

I shouted, "Why are you looking at me as though you're going to hit me or something? You want to try it, boy?"

Lester is my height but half my size. We both knew he had no hope of a successful physical confrontation with me.

Still, I taunted him, "You want to try it, punk? Please hit me. Please!" His fists trembled at his side as he peered into my face.

Afterward I retired to my study, slammed the door, fell on my knees at my chair and wept bitterly. While in my study, I overheard Lester say to Lorraine, "Ma, I know what you said, but I can't take this anymore. If he hits you again, I'm gonna pick up something and—!"

Lorraine yelled, "Don't ever let me hear you talk like that again, Lester!"

Why does Lorraine endure the unendurable and remain with me through my unbearable behavior? God, I wish that I was dead!

It was as though I had surrendered command of my soul and was occupied by an evil entity. Although it was not a total surrender. I had moments of lucidness in which I oversaw myself. Then I'd lose dominance over myself again and retreat into the enemy's control. Why have I debased myself? I am better than this! I can't continue to disgrace the name of Jesus by my involvement with the accursed thing.

Carl reared back in his chair, closed his eyes, rubbed his temples, and said to himself. "Why doesn't Morgan just say what's bothering him?"

The phone rang. Carl looked at the caller's ID. It was Peter. Carl took a deep breath, let it ring a few times, then answered.

"How have you been, brother preacher?" asked Carl.

Peter responded, "I'm good, Doc. What are you up to?"

"Just catching up on some reading while the house is quiet."

There was a three second gap of silence during which Peter waited for Carl to initiate a discussion of the diary. When Carl did not mention it, Peter said, "So... when are we getting together again?"

"I'll call you and we can set up a time. By the way, what's up with your boy?"

"You mean Arthur?"

"Yeah."

"I'm not sure. I called his cell, then the church, then his house and didn't reach him. When he finally returned my call the next day, he told me that he was at church counseling, and then he left for another appointment and got so busy that he forgot about our meeting."

"Hmm... that doesn't sound like Arthur to forget or forego a meeting about the diary."

"To top it off," Peter continued, "when I called his church his secretary said he called and said he wouldn't be in his office the whole day."

"Did you ask him about that?"

"He said that he came into his office through the rear entrance and his secretary didn't see him come in."

"That sounds kinda odd."

"Yeah, that's what I thought."

"Oh, well," said Carl. "I've got to get back to my reading."

"Carl, don't forget to call me."

"I won't."

Carl picked up the diary again. Then he cleared his throat and spoke as though Morgan could hear him. "C'mon Morgan, talk to me. Tell me what's wrong, brother."

Carl's request was granted when he read the next paragraph. After reading it, he cried out, "Oh, God, no. *No!*" Tears gushed from his eyes. He shook his head and hollered, "This can't be!" Then he said to himself, "I can't let this out." After which, he raised his head and vowed, "Morgan, I love you like a brother, and I promise that I'll keep your secret and protect your reputation."

CHAPTER THIRTEEN

On Monday night, Arthur was home, sitting on the side of his bed. With his head in his hands and his eyes flooded with tears, he asked himself, "What did I do so horrible to deserve such unhappiness?"

He got up from his bed, sauntered to Angela's bedroom, and was about to knock. His fist came within a millimeter of contact with the door when he changed his mind. He breathed a deep sigh, turned, and walked back toward his bedroom.

Angela heard his footsteps, opened the door to her bedroom, stuck her head out and asked, "Arthur, did you want something?"

Arthur stopped, looked over his shoulder and said, "Not really. It would be a waste of time, anyway."

Angela heaved a sigh and grumbled, "Arthur, I hope you don't wanna talk about the same ole' thing again. I'm tired of talking about it. Don't you have anything else to talk about?"

"Angela, when was the last time we were intimate?" he asked, determined to have his say.

Angela rolled her eyes to the ceiling and mumbled, "Here he goes again."

"What did you say?" snapped Arthur.

"Nothing worth repeating."

Shaking his head, Arthur threw up his hands as he retreated to his bedroom. "Oh, what's the use? This marriage was doomed from the start," he grumbled.

Angela, in full voice with her eyes stretched wide, countered, "If it was doomed, it was doomed because *you* refused to listen to the prophetess!"

Arthur stopped, turned to Angela and ranted, "I shouldn't have listened to any of those self-righteous, frustrated old hags in that church; none of whom were with their husbands."

Angela's nostrils flared. "See, that's what I mean. You keep talking down God's anointed!"

"You mean *Prophetess* Dora? That bloated behemoth that claimed to have had a vision of us getting married, who just *happened* to be your aunt?! Angela, we were only twenty years old and had only met two months before getting married. She told me I needed to get married if I was going to be a preacher."

"And she was right, Arthur."

"Angela, please explain to me why the so-called prophetess was always in our business—and our bedroom—after we were married!"

"She was just trying to help us stay spiritual and not lose the anointing."

Arthur's face twisted and he shouted, "By telling you that your hus-band had contracted a lust demon just because I wanted it more than once every two months? FYI, Angela—there're no such things as lust demons!"

"Perhaps if you prayed more instead of —"

"Angela, stop it! Look at us—we're married, and we've lived like room-mates for years. That's not normal! Doesn't it bother you?"

"Arthur, you're just too carnal and..."

"Answer this question for me, Angela. Did your aunt tell you how often we should have sex?"

Angela stared into Arthur's eyes but did not respond.

Arthur shook his head and replied under his breath, "Just as I suspected."

Then he walked down the stairs to the main floor.

Angela called out, "It's late. Where are you going?"

He continued walking and did not respond.

"Arthur, if you're going out, would you pick me up a pineapple soda?"

Arthur walked out of the front door, slammed it, got into his car, and drove away.

He mumbled as he drove. "My life is ruined. I let those church fools destroy my life. I have a right to be happy."

As he lamented his life, a sensation he'd experienced many times before overpowered him. There was a part of town he was determined never to visit again. Within its borders loomed the forbidden cinemas. However, when this sensation came over him, no matter which direction he drove, he ended up in this area in search of a theater whose movie suited his yearning.

Arthur circled the vicinity of the theater for ten minutes. He assumed he would not be recognized, as it was located far from where he lived. He parked and exited his car, and as he walked in the direction of the theater, he continued scouring the area. He walked past the theater three times, repeating to himself, "I'm not going in... I'm not going in."

Arthur knew from prior encounters that when the compulsion got to that point, resistance was futile. On his fourth pass of the theater, he felt the sensation of someone's hands on his back pressing him into the theater. With the exact change in hand, he purchased his ticket. He rushed inside the darkened cinema and sat in an aisle seat three rows from the back and breathed a sigh of relief, confident he had avoided detection.

Arthur slouched in his seat, dividing his attention between what was happening on the screen and those who passed by his row, making sure no one looked familiar.

He knew he shouldn't be there, but he didn't want to leave. It was a release from all the pressure, and he needed a release.

At the end of the film, Arthur hurried from the theater and got into his car. As tears flooded his eyes, he prayed, "Here I am again, Lord. I'm so sorry. *Please* forgive me! I know that I've prayed this prayer before, and I vowed I'd never do this again. Cleanse me, Lord, with hyssop and

I shall be white as snow. Lord, You know my heart." Then he thought, "I must be the worse minister in the world."

Arthur wiped his eyes, started his car, and headed home. Speaking out loud, he said, "This has got to stop! I can't continue to preach holy living and then carry on like this." He banged the steering wheel and shouted, "I thought I had this thing beat when I had quit for over a year. Then the next thing I knew, I fell off the wagon! I've prayed and fasted, and still I can't conquer this."

As he drove well below the speed limit, he recalled when he was ten years old and he and his brother Drew found their dad's X-rated VHS tapes. Drew and Arthur used to sneak and play them almost every day. That's where his appetite for pornography started. At seventeen years old, when Arthur got saved, he thought his porn problem was over. He soon found out differently when he discovered and began frequenting the peep shows in Times Square. He also believed that once he was married, he'd be "cured" because he would have sex on a regular basis and not have any further need for pornography.

"Just my luck," he thought. "I married someone who refused to have sex on the night of our honeymoon or on a regular basis. Angela wanted to spend our honeymoon praying. No wonder she wouldn't discuss the honeymoon with me before the wedding. We finally had sex a month after we were married. After we were done, she fell on her knees and repented with tears, asking God to forgive her. If I knew then what I know now, I would've gotten an annulment. As a matter of fact, I wouldn't have married her at all."

"If I get caught going to an adult theater or bookstore, I'm finished. My family, congregation, and friends will *never* talk or listen to me again."

Arthur reached home and dashed to his bedroom to avoid seeing Angela. When in his bedroom, Angela knocked on the door and asked, "Arthur, did you get the soda I asked for?"

Arthur thought, "I don't believe this. With all she's putting me through, does she actually think that I give a damn about some pineapple soda?"

"No!" snapped Arthur.

"Why are you answering me so nastily?"

Arthur said nothing else, then turned on the TV. On the program was a Christian psychologist who was speaking on addictions. At first, Arthur paid little notice to the program, but something the doctor said captured his attention. "Many of you out there are living with strongholds and addictions that you can't overcome. The first things you need to do is to acknowledge that you *have* an addiction, discover what triggers your addiction, and then recognize that you can't defeat it alone."

The host of the show said, "This is so interesting, I'm sorry, but we're out of time. We're going to have you back to talk more on this needed subject real soon." Then the host asked, "In case someone wants to contact you, Dr. Ford, where can you be reached?" Dr. Ford gave his email address and phone number. Arthur scurried to get a pad and a pen to write down the information. Arthur said to himself, "I'm going to contact him tomorrow for sure."

The next morning, Arthur lay in bed, looking up at the ceiling with his hands clasped behind his head. He was speaking out loud to himself about himself. "Reverend Arthur Wright's no sex addict. Sure, he goes to an adult theater and bookstore occasionally. But it's not like he's having sex with every woman he sees, like some of those other preachers. Reverend Wright does not need to see a psychologist."

Arthur got dressed and was about to leave for the church office when Angela shouted, "Arthur, I'm tired of you talking to me any ol' kind of way!"

"Angela, what are you talking about?"

"You know what I'm talking about; don't pretend you don't."

"Angela, I have a headache. Let's do this later."

Angela's brows gathered and she insisted, "No! I want to talk about this *now!*"

His heart pounded, his nostrils flared, and he yelled, "Angela, I *said* I have a headache!"

Angela got in his face and shouted, "Arthur, you *are* a headache!"

Arthur raised an eyebrow and in a gruff voice said, "Get out of my face, Angela!"

"Or what? What're you gonna do?"

He turned to walk away and said, "I'm warning you, Angela."

Arthur proceeded toward the front door. As he attempted to leave, Angela grabbed his jacket sleeve. Arthur snatched his arm from her grip, pushed her in the face, got into his car, and drove off.

After he arrived at church, he continued to grieve over his predicament as though mourning the death of a loved one. He walked through the office foyer and past his secretary's desk, his head down and his brow wrinkled. His secretary said, "Good morning, Pastor Wright."

His eyes still peering at the floor, he said, "Good morning, Sister Ingram."

As he opened the door to his office, she asked, "Are you feeling okay?"

Arthur responded with a grunt.

For three hours he remained in his office, staring at the walls and breathing an occasional sigh. Finally, he went to the door and said to his secretary, "Sister Ingram, I'll be out of the office for a few hours. Unless there's an urgent matter, *do not* contact me. I'll take care of whatever it is when I return."

"Yes, Pastor."

Arthur got into his car and said to himself, "I need to drive somewhere—anywhere—to think." He would not admit, not even to himself, that *somewhere* and *anywhere* were going to end up with him at a forbidden cinema.

As he drove onto the block with the theater, he said, "God, I *promise* this is my last time."

Arthur went through his ritual of driving around the area, then walking past the theater a few times, until eventually going in. Once inside, he sat and glanced at the faces of those who passed his row.

His heart skipped a beat when he noticed someone who, from the back of their head, looked like one of his parishioners. The person turned and looked straight into Arthur's face. He stared back at him and realized he was mistaken.

"Wow, that was too close," thought Arthur. His stomach rumbled, and he said to himself, "I'm getting out of here." As he hurried through the exit, he heard someone call from across the street, "Hey, Reverend Wright!"

Arthur instinctively looked in the direction of the voice. The person who called did not look familiar but ran across the street toward him. Arthur froze, and his heart raced. He said to himself, "It's too late to run. This is it. *God help me!* My ministry and life are over and done with."

CHAPTER FOURTEEN

The person Arthur heard call his name passed him, approached another man, shook his hand, and said, "Kevin Wright—man, I haven't seen you in years." Arthur rushed to his car, panting his relief as he went. He was sure he'd heard the man say Reverend Wright and was glad to be mistaken. "Thank you, Jesus, thank you Jesus," he thought. "Lord, I've learned my lesson."

Upon arriving back at church, Arthur charged into his office, collapsed into his desk chair, and turned on the TV. Coincidently, there was a replay of the show with Dr. Ford, the Christian psychologist. Arthur thought, "Oh good, I'll get to hear the things I missed."

The host of the show asked Dr. Ford, "Doctor, would you describe burnout for our audience in layman's terms?"

Dr. Ford smiled and said, "Sure. Burnout is physical or mental collapse caused by overwork or stress. It leads to the questioning of one's abilities and or the value of one's work.

"The emotional part involves feelings of depression, hopelessness, and helplessness, usually accompanied by a loss of coping skills. Often, feelings of happiness are replaced by loneliness and discouragement.

"The mental exhaustion part leads to negative attitudes toward work, life, and self. This, in turn, leads to negative attitudes toward others and feelings of inadequacy, inferiority, and incompetence."

"Doctor, what causes burnout?"

"Burnout is the result of unrelieved stress. When a person is burned out, they look for ways to escape. Some of the most common escapes are food, sleep, etc. However, there are abuses, like drugs or alcohol. The most frequent abuse of escape is sex. Sex not only involves lust and adultery, but most often, pornography.

"Pornography is an escape. Overcoming pornography starts by admitting that it's like a drug that one uses to make oneself feel good and escape the pain they feel inside.

"Overcoming pornography also requires you to realize that this sin is a downward cycle. You feel bad because you are burned out. So, you indulge in an escape to help you feel better. But then you feel guilty because of your sin. So, you feel worse than you did before; and the vicious cycle continues. Because of this, it is difficult to see whether burnout leads to pornography or if pornography leads to burnout."

The host then asked, "Dr. Ford, what advice would you give to those that say, 'I can stop whenever I want to?'"

"I would tell them, when the urge comes on you again to indulge in pornography, resist it. If you can resist and not feel a compulsion to yield, you're probably not addicted. But if you attempt to quit, promising yourself never to indulge again, and continually go back on your promise, you're in need of help."

Just then, Arthur's secretary knocked on the door. "Come in, Sister Ingram."

"Pastor, Reverend Peter Austin is on the phone."

"Ask him if it's okay if I call him back."

She went to her desk, returned a moment later and said, "Pastor, he said it's important."

Arthur thought, "Aw shucks, I want to see the rest of this program." He made an audible sigh and said, "Okay, I'll take the call."

He answered the extension on his desk and asked, "Hey, Preacher, what's happening?"

Peter said, "I'm going to call Carl so we can get together again. I wanted to know before I call him when and if you will be available."

"Pick a time between now and Saturday. I'm free all this week."

"Okay, Arthur. Don't disappear on me like the last time."

"Sorry about that. This time I'll make sure to be available."

"I'll be in touch as soon as I reach Carl."

———

After they hung up, Peter called Carl.

Carl's phone rang but before answering, he checked the caller's ID and thought, "Oh man, it's Peter. I know he wants to discuss the diary. Maybe I should answer the phone and explain why I'm not going to read anymore to him or anyone else."

The phone continued to ring, and in his mind, it seemed to get louder with each ring.

"Why hasn't my voice mail answered yet?" thought Carl.

Finally, the ringing stopped. Carl exhaled and said, "Thank God!"

His phone beeped, signaling there was a message in his voicemail. Carl sat at his desk and vowed out loud, again and again, "Nobody's going to see the rest of the diary; not Peter, not Arthur, not even Bishop Howard. As a matter fact, I'm gonna destroy it."

For the next hour, Carl grieved over his friend's death and the decision to destroy the diary. He was dozing at his desk when his phone rang. Half asleep, he answered without checking the caller's ID. It was Bishop Howard.

"How are you, son?" asked Bishop Howard

Carl gasped and said, "Oh, um... Bishop, I'm fine. How was your trip?"

"It was really good. The wife and I needed to get away. I'm back in town now. So, what was it that you wanted me to see?"

Carl said nothing for a few seconds and then asked, "So, where did ya'll go?"

"Young man, we can discuss that later. What was it that you wanted me to see?"

"Uh, I'm sorry, Bishop but I, uh, can't talk right now. Can I call you tomorrow and we set up a time?"

"I have to do the funeral of a longtime member tomorrow. I'll most likely be busy most of the day. Call me the day after."

"Okay, Bishop."

After he hung up, Carl picked up the diary and slammed it to the floor.

Then he looked in a mirror, scowled and said, "I can't take this pressure!"

Afterward, he snatched up the diary, opened it, and pulled on the pages with all his strength and attempted to rip out the pages. He heard the front door open. At that point he threw the diary in his desk drawer.

A voice called out, "Is anyone home?"

The voice was that of his son Nicholas, home on a surprise visit from college. Carl locked the drawer the diary was in and went to greet his son.

He greeted Nicholas with a smile and a hug, then asked, "What are you doing here?"

"They're testing, and all of mine are done. Besides, I missed you and Mom."

"How long are you going to be home?"

"Just until Tuesday."

"Oh good, you'll be here for church on Sunday and can help with the special youth program on Sunday night."

Nicholas frowned, then asked. "Oh, um, where's Mom?"

"She's at Sister Lorraine Kendal's house. Give her a call and let her know that you're here."

Nicholas called and said, "Hey, Mom. Guess where I am."

Trisha chuckled with excitement and asked, "Is my big college boy home?"

"Yes, Mom."

"Okay, I'll be there in a few."

————

Trisha ended the call and, still giggling, looked at Lorraine.

Lorraine smiled and said, "Girl, go home. Tell Nicholas I said hello."

"I'll be back, Lorraine, and we'll figure this mess out. They can't do this to you. Don't you worry; everything's gonna be all right. You hear me?"

"Thanks, Trish."

CHAPTER FIFTEEN

Nicholas and Carl sat in his study. Carl asked, "So how are things in school, son?"

"They're going okay and uh—"

Carl interrupted, "Good! I can't tell you how much I've missed you around the church. You know Michael is doing his best, but he can't come anywhere near you as youth leader. You coming home at *this* time is an answer to my prayers. I was worried about the youth service this Sunday, but now that you're here, I know everything's gonna be all right."

Nicholas raised an eyebrow took a deep breath and said, "Yeah, Dad."

Just then, Trisha arrived home. She opened the front door and yelled, "Where's my baby?"

When Nicholas heard her voice, he breathed a sigh of relief and said under his breath, "Thank God." Then he shouted, "I'm in here, Mom!" after which he hurried out of the study into the arms of his mother.

"Why didn't you tell me you were coming home today?" said Trisha with a full-toothed smile.

"I wanted to surprise you."

She continued smiling and said, "Mission accomplished." Then she asked, "Nicholas, are you hungry?"

"Yes, I am."

Carl walked out his office and said, "Me too. Let's go out and get something to eat. Give me a few minutes to change."

Carl went upstairs to the bedroom to get dressed, and Trisha asked Nicholas, "Does Marsha know you're home yet?"

"No, she thinks I'm coming home on Friday."

"Good answer," quipped Trisha.

They both laughed. Then Nicholas furrowed his brow and said, "Mom, I want to talk to you about something before Dad comes down."

Trisha matching his expression asked, "What's wrong, Nicholas?"

"Mom, Dad's at it again; I just got home and without asking me what I'm doing, he's already planned my activities. I haven't seen Marsha in two months, so I've made a reservation at a restaurant for us this Sunday night. But he wants me to take over the youth service. It ain't fair. Why do I always hafta change my plans to fit the church's agenda? I'm not the pastor—*he is!* He told me that he wants me to take the church someday. But I don't feel that I'm even called to preach, let alone pastor."

Then Trisha said, "Didn't you volunteer to be youth leader?"

"I didn't volunteer. I was "volun-*told*" by Dad to do it. And beside that, every time someone does not show up for a job they were supposed to do, I'm *told* by the members, 'You're the pastor's son. I know you're not going to let your dad down.' Mom, I'm tired of havin' to fill in all the time. I'm tired of being watched and told by the members, 'You should know better than that.' Especially when *their* own children get away with doing the very same things."

"Nicholas, let me say—"

"Mom, let me finish please; I *need* to say this."

Trisha raised her voice over his. "What I was about to say was, I know how you feel. As you know, your grandfather was a pastor too. And I was *always* called upon to lead testimony service—nowadays it's called praise and worship—or sing a solo or take over the children's choir when no one else wanted to do it, along with everything else."

When Carl walked down the stairs Trisha placed her index finger to her lips.

Carl grinned from ear to ear and said, "I heard y'all talking out here. What did I miss?"

"Just some mother-son talk," said Trisha.

Then Nicholas stood eye to eye with his father and stared into his face, his deep voice resonating with confidence as he said, "Dad, we need to talk!"

For the first time, Carl realized his son now stood equal to him, not just in stature, but in conviction. Carl attempted to put things back into their natural order. He stared into Nicholas's face, folded his arms and said, "So, what's the problem, boy?"

"You didn't have to answer him *that* way, Carl," protested Trisha.

"In *what* way, Trish?"

Then he looked at Nicholas, his eyes widened, and he asked, "Did I sound angry to you?"

"Well, uh, Mom seems to think so."

Carl exhaled a lung full of air, then in a patronizing tone said, "What do you want to talk to me about, son?"

Nicholas sat on the couch, and Carl remained standing with his arms folded across his chest.

"Nicholas, I thought that you were hungry," said Trisha.

"That's okay, Mom; I can eat later. This is important." Then he looked at Carl and suggested, "Why don't you and mom have a seat?"

Trisha glanced at Carl and sat on the couch next to Nicholas.

Carl said, "I'm good right here."

"C'mon, Carl, have a seat," said Trisha.

Carl paused for a few moments, then in a slow and relaxed pace he walked across the room to his black leather recliner and sat down, after which he stared at Nicholas, nodded his head and in a muted tone said, "What is it, Nicholas?"

Nicholas cleared his throat, sat at the edge of his seat and said, "First of all, you and all the church members expect me to be at every function the church has. I don't mind helping, but there is more to life than church. Ever since I was a little boy, I was forced to attend church all the time. And not just on Sundays."

Emphasizing his point with his hands he continued. "I was being pressured by the church members into acting as though I was perfect. Well, I'm far from perfect. I tried for years living up to everyone's expectations, which led to frustration and hypocrisy. I did it because I didn't want to disappoint you and Mom or disgrace the family. I know you want me to follow in your footsteps, Dad, but I'm not a preacher."

Trisha sniffled and her eyes filled with tears. Her voice cracked as she said, "Do you have anything to say, Carl?"

Carl sat back in his recliner, looked up, rubbed his chin, and gazed at the ceiling.

Trisha dried her eyes and said, "I'm so sorry, Nicholas. I know what it is to be forced into being something that you're not. I was determined, after what I went through as a pastor's daughter, that if I married a pastor, none of my children would go through what I went through. I guess I dropped the ball.

"For years, I harbored hatred toward some of the members in my dad's church. I felt that they monopolized my father's time, which cheated me and my brother from time with him.

"To make matters worse, when I was just a little girl, a woman in the church slapped my father in the face right in front of me and my brother. I wanted to say something, but my mother and father always taught us to respect our elders even when they're wrong. What outraged me is that my father didn't do anything. I mean, he just stood there!"

Trisha's breathing was erratic, perspiration forming beads on her forehead. Then she said, "Every time I think of that incident, my blood boils!"

"What happened to her, Mom?"

"That *hypocrite* left the church and died not long after that."

Carl, speaking nonchalantly, said, "Calm down, Trisha." Then Carl eased from his seat and said, "Let's go get something to eat."

Nicholas's brows came together and his lips gradually parted. As he was about to speak, Trisha touched his shoulder. When she got his attention, she shook her head and whispered, "Leave it alone for now. Let's just go and get something to eat."

Chapter Sixteen

The next day, Bishop Howard was in his office preparing to eulogize Heather Young. Heather was thirty-five years old and had attended the church ever since she was an infant. Her mother and father, who preceded her in death, were also longtime members.

Bishop Howard summoned Joel Miller, his assistant pastor, to come to his office. When Joel entered the office, he observed Bishop Howard sitting behind his desk, leaning back in his recliner with his eyes closed. Joel closed the office door, walked over to the desk, and asked, "Did you want something, Bishop?"

Bishop Howard did not respond right away but opened his eyes and stared at Joel. As he gazed, his mind reminisced about a family of five from his church who were killed in a fire while they slept in their home. He recalled how grueling it was for him when the funeral director rolled the five caskets into the church, and how he nearly passed out after he preached their eulogy.

After a minute, Bishop Howard spoke in a low, melancholy tone. "You don't know how hard it is funeralizing someone you've known since they were born."

Joel remained still and thought, "Bishop's face looks flushed. I hope he's not ill."

Bishop Howard continued speaking in a low tone, pausing in the middle of his sentences with an irregular cadence. "I dedicated... dedicated her as a baby. I... remember when she first went to um, um kindergarten. *I baptized her!* I celebrated her graduation from high school... and uh, college. I—I performed her wedding. When her husband up and left, I counseled with her all night into the early morning.

"I also buried her parents and prayed with her when she had succumbed to depression. And now I have to bury her. You can't imagine how hard it is for me to go out there, look at her casket and preach her funeral."

"If you want me to, Bishop, I could preach for you."

"Thank you, son, but this task I must do myself."

With that, Bishop Howard bowed his head and said, "Reverend Miller, please start the service. I'll be out there in a minute."

Before Joel could exit the office, he overheard Bishop Howard let out a soft moan. Hearing his mentor weep, he cringed as he fought to quell his own tears.

Bishop Howard preached the eulogy, but he was not at peak performance. He stumbled over words and misquoted a few biblical texts. When he sat down, Joel whispered in his ear, "Are you okay, Bishop?"

He nodded his head but said nothing.

At the burial site, as Bishop Howard was about to commit the body, he paused, then took a deep breath. Joel, sensing something was awry, seamlessly chimed in and finished the committal.

Carl was home alone, agonizing over the last entry he had read in the diary. His eyes widened when he glanced at a newspaper that lay on the table opened to an article titled: "*Popular Megachurch Pastor Found Dead in New York City Hotel*." He reasoned that Trisha must have left the article for him to see. Carl's eyes skipped down the article where he recognized the name of a popular Bishop of a well-known denomination who was quoted as saying:

> *We need to do something about pastors. We've swept this issue under the rug for far too long. I'm going to suggest to the presidium of our church denomination that we open a place for our ministers who find themselves overwhelmed. A place where they can find a haven to discuss their problems candidly, get help, and keep their anonymity.*

"My God." Carl thought to himself. "What in the world is going on with pastors?"

Then he reached for the diary and reread the entry he read last.

"I didn't realize that the problem was this widespread," he thought, shaking his head. "Perhaps I should let Bishop Howard read the diary and maybe with his influence, he'll reach out to other pastors."

Carl decided to call Bishop Howard right away. Bishop Howard had just returned from the gravesite when Carl called.

"Hello, Bishop. I know you asked me to call you tomorrow, but if we could get together today..."

"Well, um, I'm really not feeling my best."

"Bishop, this is important!"

Bishop Howard cleared his throat and said, "Oh, okay, son. I'm at the church right now. When can you get here?"

"I'll be on my way in five minutes. I could be there in twenty minutes."

Carl arrived at Bethlehem Cathedral, the church Bishop Howard pastored. Bethlehem was an elegant church with crystal chandeliers, blue-padded pews, and plush blue carpeting throughout the sanctuary.

He was escorted by a staff member to Bishop Howard's office, which could rival that of any Fortune 500 company CEO.

Carl entered the office and Bishop Howard, without any formal greeting, said, "Have a seat, Reverend Boston."

"Thanks for seeing me, Bishop."

"So, what is it that you wanted me to see?"

Carl reached into his attaché case and handed the diary to him.

Bishop Howard did not say anything at first. He opened the book, read a page, and then asked, "Where did you get this?"

"Lorraine gave me Morgan's entire library. The diary was nestled among his other books. I don't think she realizes that the diary even exists."

"Does anyone beside you and me know of the diary?"

"Yes, Bishop. Reverends Arthur Wright and Peter Austin."

"Did they read any of it?"

"I read some parts to them. I haven't read it all myself."

"I understand you guys are buddies, but perhaps you should've read it all before sharing it."

"You're right, Bishop."

"Well, what's done is done, but keep the rest to yourself. Everybody has a Chapter of their life they dare not read out loud. Nor will they allow anyone else to read it."

"Bishop, I'm puzzled. If he didn't want it read, why did he write it?"

"Sometimes writing things down helps us cope with our issues. I think, however, that we should keep it to ourselves for now until we read it in its entirety. Lorraine is going through enough right now. I'd hate for her to find out things about Morgan that would devastate her. She doesn't need another headache. We'll just keep this between us."

"Yes, Bishop."

Bishop Howard handed the diary back to Carl and said, "Okay, son, start reading from the beginning."

As Carl read the diary, Bishop Howard sporadically added his analysis. "The Dark Lady! That's just like the devil to send one of his temptresses... The members don't understand what the pastor goes through; they're just interested in themselves... We as pastors take on too much sometimes. We're not superhuman... We all get overwhelmed and become curt with the members at times, but that does not mean we don't love them."

Then Carl came to the part where he had left off:

> *This has been ongoing for more than a year. I have hidden it from everyone so far, but I don't know how long before someone figures out why my behavior is so erratic at times. I am hopelessly imprisoned by this evil power. Every day I plead for a divine intervention. And before my plea reaches heaven, I succumb to this evil power. The shame I feel cannot be expressed in any known dialect. I'm weakened by my yearning for release from the pressure. I pick up the phone, my trembling fingers pressing the digits. I pray: 'God please, please don't let him answer.' But his phone is never busy, and he always responds. He will be here soon. I have a desire to break free from this seedy hotel before he arrives, but I lack the power to perform that which I desire.*
>
> *The next day, I woke up in my bed, regrettably still alive. I pray I didn't do harm to Lorraine while under this evil influence. Oh, why didn't I just consume a lethal overdose? Then I'd be rid of this demon once and for all.*

"That's enough, Carl!" shouted Bishop Howard as he dabbed the tears from his eyes. "I had no idea that he was addicted to drugs. He hid it well. You see what I mean? If Lorraine had heard this, it would've destroyed her."

Carl replied, "I know what you mean, Bishop. When I first read it, it almost destroyed me."

CHAPTER SEVENTEEN

Reverend Jeremiah Riley, pastor of Mount Moriah Church, was out at a restaurant with a few of his colleagues, discussing why churches do not take in as many new converts as members like they used to.

Jeremiah smiled, then boasted, "I took in two new members this past Sunday."

"Good," said one of the pastors. "Were they new converts?"

"No, they came from another ministry."

"Are they new to your church's neighborhood?" asked another pastor.

"No, they're from Peter Austin's church."

"You mean Resurrection Temple?"

"Yeah."

Then the pastor said, "See, that's what I'm talking about. The church as a whole is not growing, just exchanging members."

Jeremiah responded, "Well, according to them, there's a mass exodus from Resurrection Temple." Then he pointed to himself and said with a giggle, "I wanted to tell them, 'Send them all right here. They got to go somewhere, so it might as well be Mount Moriah.'"

"Why do you think so many are leaving?" asked another pastor.

"From what one of them said, he's a womanizer. She told me that he made sexual advances toward her."

Then Reverend Samuel Scott, another one of the pastors, said, "Jeremiah, you must be careful about taking everyone's word for things. Some people are disgruntled and will say anything to get you to side with them. One time, I—"

Jeremiah interrupted, saying defensively, "Scott, you know that I know better than to believe everything I hear. I—"

"Preacher, I know firsthand how it feels to be wrongly accused."

"Reverend, I know when someone is lying to me. Believe me, she was telling the truth!"

"I'm just saying, Preacher..."

"I hear you talking, Scott. Trust me; I got this! Preachers, I have an appointment. I have to leave in a minute or so."

They all said, "Okay, see you later."

Then Scott said, "Hear me out, Preacher. This will only take a minute."

"Okay, hurry up."

"A few years ago, one of my members accused me of coming on to her. First of all, she was not even my type. Anyway, she spread all sorts of stuff about me that wasn't true. I was so infuriated I said to one of my deacons, 'Oh, yeah? Tell her to say that to my face.' And you know what? She did. Even though she was lying, some people concluded that she was telling the truth because she said it to my face. Even some of my 'trusted' members believed her lies. I lost more than a few members over that mess. It's amazing to me how people forget all the good you've done for them when unsupported rumors surface about you."

Jeremiah frowned and said, "I'm not sure I get your point."

Scott slapped his own forehead, closed his eyes, shook his head, and said, "Just be careful, Jeremiah."

Jeremiah left for his appointment. He was meeting with Emma and her husband at the church. It was the first of a series of counseling sessions she had requested for her and her husband. He did not mention it to the other pastors he'd met with because of what Reverend Scott alluded to. Jeremiah arrived at church a half hour before the counseling session was to begin. Emma was waiting for him in his secretary's office without her husband.

Emma was frumpy, brown skinned, five-foot-five inches tall, with short hair that she wore slicked back. Jeremiah greeted Emma and his secretary, then entered his office, which was adjoined to his secretary's office.

He said to his secretary, "Sister Marcy, escort Sister Emma in, please." Emma was wearing a lowcut blouse that revealed more than Jeremiah thought was appropriate.

His secretary escorted her into his office and asked, "Pastor, do you want the door closed?"

"Yes, please close the door, Sister Marcy."

She walked out of the office and left the door partially ajar.

He called to his secretary, "Sister Marcy, please close the door."

She raised an eyebrow, and she said, "Oh, sorry, Pastor," then shut the door.

Jeremiah greeted Emma with an embrace and asked, "Where's your husband?"

She smirked and said, "Who knows? Probably somewhere drunk."

Emma asked that the counseling sessions continue for two months, twice a week.

Jeremiah thought, "No one needs that much counseling." But he did not want her to accuse him of not being available to the members like she said of Reverend Peter Austin, so he agreed to the arrangement.

After the session, she said, "Thank you so much, Pastor. You're such a wise counselor and so easy to talk to. I feel like I can tell you anything."

She bent down to retrieve her pocketbook from the floor and paused in that position for a few moments. Jeremiah looked away and moved some papers around and pretended he was searching for something. She retrieved her pocketbook, then glanced up at him to see if she had his attention.

Then she stood with her arms stretched out and said, "Pastor, aren't you gonna give me a goodbye hug?"

Jeremiah had just risen from his chair to give her an embrace when someone knocked at the door and said, "Are you alone, Pastor?"

It was his wife Julia.

"Oh, ah, come in. I'm just about finished."

Julia was five foot ten inches tall and brown-skinned, with light brown eyes and stylish, long jet-black hair that fell past her shoulders.

"I'm sorry, I didn't mean to disturb you. Sister Marcy said that she wasn't sure if you were alone or not."

Then Jeremiah said, "Oh, um, honey, this is um, um, Emma Richards."

Julia glanced at Emma from top to bottom, smiled and said, "How are you, Sister Richards? I'm Julia Riley, the pastor's wife."

Emma smiled and said, "Glad to meet you, Sister Riley. I'm a new member here at Mount Moriah."

Julia returned the gesture. "So nice to meet you, too. Welcome to our church."

"Thank you, Sister Riley." Then she turned to Jeremiah and said, "Pastor, I'll see you next week."

"Okay, Sister Emma, same time."

Emma walked out of the office. Julia stared at her as she exited the secretary's office, then said, "Jeremiah, watch her. She's not to be trusted."

Jeremiah frowned and said, "You just met her. How do you know that she can't be trusted?"

"Women know other women. I understand you must counsel the members, just don't do it with your office door closed. That's all I'm saying."

Jeremiah sighed then said, "Okay, okay."

As they left the office and walked through the secretary's office, his eyes narrowed as he stared at his secretary until he exited the area.

Later that night, Julia called the secretary at home.

"Sister Marcy, this is Sister Riley."

"Oh, hi, Sister Riley," she said cheerfully.

"I just wanted to say thank you for the heads-up phone call."

"Sister Riley, when I saw how she was dressed and then without her husband, I knew that she was trouble. Some of these people have no respect for the church, the man of God—"

Julia, interrupting, chimed in, "Or God, for that matter."

"Sister Riley, I was raised in the South where you respected the man of God. My grandmother was what the church called a 'mother in Zion.' If a woman came to the church with a dress that was too short, my grandmother would put a sheet over her legs, and she would not be allowed to sit in the front row. Or if she hugged the pastor or held his hand too long, my grandmother would say, 'Baby, leave the man of God alone. Don't lean all over the pastor like that.' And you know what? They listened and then kept their distance. Unfortunately, we don't have church mothers like that anymore."

CHAPTER EIGHTEEN

C lyde was frustrated after Mae refused his phone call, so he decided not to call her again that night. He woke up the next day, still on his side of the bed. He kept to his side just in case Mae returned in the middle of the night from her mother's house while he was asleep. He wanted to make it as effortless as possible for her to get into bed. Without opening his eyes, he reached over to her side of the bed, expecting to feel her warm body lying beside him. Instead, he felt a cold vacant spot. Clyde thought, "Maybe she came home and slept in one of the other bedrooms. This would not be the first time she's slept in another room when angry with me."

Clyde rose from his bed and walked to the other bedrooms, including his daughter's rooms, just to find them vacant and untouched.

Talking to himself, he grumbled, "This ain't supposed to happen. I make daily positive confessions of faith over my home and family. What door did I leave open that allowed the enemy to enter my marriage?"

Then he grunted in disgust, nodded his head a few times, smirked and said, "Oh, I see what's happening. I recognize you, Satan, and I rebuke you, you foul spirit. In Jesus's name, get out of my home!"

After that, Clyde returned to his bedroom, sat on the bed, then stared out of the window. As he sighed, a tear trickled down his face. Then he called his wife's cell phone and both of his daughter's phones, but there was no answer. So, he decided to call his mother-in-law's phone, and she answered.

"Hello."

"Hello, Mother Benton, this is Clyde."

"Uh huh, hold on Clyde."

Clyde heard her in the background say, "It's Clyde, Mae. Take the phone."

Then he heard Mae say, "I don't want to speak to him."

"Take the phone, Mae. Ya'll need to talk."

Mae took the phone, took a deep breath, then muttered, "What is it, Clyde?"

"Mae, when are you coming home?"

"I hafta call you back later."

Clyde said in an indulgent tone, "Okay, okay, call me back later, then. I love you."

Without responding, Mae hung up. She then stared at her mother, sobbed and said, "Mom, I'm tired."

Mae's mother took Mae's head, held it to her bosom and said, "Baby, listen to me. I know how hard marriage can be. Before your father died, I—"

Mae railed, "Mom, I'm tired of being left alone and taken for granted. This has been going on for years! He keeps promising me things are going to change, but they never do. Maybe we should just go our own separate ways."

"Mae, you must think of Geraldine and Mary."

Mae lifted her head from her mother's chest and said, "They're sixteen and seventeen years old. They know what's going on. They hear us arguing all the time."

"So, what are you going to do?"

"Mom, let me and the girls stay here for a few more days, please, so I can think things over."

"Sure, baby."

"I don't know what I'm going to do, but I do know *I cannot and will not* continue with things as they are."

———————

The next morning, Clyde called for his maid. Mother Sommers entered the kitchen, cleared her throat, and blinking back tears, said, "Yes, Reverend?"

"Mother, are you okay?

"Yes, sir."

"You don't have to cook today. As a matter of fact, take the day off."

"Thank you, Reverend," Then she said as she sniffled, "I pray for you and Sister Jones every day."

"Thank you, mother."

————

Clyde drove to his mother-in-law's house, hoping to get a glimpse of Mae. From where he parked, he could see activity through the window of the house but could not make out who it was. He exited his car, went to her car, and left a note on the windshield that read, "Waiting for you to come home," with a heart drawn beside it.

The next day, Clyde drove past his mother-in-law's house several times during the day and even into the night. Mae's car was missing that entire time. The next morning, which was Saturday, he called Geraldine at seven-thirty and said, "Hi, Geraldine."

"Hi, Dad!"

"Is Mary near you?"

"Yes."

"Put your phone on speaker."

"Okay, Dad."

"Hey, girls, I'm coming over to pick you up today. Get ready. I'll be there at noon."

They giggled and said, "Okay."

"By the way, is your mother there?"

"No, Daddy. She said that she was going to the beauty parlor and, as you know, that can take all day. Oh yeah, Daddy, next Saturday they're giving grandma a birthday party. You should come."

"Yeah! You should!" said Mary.

"Okay, perhaps I will. Be ready when I get there."

"We will."

———

The next Saturday, Clyde arrived at his mothers-in-law's house for the birthday celebration. Mae answered the door and said, "What are you doing here?

Treading lightly, Clyde said, "You mind if I come in?"

"Well, you're here now; you might as well stay."

Clyde was greeted by the party guests. He went over to Mae's mother, kissed her on the cheek, and gave her a present. "Happy birthday, Mother Benton."

She smiled and said, "Thank you, Clyde."

Throughout the night, he noticed Mother Benton occasionally tapping on the table and staring at him. In the face of her tapping and staring, he spent most of his time chatting with his daughters. Mae entertained the party guests and conspicuously stayed away from Clyde the entire night.

When the party ended, Clyde said goodbye to everyone, kissed his daughters, and asked Mae to meet him outside because he had something to tell her. As they stood under the full moon and a low-wattage porch light, the sounds of insects filled the air with their nocturnal melodies. Clyde looked into Mae's eyes and said, "The church folks have been asking for you."

"Oh! Is that all you have to say Clyde?"

"What do you want me to say?"

Mae pouted and coolly answered, "I don't know."

"Mae, let's have a date night, like we used to."

"Why?"

"So we can talk things over."

Mae grunted. "When, Clyde?"

"Pick a time. Whenever you say, sweetheart."

"Okay. Monday." Mae said coldly

Clyde checked his phone, sucked his teeth, and said, "Ah shucks. I can't this Monday. I forgot I promised Reverend Duncan I'd fill in for him at the Bible college."

Mae heaved a sigh, frowned and in a sarcastic tone said, "Whenever you have time for your wife, give me a ring."

"No, it's not like that. Please don't be that way. I'll tell you what—how's Thursday, seven p.m. at The Spot?"

Mae exhaled and said, "Okay."

Clyde beamed and said, "What time should I pick you up?"

"That's okay. I'll drive."

————

Clyde made a reservation at Ida Kae's, nicknamed The Spot, a trendy soul food restaurant that was frequented by celebrities.

On Thursday, Clyde arrived at the restaurant exactly at seven p.m. He scoured the parking lot for Mae's car, but she had not arrived yet.

Then he thought, "Mae is probably on her way. I'll get us a table and leave a message with the maître d' that I'm expecting someone."

Once seated, Clyde rehearsed in his mind what he was going to say when she arrived. He giggled and thought, "This will be a brand-new start for us."

Earlier that day, Clyde had purchased her a diamond pendant to celebrate them getting back together. From where he sat, he could hear the maître d directing the patrons. Every time he heard the maître d speak to someone, his heartrate accelerated. Then, after fifteen minutes, he heard the maître d say, "He's already seated and waiting for you. Right this way, please."

Clyde said to himself, "This is it, Clyde."

He stood and pulled out a chair. When he turned to greet Mae, there stood a man holding a large manilla envelope.

"Are you Clyde Jones?" asked the man with the envelope.

"Yes, I am."

Then he handed him the envelope and said, "You've been served," and walked away.

"What? What is this?!" thought Clyde.

He ripped open the envelope and pulled out the documents that were inside. The first page read:

> *Supreme Court of the State of New York,*
>
> *County of Kings.*
>
> *Mae Benton Jones, Plaintiff. Clyde Jones, Defendant.*
>
> *Action for Divorce.*

After reading the court papers, he collapsed in his seat, groaned, closed his eyes, and rubbed his temples.

CHAPTER NINETEEN

Peter was watching TV in the living room when Yolanda entered the room and, donning a contemplative look, said, "I wonder why Kimberly wasn't in church Sunday."

Peter responded, "I'll assume then you haven't heard from her."

She shook her head and said, "No, I haven't heard from her. That's not like her not to show up or call. I'd better give her a call and make sure she's okay."

Yolanda called Kimberly's phone, but there was no answer. She called again but still no response, so she left a message on her voicemail.

Yolanda thought, "Something must be wrong."

She stared at Peter and said, "Kimberly calls me at least once *every* week and hardly ever misses church, especially on Sunday. I'm worried."

"Yolanda, you worry too much. I tell you this all the time. You left her a message, right?"

"Yeah."

"Then don't worry. It's only Wednesday; she's probably busy or has her phone on silent or something. I'm sure that she'll call you back before the week's over."

———

Peter could not have been more wrong. Kimberly was at home, staring at her phone, when Yolanda called, but was afraid to answer, fearing Yolanda was calling because she somehow found out that she joined Mount Moriah.

Kimberly sat on her couch and rocked back and forth, taking deep breaths. Her voice trembled as she lamented, "I thought that Pastor Austin was a man of God. And come to find out he's nothing more than a womanizer."

Her doorbell rang. She wiped her eyes and peaked out of the window. It was Emma.

"What is she doing here?" thought Kimberly.

She opened the door and said, "Hey Emma, is everything okay?"

Without being invited in, Emma came in, sat down, and said, "I don't wanna go home. Frank's drunk again and acting up. I'm gonna let him sleep it off."

Emma, blinking her eyes, raised her brows and, in a high-pitched voice, begged, "May I *please* stay here tonight?"

Kimberly thought, "Poor thing." Then she said, "Certainly."

Emma got up from the chair, kissed Kimberly on the cheek, grabbed and squeezed her, then said, "Oh, thank you! Thank you so much."

Emma released Kimberly, smiled, and asked, "So what do you think of Reverend Riley?"

"What do you mean?"

"You know. Ain't he fine?"

"He's alright, I guess."

"I counseled with him today. He gave me this firm hug as he greeted me. After the session, he was about to hug me again when his wife, the first lady, knocked on the door. I don't like her!"

"You don't even know her. How can you say..."

The corners of Emma's mouth turned downward, and her eyes narrowed, "I didn't like the way she looked me up and down, like I want her man or somethin'. Trust me, if I wanted him, he'd be mine. I ain't braggin', but I know what men like, and I can get *any* man that I want."

Kimberly thought, "My goodness, she's full of herself."

Then Emma said in a mocking tone, "I *should* take him, just to teach the first skank a lesson!"

"Calm down, sister."

"Sorry, Kimberly. It just gets me so mad when someone challenges me like that."

"Emma, how did she challenge you?"

"Oh, never mind. Forget that I said anything."

"Emma, do you want something to eat?"

Emma's eyes widened and she said, "Yeah, whatcha got?"

"I'll make you a roast beef sandwich."

"Sounds good."

Emma followed Kimberly into the kitchen. As Kimberly fixed the sandwich, Emma opened the refrigerator and moved things around.

"Um, excuse me Emma. Do you want something? All you have to do is ask."

Emma poked out her lips and snapped back, "Sorry, Ms. Kimmie. I didn't mean to impose myself. Just looking for something to drink."

"Give me a second, I'll get it for you. You can wait in the dining room."

Emma walked to the dining room, took a seat, then mumbled, "Whatever, Ms. Thang."

A few seconds later, Kimberly walked into the dining room with the sandwich and a can of soda.

"Here you go," said Kimberly as she placed the sandwich and drink on the table.

As they sat, Emma railed, "The girls at my job are jealous of me. Even when I was in high school it was the same thing. And you know something? I believe that even my sister Gwen hates me because she's jealous. That's a shame when your own sister hates you. You know what I mean?"

Kimberly yawned and stretched, then said, "Emma, I have to get up for work tomorrow. I'll show you to the spare bedroom. I have to leave by seven, okay?"

Emma responded, "Okay, I'll be ready. And thanks again."

When Kimberly rose the next morning, she checked the spare bedroom and Emma had left. The bed was not made-up, and the pillows were on the floor.

"My goodness," thought Kimberly, "Emma didn't let me know she was leaving and beside that, left the room in a mess."

When she proceeded to the kitchen to make herself a cup of coffee, she discovered an unwashed plate in the sink along with a stained coffee cup. On the dining room table there were coffee rings alongside the coaster. Kimberly's lips curled and she grumbled, "I don't believe this!" She snatched a dish rag, washed the cup and dish, then cleaned up the stains on her table before heading to work.

Kimberly returned home from work and had just sat down to eat when her doorbell rang. She looked outside and there stood Emma.

Kimberly's nostrils flared. She opened the door and said, "What are you doing here, Emma?"

Emma smiled and asked, "Can I stay just one more night, please? Frank's at it again."

"Not tonight, Emma."

"Why? What's the problem?"

Kimberly, in a bitter tone, said, "I just don't want any company tonight!"

Emma frowned, raised her voice, and replied, "Okay, okay, I'm going!"

Kimberly closed her door and grumbled, "I don't need her negative energy in my house."

Fifteen minutes later, her bell rang again. Kimberly thought, "I don't believe it; she's back here again! I ain't letting her in! I don't care if she has to sleep on a park bench!"

CHAPTER TWENTY

Kimberly peeked out of the window and, to her amazement, there stood Yolanda Austin.

"Oh God, it's Sister Austin."

Kimberly hurried back from the window and thought, "What am I gonna do? I can't face her." Then she exhaled and mumbled, "I don't think she saw me."

She kept still until Yolanda walked back to her car and she heard her drive away.

The next day, Reverend Jeremiah Riley received a call from Reverend Samuel Scott. Jeremiah answered the phone and said, "Hey, Preacher, to what do I owe this call?"

"I was just calling to make sure we're good."

"What do you mean?"

"Remember the other day when we were all at the restaurant, and I said perhaps you shouldn't take everyone's word for things? You seemed a little miffed with me. I wanted to make sure that you didn't misunderstand where I was coming from."

"No, Scott, I just wanted you to know that I am not so green as to believe everything I hear."

"I understand, but I think we as preachers sometimes do not follow the Bible as we should."

Jeremiah griped, "What are you trying to say?"

"Listen for a second, Preacher."

"I'm listening. I just ain't gonna let you insult me by telling me I don't follow the Bible!"

"Preacher, hear me out and let me ask you something. Did you follow the St. Matthew eighteenth Chapter rule when you accused Peter Austin of being a womanizer? First off, you have no proof that the accusation made by those ladies is even true. And even if you had video tape of him in the very act, according to Matthew Chapter eighteen, you're supposed to go to him in private first. If he refuses to hear you, bring some others with you. Then, if he refuses to hear them, take him before the church."

Jeremiah paused for a few seconds, then conceded, "Okay, Scott, I'll admit you do have a good point. Thanks a lot. I appreciate you."

"You're welcome."

"Scott, I have to get over to the radio station, and do my weekly broadcast."

"Okay, I'll talk with you later."

———

Later that day, Scott was driving to an appointment when he turned to Jeremiah Riley's broadcast and heard Jeremiah say, "My topic today is: 'Be Sure, Your Sins Will Find You Out.' Then he went on to say, "I don't know what we're going to do with these preachers that are molesting the members. Just a week or so ago, two ladies from another ministry came and joined Mount Moriah because the pastor of the church where they attended molested one of them. Church, pastors are supposed to p-r-a-y *for* the people, not p-r-e-y *on* the people."

Scott said to himself, "What's this idiot saying!"

When the broadcast ended, Scott called Jeremiah and said, "Jeremiah, I heard your broadcast."

"What did you think?"

"I thought you were going to abide by Matthew eighteen."

"I was, but then the anointing came over me and God began wording my mouth. You may not understand this, but when you're under the anointing, God takes over and the words are no longer *your* words, but His."

Scott exhaled in disgust and said, "Okay, Doc, do what you think you must do." Then he hung up.

———

Members from Mount Moriah also heard the broadcast and were in church the Sunday Emma and Kimberly came forward to join. A few of the members knew that Emma and Kimberly were from Resurrection Temple. They spread what Reverend Riley said on the broadcast to other members of Mount Moriah, which ignited a rumor that Reverend Austin from Resurrection Temple was a molester. Others speculated that his wife, Yolanda Austin, caught Pastor Austin and Kimberly in the middle of a passionate embrace, which resulted in Yolanda insisting Kimberly leave Resurrection Temple.

For two consecutive Sundays, Kimberly attended services at Mount Moriah, however, she kept to herself and made it her business to sit on the back pew next to the usher's station. Emma, on the other hand, sat at or near the front, blaring out "Amen" and then passing out in the aisle in the middle of Pastor Riley's sermon.

———

On Sunday after church, Kimberly sat alone in a restaurant and overheard a conversation between two members of Mount Moriah who sat in the booth behind her.

"Did you hear about Reverend Austin?" said one of the persons.

"No, I didn't."

"Well, from what I've heard, Reverend Austin got this girl in his church pregnant. She attends Mount Moriah now."

"Really? Who is she?"

"She's the new member. I don't remember her name, but she was wearing a loose-fitting blue dress this morning. Probably to hide her pregnancy."

"No, I don't remember seeing her."

"I'll tell you how you can know; this morning she sat in the back next to the usher's station."

"Hmm, I didn't notice."

"I'll point her out to you next Sunday."

At that instant, Kimberly sprang from her seat and left the restaurant, undetected by those who sat in the booth behind her. Her lips curled as she murmured to herself, "I'm never going back to Mount Moriah ever again!"

———

Peter was at church for the annual business meeting Monday night, which was attended by half of the congregation. The meeting began with the oldest deacon in the church, Deacon Halsey, giving the invocation. Deacon Halsey stood at his seat, cleared his throat, and then uttered, "God, we come to You tonight as humble as we know how, knee bent, and body bowed. You said in Your Word that everything that's done in the dark will come to the light. We're asking You to expose the evil in this your holy church and expel the dark forces. In the Name of the Father, and of the Son, and of the Holy Ghost. Amen."

Peter overlooked the peculiar prayer as he had done in the past. Deacon Halsey was known for his awkward remarks. However, deference was granted to him because of his advanced age and because he was the patriarch of the church's largest and most prominent family.

The treasurer read the expenditures from the previous year and the projected budget for the coming year. After he read the expenditures for the pastor's home and car expenses, someone from the audience was overheard saying in a sarcastic tone, "We sure take real good care of the pastor."

The treasurer was about to take his seat when he stopped and said, "Excuse me, did someone have a question?"

The same person who made the remarks raised his hand, stood, and said, "I was just thinking, does the pastor *really* need a new car every four years? And why does he have to take a month of vacation every year, at the church's expense? My job gives me two weeks' vacation, and my car is seven years old and still runs good."

The treasurer said, "Um, brother—"

He interrupted the treasurer and continued to rant. "And another thing—I think we spent too much money on all these revivals! We don't need all that stuff. I heard what you said about the church's bank account. With all the people that give to this church, we should have millions in the bank."

A woman stood and shouted, "Now, hold up, brother! Do you know the toll stress takes on the mind and body that a pastor must endure? I know you think all he does is preach on Sunday and then vacation from Monday through Saturday! You have no idea what it takes to run a church! Especially with people like you in it!"

Peter stood with his hands raised and said, "Okay, sister, that's enough."

"No, Pastor, please let me say just one more thing!"

Peter shook his head, but she continued despite his objection. "And another thing—as far as revivals go, I got saved in one of those revivals, sir! So, don't you *dare* go there!"

Then Peter said, "Okay. With that, we'll be dismissed."

Deacon Halsey smiled and asked, "Reverend Austin, may I ask a question before we dismiss the meeting?"

Peter bowed his head and said, "Sure, go right ahead Deacon."

"Where's Sister Kimberly?"

Peter's eyes narrowed, his brows came together, and he replied, "Excuse me, Deacon?"

"I want to know where Sister Kimberly is!"

"What... um, why do you want to know?"

"I heard she now attends Mount Moriah because of some stuff going on between you and her."

Someone in the audience yelled, "Deacon, sit down!"

Deacon Halsey looked in the direction of the voice, his veins protruded on his forehead, and he shouted, "Don't tell me to sit down! I just want to know what the hell is going on!"

At that point, one of Deacon Halsey's nieces stood with her hands on her hips and fumed, "Well, my girlfriend from Mount Moriah told me that it is all over Mount Moriah that Kimberly joined because Reverend Austin molested her. As a matter of fact, my friend told me that Pastor Riley talked about it on the radio and mentioned Reverend Austin by name. Now, he couldn't call his name on the radio if it weren't true!"

The room was silent. Someone remarked, "Lord have mercy!"

Peter stood at the podium and said, "I don't know anything about what you're talking about."

"So, *you* say!" railed Deacon Halsey's niece.

Then a woman in a grey dress stood and blared, "You just need to sit down and shut up!"

Deacon Halsey's niece pointed her finger at the woman in the grey dress, shook her head, then yelled, "Don't you tell me to shut up!"

Peter's eyes bulged, his veins protruding on his forehead as he banged the podium with his fist and shouted, "Everybody shut up! This business meeting is over! All y'all get outta here!"

Peter focused his eyes on the doors leading to the parking lot and, without saying another word, exited the church.

When he arrived home, Yolanda asked, "So, how did the meeting go?"

"Hmm!" answered Peter, as he slammed his briefcase on the table. Then he said in a gruff voice, "Guess what I found out tonight!" Then, in a cynical tone, he said, "Your sweet little, innocent Kimberly joined another church. And instead of just leaving, she thought it necessary to start a rumor that I molested her!"

"Honey, I know her. She wouldn't say anything like that," said Yolanda.

"Now it makes sense why she left without so much as a 'thank you, suckas, for helping me with my schooling and all the other stuff y'all done for me!'"

"Baby, listen to me. You can't believe everything malicious church folk have to say."

"Then explain to me why she hasn't contacted you in weeks!"

Yolanda beckoned him with her arms to lay his head against her breast. "Peter, don't worry yourself about it."

Peter stood in place and ranted, "See, that's what happens when you do stuff for nig—!"

Peter paused, exhaled, and mumbled, "That's it! I ain't gonna let any more of those leeches get close to me again! And I ain't going out of my way anymore for *nobody*! All you do is get kicked in the..."

Yolanda, with a raised eyebrow, asked, "Anything else happen tonight?"

"Yolanda, you ain't fooling anyone. I know somebody called you about the meeting."

"Peter, everybody knows how off the rail Deacon Halsey is. Just don't call on him to do anything else." Yolanda yawned and said, "Come to bed."

Peter released a lung full of air and said, "I'll be there in a few."

Peter sat in his living room, his lips curled as he banged the arm of the couch and grumbled, "This is it! I can't take this crap anymore! First thing tomorrow, I'm going to call Riley, and if he mentioned my name in relation to a molestation on the radio, I'm going to sue him for defamation of character.

"Next, I'm going to fire Deacon Halsey. I don't care how many relatives he has in the church, nor how respected he is. It's time someone else took that position on the board anyway."

Peter sat on his couch and remained there until just before dawn, after which he retired to bed.

Chapter Twenty-One

C arl spent the night tossing in bed, bemoaning Morgan's drug addiction. He had just drifted off when he felt Trisha shake him, rousing him from his sleep.

"Carl, wake up! Wake up!" she shouted.

Carl grumbled, "Why are you yelling like that? You almost scared me ta' death."

"I'm sorry. You were groaning and crying in your sleep."

"I'm fine, Trish. Now that you woke me up, I'm not sure if I can get back to sleep right away."

"I'm sorry, Carl. I just thought that you were..."

"It's okay, babe. I'll watch some TV until I get sleepy."

"Please don't make it too loud."

"I'll watch it in my study."

Carl went to his study and turned on the TV. While the TV played, Carl stared at the desk drawer where the diary was and scratched his head. After five minutes, he opened the drawer. At first, he listened for Trisha, then glanced from side to side. When he determined that the coast was clear, he opened the book. Then he heard the front door open. "Nicholas, is that you?" he called.

"Yeah, Dad," Nicholas said in a muted tone.

Carl put the diary back into the drawer and said, "Come here, Son."

Nicholas stood by the office door, exhaled, and said, "Yes, Dad?"

"Nicholas, I didn't know you felt the way you did. I'm sorry. I..."

"It's okay, Dad. Can we talk about this another time? I'm kinda sleepy right now."

"Sure, we'll talk later. Good night."

Nicholas yawned, waved, then retired to his bedroom.

Carl recovered the diary from the drawer. It slipped from his hand, fell to the floor, and opened to the page where he had left off, enticing him to read further to reveal more of the mystery of Morgan's soul.

Carl picked up the diary, opened it, exhaled, then read:

> *It was another Lord's Day in which my congregation expected to be lifted from their doldrums via the 'voice of God' by way of a compelling sermon. I addressed them from the sacred desk and peered into their eager faces, being egged on with shouts of 'amen' and 'preach pastor', knowing they determined their lives by my words. At that moment, I felt that I was no longer human but divine, or at the least a chosen vessel.*

However, I am not divine. I am a man, a mere man. And when the euphoria ends, I am faced with the demons that plague my mind. After the service, three of the young ministers approached me and, with youthful zeal and age-appropriate naivety, said, 'Pastor, how long will it take for us to preach like you?'

What they really meant was, 'When will we receive the accolades and adoration from the congregation?'

I was tempted to say to them that they did not know what they were asking. Not wanting to douse their zeal, I told them to just remain faithful.

They grinned and said in unison, 'We will!' They continued to smile as they left my office, ready to take on the world. As with young, inexperienced ministers, they were under the delusion that ministry is free from difficulty and the minister free from problems.

I recalled as a novice, hearing in the deepest region of my soul what I believed to be Jesus beckoning me, as He did with His disciple, to 'step out of the boat and onto the pastoral sea.' Moreover, I was persuaded by the testimonies of others who claimed to have stepped onto the sea and, despite the turbulent currents, did not sink. Why have I sunk into an ocean of despair when others, no better than me, remained afloat?

I've heard that God has ordained a season when one reaps the benefits of their faithfulness to ministry. I believed my season had arrived, so I ventured out in faith toward the promised land, just to end up in the wilderness by season's end. I refuse to continue meandering from the joy of pregnancy just to end up with the heartbreak of a miscarriage.

I'm finished. I'm through. I give up! I will not continue to take part in this charade any longer.

I feel as though I've been played like a pawn on a celestial board game for the amusement of the gods. I am pitied by some of my peers as an orphan and ridiculed by other of my peers like the son of a harlot. Why am I deprived of God's blessings?

Jeremiah, the Old Testament prophet, expressed my sentiments best. "You deceived me, Lord, and I was deceived; you overpowered me and prevailed. I am ridiculed all day long..."

My Friday night evangelistic service is when I invited guest preachers to minister to the congregation.

Carl introduced me to a preacher that was visiting from out of town named Gary Bonds. Carl told me that Bonds was some preacher. He said he had preached for him, and the church is still reelin' and that I should have him preach for me.

Carl knew what I liked and has recommended other preachers to me in the past, which worked out well. However, I accepted Carl's recommendation more out of desperation than respect for his judgment. My week had been riddled with sentiments of abandonment, disillusionment, and depression. I prayed, 'Lord, I need a word from you tonight!'

Rev. Bonds came out the gate proclaiming God's eternal and immutable love for His people. "There's nothing you can do to make God love you any more or any less," he said. "God forgives and will restore your soul. And when God restores you, your spiritual cup will overflow."

Tears filled my eyes, and I pleaded, "God, please overflow my cup tonight."

Then Bonds said, "However, in the case of the under shepherds, there're limits. For example, if the pastor engaged in an adulterous affair or sinful addictive behavior, while God forgives, the pastor has forfeited the right to pastor any longer. I know that sounds harsh, but that's the way it is."

I choked at his statement, feeling trapped between the higher moral standard pastors are held to and if they fail, cannot be restored–which was instilled in me as a young minister– and life's experiences, which have taught me sincerity is no guarantee one will not be overtaken in a sin.

Still, I am ready to resign my position, however, on my terms and not because some judgmental, sanctimonious church folks deemed me unfit to be pastor. After service, many of the congregants said, "Pastor, we really enjoyed the minister. When are you going to have Reverend Bonds back?"

I told them that I'd work something out with the preacher. Suddenly, I felt eyes peering at my back. I tried ignoring it, but the feeling overpowered me; I had to get out of there and search for whoever it was staring at me. I was chatting with one of the parishioners at the time. Then I said to the person

I was talking to that I had to attend to something and asked if she'd mind if we continue our conversation later. She said, "Sure, Pastor."

I rushed to the parking lot, looking for God knows who. Once outside, I caught a glimpse of the back lights of a car hurtling from the parking lot.

"Carl, you're *still* up?" said Trisha.

Carl jerked at the sound of her voice and responded, "I, uh, am about to call it a night, Trish."

Trisha lingered at the office door, yawning and rubbing her eyes.

"Well, hurry up. I don't sleep good when you're not in bed with me."

As Trisha sauntered back to the bedroom, Carl placed the diary into the drawer, closed the drawer, and followed her to bed.

———

At 3 a.m. Trisha was awakened by a noise coming from their backyard and the flash of red and blue lights through their bedroom windows.

Trisha shook Carl. "Carl, wake up!"

"Was I making noise in my sleep again? I'm sorry. Go back to sleep."

"No, there are lights flashing in front of the house, and I hear something in the backyard."

Chapter Twenty-one

Carl leaped from his bed and rushed to the window.

"What in the world is going on?" he fumed.

He proceeded to the front door and grabbed the doorknob.

"Don't open it, Carl!" begged Trisha.

Carl opened the door despite her objection. To his shock, he saw three police squad cars, flashing their lights. Appearing from the back of the house and walking toward the front door with his flashlight shining in Carl's face, was a police officer. Carl squinted, shaded his eyes, then asked, "What's the problem, Officer?"

"Does Nicholas Boston live here?" asked the policeman.

"He's my son. What's the problem?"

"Is he home?"

"He's in bed."

"I'd like to speak to him."

"What for?" asked Carl.

"I just need to ask him a few questions."

Trisha stood on her toes behind Carl, holding and peeking over his shoulder. "Nicholas!" Trisha yelled toward her son's bedroom.

There was no answer. Trisha yelled again, "Nicholas, come here!"

Still no response. Then she said, "I'll go get him."

Trisha returned a moment later, shaking her head, and with a nervous stutter said, "He, he's, um, not in his room."

"Do you have any idea where he could be? Like at a friend's house or something?"

"No, Officer. I don't."

The officer reached into his jacket pocket, pulled out a card and said, "When you hear from him, make sure he contacts me."

"Okay, I will."

The squad cars drove off. Trisha went back into the bedroom. As the tears overflowed, she murmured, "What has Nicholas gotten himself into?"

Carl followed her and called Nicholas's cell phone, but it went directly to voicemail. Then he banged the mattress with his fist and ranted. "Boy, where in the world are you? *Call me right away! It's urgent!*"

Trisha sat on the edge of the bed with her head in her hands and wept. Carl laid on the bed, cuddled Trisha's head, and placed it on his chest.

She placed her hand in his and said as she sniffled, "Lord, please protect my baby."

CHAPTER TWENTY-TWO

At 5 a.m. Trisha rose from the bed. She had not slept all night. On her way to the bathroom, she heard the front door open and called, "Nicholas, is that you?"

"Yeah, Mom."

"Where were you?"

"I was out with some friends."

"Where?!"

Nicholas sighed, "Just out, Ma!"

Carl heard their voices and rushed into the room. Pointing his finger at Nicholas, he said, "Boy, don't ever let me hear you raise your voice like that at your mother again!" Carl stared at Nicholas and in a sarcastic tone said, "Um, by the way, the cops were here last night looking for you. Is there anything you want to tell us?"

Nicholas stared at Carl but did not respond.

"Carl, remember, the cop said that Nicholas should call him when he gets home."

"He ain't callin'; we're going to the precinct!"

Carl took out his phone and pushed the speed dial. Trisha frowned and asked, "Carl, who are you calling?"

"Brother Mallard. I want him to meet us at the precinct."

"Don't you think it's a bit too early in the morning to call?"

"After he was sworn in as a lawyer, he said, 'Pastor if you need me, call me, no matter what time of the morning or night.' Well, we need him."

Carl called Mallard and they arranged to meet at the precinct. Mallard instructed Carl, "Don't go into the police station until I arrive. I want to talk with Nicholas before they question him."

Carl hung up, stared at Nicholas, and shouted. "Boy, get in the car!"

"Carl, please!" said Trisha. "This is not helping."

They got into the car and headed for the precinct.

Carl mumbled as they drove. "This doesn't make no sense. Got me going to the police, like I don't have better things to do. What if I see one of the members of the church at the police station? That's going to make me look terrible. This is so embarrassing."

Trisha and Nicholas remained still as Carl continued to rant.

When they arrived at the station, Mallard was already there waiting for them. Carl spotted him and rolled down the window. Mallard walked to their car and said, "Good morning, Pastor and Sister Boston."

Mallard looked in the backseat and waved to Nicholas. Nicholas nodded his head.

Carl shook Mallard's hand, then opened the door and was about to get out when Mallard said, "Pastor, let me speak with Nicholas alone for a minute."

Carl closed the door and sat shaking his leg and tapping the steering wheel.

Nicholas got out of the car, and he and Mallard walked behind the car. After Mallard spoke with Nicholas, they returned with blank looks. Then Mallard said, "Let's go inside, y'all."

They went inside and asked for the police officer who had given them his card. The officer at the front desk said, "Please be seated. I'll call him."

After twenty minutes, Carl exhaled then complained, "What's taking so long?"

Trisha's face winced as she bowed her head and mumbled a prayer under her breath. Soon after, the police officer came to where they were seated and said, "Hello, Mr. and Mrs. Boston. Come into my office, please."

Carl pointed to Mallard and said to the officer. "This is our lawyer. We would like him to come too."

"Sure, no problem."

They entered the office and he said, "Have a seat, please."

The officer read Nicholas the Miranda Rights, then asked, "Nicholas, do you know Billy Streeter?"

Nicholas glanced at Mallard. Mallard nodded his head then Nicholas answered, "Yes, I do."

"When was the last time you saw him?"

"Last night."

"Where and about what time?"

"About 9 p.m. We ate together at the Burger Stop."

Carl and Trisha gasped. Billy Streeter had a notorious reputation. They had no idea Nicholas knew Billy, let alone associated with him.

"Are you sure of the time?" the officer asked with a raised brow.

"I'm positive."

Then he sighed, rose from his seat and said, "I'll be back in a minute."

After he left, Carl grumbled, "You've been hanging with that thug?! How many times have I told you to watch your company!"

"Carl, please, let's discuss this later at home," said Trisha.

"Hmm. That's *if* he's going home!"

"Please calm down, everyone," Mallard interjected. "So far it doesn't appear as though they have anything on Nicholas."

The officer returned and asked, "Nicholas, where were you at 10 p.m. last night?"

Carl answered, "Officer, he came home at ten. We had some words, then he went to bed."

"Then where was he at three this morning when I was at your house?"

All eyes were on Nicholas. Nicholas glanced at Mallard. Mallard nodded his head, then Nicholas stared at the officer and said, "Billy called and asked me and some guys I know to meet him at his house at midnight. He said we were going to hang out. We waited and when he didn't show up, we went to a club and hung out there for a few hours. Then we left."

"What time did you arrive home?"

"About 5 a.m."

"Do you know where Billy is now?"

"No, officer. I don't."

"He's in the hospital in critical condition. About ten-thirty last night he was shot while attempting to rob a gas station. He gave us your name, along with some others, as accomplices to the robbery. We contacted the other boys, and all your stories line up. You're free to leave. But before you go, I want to say something. Clearly, you come from a family that cares for you. How old are you, Nicholas?"

"Eighteen."

"Billy Streeter is thirty. Why would you associate with him? First off, he's too old for you, and secondly, he's a low life. If he lives, and after he serves time in prison, when he gets out, he's not going to change his ways. Someone needs to slap you into reality for taking your parents through this crap."

The officer ordered Nicholas to stand. As Nicholas rose from the chair, the officer stood with his nose within an inch of Nicholas's face, the muscles in his neck strained as he shouted like a Marine drill sergeant. *"Get outta my sight! Stay outta trouble and thank your personal god for parents who care!"*

Nicholas turned from the police officer and walked out of the office. The others followed. Carl glanced at the officer as he left, who gave him a wink. Carl turned back, shook his hand, and whispered, "Thank you" and walked out of the office.

Once outside, Carl said, "Thank you, Brother Mallard."

"You're welcome, Pastor. I'm glad everything worked out."

"Thank you so much, Brother Mallard," said Trisha as she hugged him.

"Glad to help."

Then Mallard said, "Nicholas, you were fortunate this time. What the policeman told you is right. Stay away from people like this Billy character. I hope that you've learned from this experience."

Nicholas nodded his head and got into the car. Everyone in the car stared ahead and remained silent as they rode. When they arrived home, Trisha asked, "Does anyone want to eat?"

Chapter Twenty-two

They responded with an apathetic, "Yeah."

As they ate, the only sound heard was the clinking of forks against their plates.

Chapter Twenty-Three

After they finished eating, Carl and Trisha retired to their bedroom. Trisha stared at Carl and said, "Are you going to speak to your son?"

"Eventually. I need to calm down first."

Trisha sneered and said, "C'mon, Carl, everyone makes mistakes."

"This was not a mistake, Trisha. This was a blunder! Don't you realize he could've gone to prison or even worse?"

"I believe he's learned his lesson. When you speak with him, try not to be so negative."

Carl sucked his teeth and stared at Trisha. Just then, Trisha's phone rang. She looked at the caller's ID and said, "It's Marsha."

"Marsha who?"

"Nicholas's girlfriend. I wonder what she wants."

Carl left the room to go into the kitchen. Trisha answered the phone. "Hello, Marsha, how are you?"

"I'm well, Sister Boston. And how are you doing?"

"I'm good.

"Is Nicholas near you?"

"No, he isn't."

"Good, I want to talk to you about him."

Trisha's heart skipped a beat and she said, "What's wrong?"

"Nicholas asked me not to say anything."

"What's wrong, Marsha?"

"He told me that he's leaving the church."

"He's leaving Ephesians to join another church?"

"No, not just his father's church, but all churches. He said that he's tired of the church scene and he doesn't want to be a hypocrite. Also, I'm afraid that he's caught up with the wrong crowd and is smoking pot. He said that he was going to tell you he was leaving the church, but I thought that I'd give you a heads-up."

"Thank you so much, Marsha."

"You're welcome, Sister Boston."

Trisha ended the call. As her tears flowed down her cheek she thought, "I can't tell Carl about this; he'd be devastated. God, I can't handle this."

Trisha felt her heart flutter and could hear her pulse beating in her ears. She cried, *"Oh Jesus! Oh God, help me!"*

Carl and Nicholas heard her cries and ran to the bedroom. By the time they reached her, she was heaving short rapid breaths.

Carl shouted, *"She's hyperventilating, Nicholas get me a paper bag! Now!"*

Nicholas returned with a paper bag. Carl opened the bag and placed it over her mouth and nose. She inhaled and exhaled into the bag until she began breathing normally.

Carl caressed her cheeks, kissed her on her forehead and said, "Darling are you okay?! What happened?"

As tears ran down Nicholas's face, he said, "Mom, you need to go to the hospital."

"No, I'm all right now," she responded.

"What happened, Trish? Maybe you should lie down."

Trisha laid on the bed and said, "I'll be alright."

"Nicholas, let me talk to your mom alone."

Nicholas walked out of the bedroom, staring at his mother as he went.

Carl peered into Trisha's face. His voice cracked as he said, "Babe, what happened?"

"I'm fine."

"Trisha, did it have anything to do with the way I've been acting?"

She shook her head.

Carl sniffled and said, "Trish, I don't want to lose you. Do you hear me? I *can't* lose you!" Carl bowed his head in his hands, weeping, then hugged her around her neck and said, "I love you, Trisha."

Trisha smiled, patted him on the back and said, "Carl, I ain't going nowhere. You ain't gonna get rid of me that easy. And besides, I don't want your next wife to come in here and wear my clothes."

Carl chuckled, then wiped his tears.

"Carl, we need to talk with Nicholas though."

"Nicholas, come in here, please," Carl called.

Nicholas walked into the room.

"Have a seat, Nicholas," said Trisha. Then she asked, "Is there something you want to tell your parents?"

"What do you mean?"

Carl, interrupting, said, "Excuse me, Trish, but before you continue, I want to say something.

Carl stared at Nicholas and said, "I'm sorry, son, if I was harsh with you. You don't understand how it is to be a parent of a young black man nowadays. Every time you step out the door, your mother and I worry and pray you get home safe. You're an endangered species. A stop by a policeman for a simple jaywalking violation could escalate into an execution. I hope you see where I'm coming from."

"Dad, I have worries too."

"I understand, Son."

"No, you *don't* understand! You think you're the only one with fears? I worry about you and the stresses you are under as a pastor. Dad, I remember when I was a kid, one time the members didn't pay their pledges. I witnessed you pulling your hair out, wondering where you were going to get the money. I've observed you so preoccupied with church stuff that you mumbled to yourself until you fell asleep right in the middle of our conversation."

Nicholas's voice cracked. "I hurt when I hear the spiteful things some in the church say about you behind your back when they think I'm not listening.

"Also, I was terrified after my godfather committed suicide. I became sick thinking that the same thing would happen to you. I cried when I told Richard, my roomie who's also a preacher's kid, about Reverend Kendal's suicide. He, in turn, showed me an article about a preacher who was found dead of a drug overdose in his hotel room. We concluded that he was under all sorts of stresses and that's why he took drugs. I left the article on your desk, hoping you'd read it."

"I read it. I thought your mother had left it."

"Dad, I'm surprised that more pastors don't take drugs, commit suicide, or suffer a nervous breakdown or a heart attack."

"I didn't know Pastor Kendal's death affected you like that."

Nicholas shook his head and said with a sigh, "And neither did you ask."

"Nicholas, other than I'm sorry, I don't know what else to say."

Trisha remained still and inwardly applauded Nicholas's cathartic episode.

"I'm sorry, Dad, but that's not the life for me, my future wife, or my kids."

Carl's brows gathered and he said, "I'm sorry I wasn't a good enough father to you. I know I wasn't perfect, but I didn't realize I was *that* bad."

"Carl, don't make it personal. He didn't say you were not a good father."

"Yeah, Dad, please don't take it there."

Carl checked his watch and said, "Please excuse me, I have an appointment at the church in a half hour. I'll be back as soon as I can."

"Dad, I may not be here when you return. I'm meeting Marsha this afternoon."

Carl exhaled, and speaking in a low tone said, "Okay."

Carl kissed Trisha on her cheek and tapped Nicholas on the shoulder. Then he dragged his feet as he exited the room with his hands in his pockets and shoulders sagging.

CHAPTER TWENTY-FOUR

After Carl left for the church Trisha fixed her eyes on Nicholas. Nicholas glanced back at Trisha and asked, "What's wrong, Mom?"

Trisha responded in a measured tone, "Nicholas, what's going on with you?"

"What do you mean?"

"First of all, you were hanging out with that criminal Billy Streeter. I've always told you that you can't lay down with dogs and not get fleas."

"Aww, mom. That was nothin'."

"Don't *tell* me it was nothing!" Trisha ranted. "He wouldn't let you hang with him unless you are into what he's into! Now tell me—what are you into, Nicholas?"

They stared into each other's eyes for three seconds, without as much as a blink.

Trisha took deep breaths and her eyes tightened. Finally, Nicholas looked away from Trisha and said, "Mom, me and Richard experimented with a little pot."

Trisha, with a raised brow, said, "Go on!"

"We only tried it twice."

"What made you try it even once?!"

"I don't know," he said nonchalantly.

"Why have you paired up with Richard?"

"His mother is a pastor, and he goes through the same things that I do. His mother depends on him for everything."

"What about his father?"

"His father is not in the picture."

"Where is he?"

"They're separated."

"Oh, I see. Nicholas, you still haven't explained to me why you were hanging with Billy."

"He was supposed to have the hook-up to this exclusive club where many of the rap artists frequent. He told us he could get us in."

"For how much?"

Nicholas lowered his head and said, "A hundred and fifty dollars—"

"A piece?!"

"Yeah."

"Where were you going to get that kind of money?"

"I borrowed some of it from Marsha."

"I didn't know that you saw her."

"I stopped by her house before I met my friends."

"How much did you borrow?"

"A C-note."

"Nicholas, I am too disappointed in you right now. I—"

"I'm going to see her this afternoon, Mom. I have her money."

Trisha stood, and shook her finger in his face and raged, "Don't you *ever* borrow money from her again!"

"Are you going to tell Dad?"

Trisha looked away from Nicholas and sat on the bed.

"Mom!"

Still peering away, she waved him off.

Nicholas drifted from her room like a condemned man headed for the gallows without being given an opportunity for an appeal. When he reached his room, he laid across his bed facedown. His phone rang. It was Morgan Kendal's son, Lester.

"Hey, Lester, what's up?"

"Hey, Nicholas! My mother told me you were in town. I hope we will get together before you go back."

"Yeah."

"Is everything okay?"

"Yeah. What are you doing this afternoon?"

"I'm free."

"I'm meeting with Marsha this afternoon. Why don't you and uh... Shirley? Are you still seeing her?"

"Yeah."

"Why don't we all get together at the Burger Stop about three?"

"Sounds good. I spoke with Shirley earlier; she's not doing anything."

"Good, see you there."

Nicholas remained in his room to avoid confronting with his mother.

At two-thirty he called out as he was leaving, "Mom, I'm headed out. I'm going to meet with Marsha at the Burger Stop."

Trisha responded with a dull, "Okay."

"That's it, Mom?" he thought. "Not even a 'have a nice time' or a 'tell Marsha I said hello?'"

Nicholas wiped his eyes and left for the restaurant. When he arrived, Lester, Marsha, and Shirley were standing in front of the restaurant talking. Nicholas greeted everyone and then they convened inside. Once seated, Nicholas asked Lester, "Les, how have you been, man?"

"I miss my dad a lot. I have my good and bad days."

"How's your mom doing?"

"About the same."

Marsha cuddled Nicholas's hand and said, "Nicholas, you're so worried about everyone else. How are you handling it?"

"You know me."

"Yes, I do know you."

Shirley said, "Like Marsha said before you arrived, 'Nicholas wants to be brave for everyone else.'"

"Thank you for your concern everybody, but I'm fine."

Marsha giggled and said, "Okay, Superman."

Lester paused, stared at Nicholas for a few seconds and said, "Speaking of my father, I can still see him mumbling to himself as he wrote in his journal. I'd sure love to get a hold of it. I believe it will reveal why he took his life."

"Do you know where his journal is?" asked Nicholas.

"No. The last time I saw the journal was about a month before he died. I've searched all over the house for it. When I asked my mother what happened to all of my dad's books, she shook her head as she walked away and said, 'I gave them away.' When I asked her to who, she said, 'They're gone.'"

Nicholas's brow furrowed and he said, "Think about it, Lester. You said that you searched the entire house for the journal, right?"

"Yeah."

"Hmm," said Nicholas. "Your mother said that she *gave* the books away, not sold or threw them out. Who then would she most likely give the books to?"

Lester answered, "A preacher."

Nicholas grinned and asked, "And what preacher would she likely *give* your father's books to?"

"A preacher that was a good friend of my dad."

"And who was your father's best friend?" he said as he slowly grinned.

"Your father, Reverend Carl Boston."

Nicholas and Lester high-fived each other and Nicholas shouted, "*Bingo!* That means the journal is in *my* house and probably in my father's study."

Then Lester said, "Listen, bro, if you run across the journal, *please* let me know."

"You got it, Lester."

CHAPTER TWENTY-FIVE

After they ate and said goodbye to their friends, Nicholas and Marsha strolled hand in hand through a nearby park. Nicholas was unusually quiet as they walked, answering Marsha's questions with short responses.

Finally, Marsha asked, "Nicholas, what has you so preoccupied?"

"Nothing."

Marsha smirked and said, "I know you; you're thinking how you can get your hands on the journal."

"Not really, I was just—"

"Spare me your lies, Nicholas. I saw the look in your eyes when Lester brought up the subject of the journal."

"Marsha, what if there's something in the journal that could save the life of someone considering suicide? Wouldn't it be worth me reading it?" Nicholas was now blinking back tears. "I loved my godfather and had the highest respect for him. It's killing me not knowing why he killed himself. Can you understand that?"

"I hear you, but what if the journal turns out to be a Pandora's Box and reveals things you don't want or need to know about your godfather?

What if reading the journal does permanent damage to your image of him? Do you think you can handle that? Are you willing to take that risk? And besides, you have no right to look into his private notes. Would you like it if someone read your personal journal?"

Nicholas did not respond but stared into Marsha's eyes. They continued to stroll through the park when suddenly Nicholas snapped his finger and said, "Oh yeah, Marsha, I have your money." He reached into his pocket for his wallet. In it was a hundred-dollar bill, and he handed it to her.

"You sure you don't still need it?"

"No, I ended up not needing it. But thanks anyway. Marsha, I'm going to walk you home, then head home and spend time with my parents before going back to school. We're still on for tomorrow night, right?"

"I thought you said that your father wanted you to take over the youth service tomorrow night."

"He does, but uh, we talked and it's cool."

———

Meanwhile, Reverend Carl Boston was at the church, meeting with the trustee board members and the church's accountant. As they sat at a conference table, the accountant took a deep breath before revealing the grim news. "Reverend Boston, I'm afraid you're going to have to cut back on many of the activities of the church or else."

"Or else what?" asked the trustee board chairman nervously.

"Or else the church will have to file for bankruptcy."

Carl stared away as the accountant continued. "The church has been operating at a deficit, scarcely making payroll for months. To make matters worse, the mortgage is two months in arrears. Uh, Pastor Boston, do you have a question?"

Carl was shaken from his musings. "Hmm? Oh, um, I guess we have to renovate. How much will it cost?"

Everyone's eyes narrowed and they glanced at each other. "Pastor, are you with us?" asked the board chairman.

"Yeah, ah, sorry. What was the question again?"

They stared at each other again and then at Carl. The board chairman asked, "Pastor, are you, alright?"

"Hmm?"

"Pastor, perhaps you should go home and get some rest," the board chairman suggested. Then he looked at the others and said, "This meeting is postponed until later next week."

"It's important that we make some decisions very soon," said the accountant, "I hope you feel better, Reverend."

"Thanks," Carl said absently.

"Do you need someone to drive you home, Pastor?" asked the chairman

Carl's speech dragged. "Nah, I'll be okay. I just need a little rest, that's all."

As he wandered to the door, they all said, "Feel better."

Carl left the church and decided to go to a restaurant for a late lunch. He occasionally drank a glass of wine with his lunch. This time, in addition to wine with lunch, he drank a couple of glasses of wine after lunch. After he finished the third glass, he lamented to himself, "I'm a bewildered pastor of a declining ministry, my son thinks I'm a rotten father, and my wife no longer respects me."

When he arrived home, he went straight to the bedroom and collapsed on the bed without giving notice he was home.

Trisha was in the kitchen cooking dinner. She heard the front door open and called out, "Carl, is that you?"

He slurred, "Yeah, Trish."

Before Trisha could reply, Carl was unconscious.

"Okay, I'll call you when dinner's ready."

Soon after, Nicholas returned home. He walked into the kitchen, his face plastered with a cautious smile as he deliberated whether or not Trisha was still angry with him. Then he said, "Mom, something sure smells good. Whatcha cookin'?" He smiled and said, "I can't tell you how much I've missed your cooking while at school."

"Uh huh," Trisha said casually.

"I brag about your roast beef all the time." Then he chuckled and said, "Me and my roomie Richard tease each other about whose mom is the best cook."

Trisha stirred a pot of stew, then sighed. Nicholas shook his head and said, "Ah, c'mon, Ma, speak to me! I'm sorry, okay? I admit I shouldn't have borrowed money from Marsha. I gave her the money back."

"I would think so. We didn't raise you that way."

"I know and I'm sorry. I'll never do that again."

Trisha poked out her lips and said, "What about the reefer, Nicholas?"

"Mom, like I said, it was just twice. After that I did not, nor will I ever, do it again."

Trisha rolled her eyes and grunted, "Hmm."

"Did you tell Dad?"

"No, I didn't."

"Thank you, Mom. You know him; he'll never let me forget it."

"Nicholas, I strongly suggest that you don't say anything negative about your father. By all rights, I should've told him."

"Sorry, Mom. By the way, where's Dad?"

"I think he's in the bedroom."

"I'm surprised that he's not in his study. Do you think Dad would mind me watching TV in his study?"

"Go ahead, just don't touch anything. You know how particular your father is. He can tell when the least little thing is out of place."

————

As Nicholas sat watching TV at his father's desk, he looked around and thought, "I wonder if Reverend Kendal's journal is in the desk."

His hands shook as he touched the drawer handle. He tugged a bit, and it came ajar. He looked around, then opened it more. "I ain't gonna read the journal, I just want to see if it's here."

Nicholas continued to open the drawer, little by little. He peeked and saw what appeared to be a book, but he could not make out the words on the cover. So, he opened the drawer further, slipped his hand in, and pulled the book out. The cover read, "The Holy Bible." He sucked his teeth and said, "Ah, man, it's just my dad's Bible. I guess this is God's way of showing me that Marsha was right. I shouldn't read Reverend Kendal's personal journal."

But then he had a sneaking suspicion the journal was in one of the other drawers. He grabbed the handle of another drawer.

"What are you doing, Nicholas?" Trisha glared at him as she stood by the office door.

"Oh, nothing."

"Dinner's ready. Come eat."

She went upstairs to the bedroom, stood at the door and said, "Carl, dinner's ready."

Carl lay lifeless, like a prop used on the set of a play. Then she said, "Carl, your dinner is going to get cold."

Carl groaned and said, "I'm not hungry right now. Let me sleep, please."

"Okay, your food will be on the stove."

As she left, he dozed off again and slept through the night.

In the morning, Trisha woke, pulled back the curtains, and invited the radiance of the sun to invade their bedroom. Carl shaded his face with his hands and, in a raspy voice, said, "Trisha, what time is it?"

"It's time for you to shower and get ready for church."

He looked at his watch on the nightstand. "We've got plenty of time. Why did you wake me so early?"

"I thought if you got up at your usual time, you'd be late for church. You were so out of it last night, and you didn't eat your dinner. What had you so drained?"

"I don't know. I guess I needed the rest."

On their way to church, Carl made a few wrong turns. He stopped at a corner, where he had driven hundreds of times, and paused for a few seconds, confused.

"Are you okay, Carl?" asked Trisha.

"Yeah, I'm good. I was just turned around for a second."

At church, Carl stammered through his sermon, bolstering his ramblings with mixed metaphors and convoluted logic. The stunned audience, that had celebrated his preaching in the past with shouts of 'amen' and 'preach pastor,' was silent.

Trisha rose from her seat and beckoned one of the ushers, who was a nurse, to follow her. The nurse joined her on the pulpit. Trisha approached Carl while he was speaking and tapped him on the shoulder, then whispered, "Carl, have a seat."

Carl shrugged his shoulders, turned, and stared with widened eyes. The congregation murmured as Carl was escorted to his office by the nurse and Trisha. One of the ministers addressed the audience from the podium, "Saints, we need to pray for our pastor."

They replied, "Amen!"

"I don't mean later. *I mean pray right now!* Hold your neighbor's hand; let's intercede for our leader."

Once in his office the nurse said to Trisha, "We'd better call an ambulance."

Trisha responded, "Yes, yes... call them."

Trisha looked at Carl and said, "Carl, please lie down."

Carl's hands trembled, and he stumbled as she guided him to the couch. He laid down, then groaned.

Trisha called Nicholas, but there was no answer. The ambulance arrived. While in the ambulance on the way to the hospital, Nicholas called,

"Hey, Mom, I see you called. I know I'm late, but I'm on my way. I'm riding with Marsha."

Trisha said, "Nicholas, listen to me. Go back home, go to your dad's study, and look in the middle drawer. If it's locked, the keys are in the cabinet next to the green vase. Bring the medical card to the emergency room."

"Why? What's wrong, Mom? *Where's Dad?!*"

"Your father had an incident. He'll be fine."

"What in the world does that mean?!"

"Just do as I say! Your father's fine."

Marsha asked Nicholas, "What's wrong?"

"My father is being rushed to the hospital."

"What happened?"

"I don't know. My mother said he's fine."

"Well, maybe he is."

"No, he ain't! My father would *never* miss a Sunday service, no matter how he felt! Marsha, please take me home. I have to get something. And after that, take me to the hospital."

Sweat dripped from Nicholas's forehead as he prayed, "God, *please* spare my father!"

Nicholas rushed into the house and straight to his father's office. He tried to open the desk drawer, but it was locked. He went to the cabinet, found the key, and opened the middle drawer. In it lay a black book. He removed the book, found the medical card, and put it in his pocket. As he rushed to put the book back into the drawer, his thumb got caught between the front cover and the first page. He pulled his thumb out of the book, and the cover flipped open. He glanced at the first page which read, "The Me Nobody Knows." At the bottom of the page it said, "Morgan Kendal."

Nicholas froze, his heart raced, and he cried, *"The journal!"*

CHAPTER TWENTY-SIX

Nicholas thought, "I need to get to the hospital and see about my father. I don't have time for this right now." He placed the diary back into the drawer, then ran out of the house and into Marsha's car.

"Marsha, let's go!" he said, rushing her.

Meanwhile, Trisha conversed with the doctor. "Mrs. Boston, has your husband been under any extreme stress lately?" asked the physician.

"He recently lost his closest friend to suicide, which was stressful enough. And on top of everything else, he's a pastor. So, I guess it's safe to say, yes, he's been under more than enough stress."

The doctor said, "It appears that your husband has had a nervous collapse."

"My father was a pastor too, who also suffered a mental breakdown," Trisha said.

"I'm going to recommend a therapist for your husband," the doctor continued. "Pastors, police, and others who are in the people-servicing professions are under tremendous pressure. They need servicing themselves. Not unlike a caretaker who's so busy caring for others that they ignore the warning signs that a mental breakdown is looming."

Trisha sighed heavily and thought, "Carl ain't going to some therapist. I can hear him now, 'Trisha, I ain't crazy!'"

As if reading her mind, the doctor interrupted her thoughts. "Mrs. Boston, I know the stigma attached to getting therapy, especially for pastors. Your husband is not the only pastor I've seen with a mental collapse. When I speak to the pastors I've treated, I ask them, 'If you broke your leg and needed crutches, would you use them?' They say, 'Sure.'"

"Then I ask, 'And when your leg heals, what do you do with the crutches?'

"They say, 'I throw them away.'

"Then I say, 'Well, apply that same principle to the therapist. When you no longer need one you—'"

"Doctor, you don't know my husband."

"I'll talk to him, Mrs. Boston."

———

Nicholas arrived at the hospital and ran into the emergency room. He asked the person at the front desk, "Is there a Reverend Carl Boston here?"

She checked the register and said, "Yes, he's in bed number seven."

The beds were lined up perpendicularly on one side of the walkway. Each bed was enclosed on three sides with a white opaque curtain. On the other side of the walkway were three nurses' stations and a doctor's office. Nicholas dashed down the walkway and nearly bumped into Trisha as she exited the doctor's office.

Catching his breath, he asked, "Mom, how's Dad?!"

"Calm down, Nicholas, your dad is fine."

"What happened?"

As she was about to explain, Trisha noticed Marsha walking toward them. Alerting Nicholas to her presence, she said, "Oh, hi Marsha. Thanks for bringing Nicholas."

"You're welcome. How is Pastor Boston?"

"He's in with the doctor right now."

"Can I see him?" asked Nicholas

"Wait here. I'll check."

Trisha pulled back the curtain and entered the stall where Carl lay. The doctor stood over Carl, reading his chart. Then he said, "Reverend, are you awake?"

Carl coughed and said, "Yes, Doctor."

"I spoke with your wife earlier. She said that you've been under intense pressure lately."

"No more than usual," Carl said nonchalantly.

"I want to ask you a few questions."

Carl smiled and said, "Shoot, Doc."

"Have you been feeling overwhelmed lately?"

"What do you mean?"

"I mean unable to carry on daily activities."

"Not really."

"What about depression?"

"I felt bad at times, but I wouldn't call it depression."

"What happened at church this morning? Why did your wife bring you into the emergency room?"

Trisha stared at Carl and said to herself, "Oh, he's got you now, Carl."

"Oh, that? I was just extremely tired, that's all. I probably need to get away."

The doctor recommended Carl go to therapy, and as promised, he gave Carl the same spiel he gave his other clergy patients. Carl stared at the wall.

Trisha thought, "Nice try, Doc, but your pitch is falling on deaf ears."

The doctor said, "I gave the contact information of a therapist to your wife."

"Thank you, Doctor. Can I leave now?"

"Sure."

"Nicholas is waiting to see you, Carl," said Trisha.

Carl smiled and said, "Oh! My boy. Tell him to come in."

Trisha stuck her head out of the curtain and said, "Come in, Nicholas."

Nicholas eased through the opening of the curtain, looked around, and then broke down in tears. As he sniffled, he said, "I'm sorry, Dad."

"It's okay, Nicholas. Don't worry; I'm fine."

————

Marsha drove Nicholas and his parents to their house. Then she drove Nicholas to the church to retrieve Carl's car. When Carl entered the house, he headed straight to his study.

"Carl, *where* are you going?" asked Trisha. "The doctor said that you should go to bed right away and rest."

Carl suspected that the hiding place for the diary had been compromised, so he went to his desk, retrieved the diary, and hid it behind a bookcase until he could find a new hiding place.

As Carl entered his bedroom, his phone rang. Trisha snatched the phone and said, "You ain't taking any phone calls. You have a choice: either I answer your calls or whoever it is can leave a message."

Carl laid back on his bed, smiled, and closed his eyes.

Chapter Twenty-Seven

F our days had passed since Clyde was served with divorce papers and still no word from Mae.

He rocked back and forth in the dark on his couch, praying Mae would reconsider. As he contemplated how he would cope with the humiliation of a divorce, his phone rang. It was Mae.

"How are you Clyde?" she asked coldly.

Clyde responded in a monotone. "I'm well, and you?"

Mae paused for a few seconds, then said, "I think that we should talk to the girls together."

"About what?"

"Weren't you served the divorced papers?"

Clyde erupted, *"Why did you tell me we were going to meet and then slap me with divorce papers?"*

"If you had treated me better, there wouldn't have been any need for a divorce!" Mae countered.

"What do you mean by, 'If you had treated me better?!'"

Mae sucked her teeth and said, "So, when can you meet with me and the girls?"

"Mae, answer my question. What did you mean by that statement?!"

"Clyde, I ain't gonna argue with you. Are you going to meet with us or not?"

Clyde squeezed his eyes shut, gritted his teeth, and hurled the phone to the couch. Then he snatched the phone off the couch and shouted, "Mae!"

"Yeah, Clyde!"

"Are you trying to hurt me, or something?! Why would you destroy our family?"

"Look, Clyde—"

"No, you look Mae!"

"Clyde, I swear on my father's grave, if you yell at me again, I'll hang this phone up!"

"Mae, why are you acting like this?"

"I'm tired. I've tried for years to keep this marriage together. You don't love me. Perhaps you never have."

"Where did *that* come from?"

"My mind is made up. I'm going forward with the divorce."

"Are you saying there's no hope for us?"

"I'm saying that I've had enough, and I'm fed up."

Clyde made an audible sigh then said, "Okay, then that's it. It's your decision."

Mae said, "When are we going to tell Geraldine and Mary? And don't say anything to anyone before we tell them. I want them to hear it from us first and not from those gossiping church folks."

Clyde contemplated the possibility Mae would change her mind, so he suggested, "No need to rush. There's plenty of time for that."

"Clyde, I'm not going to change my mind..."

"I know... I know. Like you said, your mind is made up."

"Yes, it is."

"I'll get back to you tomorrow."

"Make sure that you do!" she demanded, then hung up.

Clyde called his mother-in-law. "Hello, Mother Benton."

"Hello, Clyde."

"Sorry to call you at this hour. Do you have time to talk?"

"Sure."

"Mae has filed for divorce."

Mother Benton remained silent and waited to hear what else he had to say.

After three seconds he asked, "Are you aware of that?"

"Clyde, she expressed to me her displeasure with the marriage."

"Did she give you a reason for her displeasure?"

Mother Benton simply asked, "What did she say to you?"

"She said that I don't love her. Mother, I love her with all my heart. Neither her nor our kids have *ever* wanted for anything. I just can't figure out why she's doing this."

"Well, Clyde, all I can do is talk to her. But you know once she makes her mind up, no one can change it. Her father was the same way."

"She told me before we were married, she didn't believe in divorce and that she wanted her family to always remain intact."

"All I can say is that life's experiences have a way of changing the way we think about things."

Realizing that he was getting nowhere, he said, "Thank you for your time, Mother. Good night."

"Good night, Clyde."

The next morning, Clyde went to the church office. He sat at his desk for three hours, staring at the walls and shuffling papers around. He instructed his secretary that he was not receiving any visitors or phone calls. Finally, he decided to leave the office early. As he drove up to his house, his heart skipped a beat. Parked in front of the house was Mae's car.

He said to himself, "Clyde, don't get excited. She was not expecting you to be home. This probably means nothing."

He got out of his car and eased open the front door. The house was still, as though it had been abandoned. For reasons not even he could explain, he tiptoed to the bedroom. When he opened the door, his eyes bulged, and he was unable to breathe or speak. Lying across the bed, fully clothed and fast asleep, was Mae.

Clyde walked to his side of the bed and was tempted to slide into bed next to her. He decided against it, fearful of what her reaction would be when she woke and found him lying there.

He slipped out of the bedroom and into the living room, then sat and stared at a blank TV screen. Soon after, he heard the front door rattling. It was Geraldine and Mary coming home from school.

"Hey, girls!" said Clyde as he leaped from the couch, his face beaming.

They ran into his arms and hugged him as though he would leave them forever if they let go.

"Hey, Dad, it's good to see you. It's just like old times," said Mary with a chuckle.

Geraldine laughed. "Where have you been hiding?"

Mae heard the commotion and came into the living room.

She said, "Hey girls. How was school?"

"Fine," they said as they continued to grin.

"How are you, Mae?" said Clyde as he smiled.

"Fine, and you?" she said in a casual tone.

After that cold response, Clyde knew he made the right decision not to lie next to her as she slept.

Mae turned her attention to their daughters. "Go up to your rooms, girls. Let me speak to your father for a minute."

"Okay, Mom." Their faces gleamed as they walked upstairs to their rooms.

"Clyde, I didn't think you'd be home. What happened at the office?"

"Nothing; I just decided to leave early."

"Since you're here, we might as well tell them tonight."

"What did you tell them? They were all hyped when they saw me."

"I just said to them, before they left for school, not to go to my mother's but to meet me at home."

Clyde sneered and said, "Oh. I see."

Chapter Twenty-seven

"I'll fix dinner later, and we can tell them after we eat."

Clyde shook his head. "How can she be so cavalier when our lives are about to be destroyed?" he thought.

———

After dinner, they remained at the table. Geraldine and Mary reminisced, touching on happy times the family had spent together. They prefaced their memories with "remember when...?" before they convulsed with laughter. Clyde feigned a giggle to keep up appearances. Mae, however, looked at everyone with a blank stare.

"Geraldine, Mary," Mae said, "I need you to listen to me and your father. First of all, we love you both very much."

Clyde said, "Ya'll will always be our babies."

Geraldine sat up in her chair and her body stiffened. "What's going on?"

Mae sniffled, stared at them, and said, "Me and your father are getting a divorce."

Geraldine's eyes teared and her hands trembled. Mary screamed, *"What are you saying?! What are you saying?!"*

"Calm down, Mary," said Clyde as he fought to hold back tears.

Mary continued to scream, *"Dad! Mom! Y'all can't do this! Please, please, don't do this to us!"*

Geraldine's eyes flooded and her voice quivered, "Maybe, ah, maybe y'all should pray!" Then Geraldine leaped from her seat, ran upstairs, dropped on her bed, and let out a loud, piercing cry.

Mary stared at the floor, shook her head, and cried, "No... no, this can't be happening!"

Mae went to give her a hug. Mary shied away and said, "This is all your fault, Ma! Dad wanted to stay married, but *you* wanted a divorce!"

"Mary, that's your mother!" scolded Clyde.

"It's okay, Clyde," said Mae. "Go see about Geraldine. I'll talk to Mary."

Mary sat stoned-faced and stared away from Mae. Mae looked at Mary and said in a calm voice, "Mary, listen to me. Sometimes things don't work out. Life isn't always pleasant."

Mary's face remained stoic, and she continued to look away. Then she got up to get a tissue, dried her eyes and wiped her nose. As she wiped her nose she said, "Ma, I don't understand why you want to divorce Dad. You don't love him anymore or somethin'?"

"Mary, it's not that simple."

"Yes, it is! If you loved him, you wouldn't get a divorce."

"Look at me, Mary."

Mary covered her face with her hands and shook her head. Mae grabbed her shoulders and turned her around so that she would face her. Mary kept her hands over her face and her head bowed.

As Mae talked with Mary, Clyde and Geraldine walked down the stairs and back into the kitchen. Her arms were locked around his waist and her face buried in his chest.

"We need to go to the living room and sit down," Clyde said.

Mary sniffled and sighed. "I just want to be alone right now."

"Mary, *please* come sit with the family!" begged Geraldine.

Mary ignored her sister's pleas and started heading upstairs to her bedroom. Geraldine stood and took steps toward Mary. Then Mae said, "Hold up, Geraldine, give her some space. Let's call it a night. We'll talk tomorrow."

Geraldine continued to her bedroom. Mae walked toward the bedroom, which was located on the first floor, turned, looked at Clyde and said, "You comin', Clyde?"

Clyde followed her into the bedroom and said under his breath, "What's *this* about?"

They got dressed for bed and he laid next to Mae, his body stiffened, as though she was a stranger. Mae pulled the cover over her shoulders and laid on her side, facing away from Clyde.

Clyde laid on his back with his hands clasped behind his head and remained still, careful not to disturb Mae. As he stared at the ceiling, he reminisced about the time when they were first married. Everything they did had a newness to it. They could not wait to wake up and do something together, like walk in the park or take in a movie.

Even if they stayed home, it was brand new, because the marriage was brand new.

Clyde chuckled when he recalled the birth of their daughters. He glanced at Mae, hoping to sense the slightest clue that she shared his sentimentalities. When there was no indication she was in sync with his feelings, he turned to his side and continued to ponder his life with Mae. After what to him seemed like hours, he felt a hand touch his shoulder and heard a voice whisper, "Clyde, are you awake?"

"Yes."

"Clyde, honey, I don't want a divorce."

"Neither do I."

"All I wanted was your attention. I'm so sorry that I hurt you in the process."

"That's okay, Mae. I promise you'll have my full attention from now on. I was thinking about—"

"Let me finish, please."

"I'm sorry. Go ahead."

"I don't want to stand in the way of your ministry."

"I know, babe."

"I'm going to tell you the real reason I filed for divorce. I want you to know something about me that I've never told you. You may not want me after you hear this."

"Mae, what is it…?"

"Dad," whispered a familiar voice that was close enough for Clyde to feel breath on his ear. It was Geraldine. "Mom said to wake you."

Clyde rubbed his eyes and said in a raspy voice, "What, what?"

"Get up, Dad. Mom made breakfast."

"Okay, Geraldine, I'm coming."

Clyde lamented as he proceeded to the bathroom, "It was all just a dream. I can't take this torture any longer."

A tear trickled down his face, and he murmured, "I give up. She can have the house and anything else she wants. I'll just sign whatever."

CHAPTER TWENTY-EIGHT

E mma arrived at church for her counseling session with Jeremiah that Tuesday. Jeremiah was sitting behind his desk when the secretary escorted Emma into the office and left the door ajar.

Before she sat down, she asked, "Do you mind if I close the door, Reverend? I have some extremely sensitive things I want to say."

Jeremiah said, "No one can hear us."

"Your secretary's right outside the door. She kinda makes me nervous."

"It's okay, Sister Emma. She can't hear us."

"I want to share some personal things with you, that's all. I hope that you don't share my business with anyone, not even with your wife."

"Sister Emma, what I say to my wife is my business. If you have a problem with that then…"

"I'm sorry, Pastor, I didn't mean anything by it. I'm just a very private person, that's all."

"I won't discuss anything with my wife I deem unnecessary for her to know."

"That's good enough for me," she said with a satisfied look.

"What's troubling you, Sister?"

"My husband's so preoccupied with getting drunk that he spends no time with me." Then she glanced at the office door and in a muffled tone said, "I'm still young and vibrant, if you know what I mean. So, where does that leave me?"

"Have you spoken to your husband about getting help for his drinking problem?"

"He says that he doesn't have a drinking problem."

"Would he come to counseling along with you?"

"He won't come."

"Did you ask him?"

"Believe me, I know he won't come."

Emma paused, took a breath and said, "Pastor, I'm sorry. I'm still uncomfortable with the door open and your secretary's desk just a few feet from the door."

"Like I said, she can't hear us."

Emma raised her brows and asked, "Pastor, since Frank won't come to church, what if I asked him if he would let you counsel us in our home?"

"Well, uh... Sister Emma, I don't know about that."

She smiled and said, "But what if he consented?"

"Let me think about it. You'll have to get back to me."

Emma grinned and said, "Oh good! I'll even cook a little somethin.'"

"I didn't say I would. I said I'd think about it."

She continued to grin and said, "Okay, Pastor. I'm just so excited. When should I call you?"

"Call me in a couple of days."

She giggled and said, "Okay, Reverend. You're the best pastor in the world and believe me, I've known plenty of 'em."

Emma stood with her arms outstretched, inviting an embrace. Reverend Riley pulled open his desk drawer, looked into it, and pretended not to see her. Still looking into his drawer, he said, "I'll wait for your call."

Emma lowered her arms and said, "Goodbye, Pastor," then exited the office.

Sister Marcy smirked and said in a sarcastic tone to Emma as she left, "Have a nice day, Sister Richards."

Emma flashed a wave but did not speak or look in her direction.

Two days later, Emma called the church's office. The secretary answered. "Reverend Riley's office."

"May I speak with Reverend Riley, please?"

"Who may I say is calling?"

"Emma Richards. He's expecting my call."

"Hold on, please." She switched over to Jeremiah and said, "Reverend, Ms. um... Richards is on the line. Are you available?"

"Yes, I'll take the call."

Before she connected the call, she said, "Pastor, did I tell you your wife called earlier?"

"Yes, you did. Thank you, Sister Marcy."

Sister Marcy was tempted to disconnect the call but changed her mind.

"Hello, Sister Emma," Jeremiah said.

"How're you, Pastor?"

"I'm good, thanks for asking. And you?"

"I'm great. So, have you thought about whether you will make a house call or not?" she said with a giggle.

"Since he won't come to church, I guess I'll come *this* time."

"Oh good!"

"Ask your husband if it's okay first before we set a time and date."

"Forgive me, Pastor, but I already have. I prayed that you would consent, so I asked Frank and he said yes. He's looking forward to meeting you. I hope you're not angry with me for jumping the gun."

"It's okay as long as he knows I'm coming."

"Thank you so *very* much, Pastor."

They agreed to meet at noon on Wednesday of the following week.

When Wednesday came, Jeremiah was in his office preparing to go to Emma's house. Before he left, his secretary called and said, "There's a woman here who says it's urgent that she speak with you."

"What's her name?"

"Her name is Gwendolyn Crown."

"Give me a minute."

"Yes, Pastor."

A minute later, Sister Marcy knocked on the door and asked, "Are you ready to receive Ms. Crown?"

"Yes, please send her in."

Gwendolyn Crown was a petite five-foot-five, frumpy twenty-six-year-old with a perpetual smile and soft voice. Her hair was disheveled, and she wore an oversized sweater that was stretched to twice its original size. Sister Marcy escorted her to the chair in front of his desk and left the door partly open when she left.

Jeremiah asked, "How may I help you, sister? And make it quick please; I have an appointment."

"Pastor, I'm here to help *you*."

"Excuse me?"

"Do you know Emma Richards?"

Jeremiah hesitated for a moment and then answered, "Yes."

"I understand she's a member of your church."

"What is it that you want?" he asked impatiently.

"Emma is my sister. I came to warn you not to trust her. She has serious problems."

"You mean mental problems?"

"Some might say that. However, I *know* her. She's just evil. If she hasn't already, she's going to try to seduce you. She's done this in other churches and then bragged about her conquests. Pastor, do not have anything to do with her. Please heed my warning."

Jeremiah rose from his seat and walked to where she sat and said, "I'm sorry, sister, but I'm in a hurry." Then he gestured to the office door and in a dismissive tone said, "Thank you so much."

———

When Jeremiah arrived at Emma's house, he rang the bell. Emma answered the door wearing a low-cut, loose-fitting lounge dress. Before he entered the house, he asked, "Where's Mr. Richards?"

"He's caught in traffic."

"Maybe I should wait in my car until he arrives."

"No need for that, Pastor; he'll be here soon. Come into the living room and sit down. I have something cooking on the stove. I'll be out in a minute."

Jeremiah sat, his heart pounding as he tapped the arm of the chair with the tips of his fingers. Then he heard the front door open. He sighed heavily and said under his breath. "Good, her husband is home."

As Frank walked in, Jeremiah stood, stretched out his right hand, expecting Frank to reciprocate, smiled, and said, "I'm Reverend Jeremiah Riley. Nice to meet you."

Frank froze, curled his lips, and shouted, *"What the hell are you doing here?!"*

Emma, rushed from the kitchen, covering her low-cut neckline, and screamed, *"Frank!"*

Chapter Twenty-Nine

Emma gasped and said, "Frank, this is ah... ah, Pastor Riley, the pastor of Mount Moriah, the church I told you about. He's here to um... um, visit with me because um... I'm a new member. Do you remember I told you that I joined?"

Jeremiah stood with his left foot forward, braced for a possible physical confrontation. Then he said, "Mr. Richards, I think there's a misunderstanding. I was under the impression you knew I was coming."

Frank didn't say anything and snatched Emma by the arm and pulled her into the kitchen and slammed the door. However, nothing short of a soundproof vault could mute the roar of his voice.

"Emma, why are you dressed like a whore?!"

"I ain't dressed like no—"

"Is this what you do while I'm at work?! The neighbors told me that men come here after I leave for work!"

"They're all liars!"

"You have the *nerve* to deny it when I just caught you with a man in the house while you thought I was at work?! Look at you, all exposed! *You think I'm an idiot or something!*"

"He's the pastor!"

"I don't care who he is! What is it with you and preachers, anyway? First there was that Pastor creep from Resurrection church, and now this guy!"

As they argued, Jeremiah stood in the living room with his arms folded, regretting ever having laid eyes on Emma.

Frank rushed out the kitchen and said, "Reverend, you need to leave right *now*!"

Jeremiah went toward the door, and afterward thought, "He may hurt her."

Then he turned back around. Frank's eyes stretched and he said, "Are you deaf or something? I said, leave my house!"

"Mr. Richards, please allow me to say something."

Frank's hands were balled into fists, and his chest heaved. He leered at Jeremiah and said incessantly, *"Reverend, get out of my house! Get out of my house...!"*

Jeremiah stood his ground and said, "I know you're angry, but don't do something you'll regret for the rest of your life."

Then he turned and walked out of the house. He got into his car, sat there for a few moments, and thought about what had just transpired, concluding, "I could've been killed messing around with that wretched woman."

As he drove off, his heart raced, he took a deep breath, shook his head, and said, "Lesson learned."

He went back to his office, leaned back in his chair, covered his face with his hands and prayed, "Lord, forgive me for my stubborn pride. I promise I will listen to wise counsel from now on and not judge the messenger You send to deliver the message."

Sister Marcy called him and said, "Pastor you have a call from Reverend Peter Austin of Resurrection Temple."

"I'll take it, thanks."

"Hey, Preacher, how are you?"

Peter answered with a cool response. "I'm good."

"To what do I owe this call?"

"I hear a couple of my members joined Mount Moriah the other Sunday."

"Yes, they did. Emma and Kimberly."

"I see. And what was the reason they gave you for why they left Resurrection Temple?"

"What's this, the third degree or something?!"

"I just have one question, my *brother!* Did you call my name on your broadcast and accuse me of molesting them? That's all I want to know."

"I'm not sure what you're talking about, but I sure don't like your attitude. And besides, where did you get that from?"

"I heard it from some people."

"Reverend, I suggest you not listen to everything *some people* have to say!"

Peter retorted, "I could say the same thing to you. I heard that you're spreading rumors I molested Kimberly!"

"I said no such thing!"

"Then who were you referring to on your broadcast?"

Jeremiah stopped, took a deep breath and said, "Preacher, we need to talk."

"We're talking right now!"

"Doc, I want to talk to you in person."

"Why?"

"I'll tell you when I see you."

"I don't see why you can't tell me over the phone."

"C'mon, Doc, meet me at Sara's."

Peter relented, and he and Jeremiah met at Sara's, a restaurant where preachers frequented. Peter arrived first and soon after Jeremiah came. Peter greeted Jeremiah with a frigid stare, nodded his head and said, "Pastor."

"Thanks for coming. Let me start off by saying I owe you an apology," said Jeremiah.

Then he related the story Emma had told him in his office about Peter attempting to force himself on her.

Peter said, "I heard Kimberly also said I molested her."

"Kimberly never said any such thing. As a matter of fact, she was reluctant to join. Emma and I pressured her into joining."

"So that lying Emma is the main cause for all of this," Peter grumbled.

Jeremiah went on to tell him what occurred at Emma's house. "I should've listened to my wife," Jeremiah confessed. "She didn't trust her from the start. Doc, she's dangerous. Earlier today, a lady came to my office claiming to be Emma's sister and warned me to stay clear of her.

"Reverend I can't tell you how sorry I am for this misunderstanding. I'm partially to blame. I shouldn't have listened to her."

"It's fine, Jeremiah. I accept your apology; we're good."

Then Jeremiah smiled and said, "We haven't fellowshipped in a while. Let's set up a date for you to come and preach. I'm going to check my calendar and get back to you."

Peter smiled and said, "Sounds good."

Then they shook hands. The server came to the table and asked, "Are you ready to order?"

Jeremiah said, "Order what you want, Preacher, it's on me."

Peter smiled, looked at the server and said, "In that case, I'll have the most expensive steak on the menu."

They all chuckled. After that Jeremiah and Peter placed their orders.

CHAPTER THIRTY

After lunch, Peter left the restaurant. As he drove home, he mumbled to himself, "Nothing *just* happens without a reason. God's just letting me know who the traitors in the congregation are. Thank you, Lord. I'm going to do some house cleaning."

Peter arrived home and told Yolanda what happened between him and Jeremiah and the lies Emma had told.

"Yolanda, I'm going to fix this!"

"What are you going to do?" Yolanda asked.

"First of all, I'm going to fire Deacon Halsey."

"Peter, you'd better give this some prayerful consideration; this could backfire."

"Like I said before, it's time he gave up that position."

"It's not just him I'm talking about. His relatives are in key positions in the church. Like his nephew Tyrone, for example, whom you assigned as youth pastor. The young people love him, especially the way he excites them when he preaches."

Peter took a deep breath and looked pointedly at his wife. "Yolanda, Deacon Halsey is out!"

"Peter, you're too angry to make any rational decisions right now. Perhaps you shouldn't make any changes just yet. First, calm down, then call a special church meeting and inform the congregation of Emma's lies and what Reverend Riley told you."

Peter paused, then said, "Okay, maybe you're right. I'll announce the meeting this Sunday."

Sunday came and Peter said to the congregation, "This Thursday I'm calling an urgent member-only meeting at seven p.m. I need to clear up a few things and it's imperative that every member attends."

Several of the members were not in service that morning, including Deacon Halsey. Peter met with Tyrone after church service in the sanctuary and asked, "Brother Tyrone, is the deacon okay?"

"Yeah, I spoke with him last night. He's fine."

"Oh, okay. Would you do me a favor and tell him about the church meeting this Thursday?"

"I will, Pastor."

A few of the leaders of the youth auxiliary came to where they were standing, greeted Peter, then said, "Brother Tyrone, do you still want to see us today?"

"Yeah, meet me in my office. I'll be there in a minute."

Peter said, "Tyrone, how are the plans for the youth banquet coming?"

"Fine, Pastor. I'm meeting with a few of the committee heads right now."

Peter smiled, patted him on his back and said, "Good. Good work."

––––––––

Peter tried for two days to reach Deacon Halsey with no response. Finally, on Wednesday, the deacon called the office to speak with Peter. Without any formal greeting he said, "Reverend Austin, I have something to discuss with you."

"Hello, Deacon, how are you? What is it that you want to discuss?"

"I will not be at the meeting."

"Are you ill?"

"No, I'm leaving Resurrection Temple. I feel it's time that I moved on."

"Well, Deacon, this comes as a surprise."

Peter was careful not to give the impression he was elated. He waited for the deacon to give an explanation and when he didn't, Peter said, "Deacon, why are you leaving?"

"Like I said, it's time for me to leave."

Responding more out of protocol than sincerity, Peter said, "Well, you have my prayers, Deacon. You'll be missed."

"Yeah." He hung up abruptly.

A half hour later another member, Edward Victor, called. Edward was sixteen years old and a convert of five years. He was one of those on the banquet committee working with Tyrone.

"Hello, Pastor Austin. How are you?"

"I'm well. How may I help you, son?"

"I will not be returning to Resurrection Temple." In the same breath he continued, "It has nothing to do with you or any of the church members. You have taught me so much. I just feel that God is leading me somewhere else."

"Are you sure?" Peter asked with skepticism.

"Yes, I am."

"How do you know?"

"I dreamed I was in a burning house. In the dream, I heard something say, 'Get ye up from here.'"

Peter sighed, "Dear God." Then he said, "Edward, we need to talk. Meet me at church tomorrow at six before the meeting."

"I'm going to try, Pastor."

After they hung up, Peter called Tyrone and said, "Brother Tyrone, this is Pastor."

"Yes, Pastor."

"Tyrone, did you know your uncle was leaving the church?"

"Yes, I did."

"Why didn't you tell me?"

"I thought it was better that you hear it from him."

"Uh huh. By the way, I want you to know that I heard from one of the committee members, Edward Victor, that he's leaving too."

"Yes, he told me."

"Tyrone, why didn't you tell me about Edward leaving?!"

"Pastor, I'm going to be honest. A few of us are leaving Resurrection Temple. I spoke with many of the members, and they were hurt when they found out what happened with you and Sister Kimberly."

"Have you *spoken* with Kimberly?!"

"No, I haven't but my cousin told me—"

Peter raised his voice and said, "Then how do you know that the rumors are true?!"

"Pastor, it's not just that. The Lord has been leading me for six months to start my own church. I'm finally going to do what the Lord wants me to do."

"So, you've been planning this split for months?"

"No, Pastor, it ain't like that. I just want to obey God."

In a measured tone, Peter said, "Boy, you're starting out wrong! You don't build a work by breaking up someone else's work If you believed that God wanted you to pastor, you should've done it the *right* way. I would've mentored you and gave you advice along with help. A *real* son would *never* stab his dad in the back!"

Tyrone remained silent. After a few moments, Peter said, "I suppose that Edward and your uncle are going with you."

"Yes, Pastor, and most of my family too."

Peter never dreamed Tyrone would backstab him, nor the dreaded words, *church split* would ever be associated with Resurrection Temple.

CHAPTER THIRTY-ONE

Carl tossed and turned in his bed, sweat dripping from his forehead. His anxiety intensified as he imagined Trisha or Nicholas wandering into his study and discovering the diary.

"I need to get to the diary and make sure it's secure."

Trisha was in the living room, lying across the couch, when the house phone rang. She went into the kitchen and answered the phone.

While Trisha was on the phone Carl eased down the stairs past the kitchen into his study and retrieved the diary. He crept back upstairs to the bedroom and opened the diary.

Then he heard footsteps ascending the stairs. He rushed to his closet, grabbed an empty shoe box, placed the diary inside the box, and shoved the box under the bed.

There was a knock at the door. "Hey, Dad, Mom said to check on you. Are you alright?" asked Nicholas.

"Yeah, I'm good."

"Okay, just checking."

Trisha had answered the phone, and the person on the other end said, "Hello, I'm Pastor Joan Sneed. Is this Nicholas's mother?"

Trisha's heart fluttered, and she said, "Yes, it is."

"My son Richard and Nicholas are college roommates."

Trisha breathed a sigh of relief and said, "Oh yeah. How are you?"

"I'm fine, thanks. I hope you don't mind me calling. I got your number from Richard. He talks about his PK roommate all the time."

"Yes, Nicholas mentioned Richard to me too."

Trisha was in a quandary wondering whether she should reveal to her that Richard and Nicholas smoked pot.

As Trisha mulled over her indecisiveness, Joan blurted without hesitation, "Mrs. Boston, I found traces of marijuana in Richard's pocket and after I interrogated him, he confessed to me that he and your son had been experimenting with reefer."

Joan continued in an irate tone. "I told my son I will not house a drug addict and that I was going to tell you, just in case you didn't know, that Nicholas and he smoked a reefer!"

Trisha said, "Nicholas told me that they only tried it twice and were not going to do it again."

"Yeah, that's what Richard told me too. Hmm... what did your husband say?"

"I didn't tell him."

"I didn't tell my husband either. We're separated."

Joan cleared her throat and said, "It's hard enough being a woman pastor with no husband and uh—" She abruptly stopped in mid-sentence. A moment later she sniffled and continued, "Along with raising a child with no help."

Trisha dabbed a tear from her eye. "Poor thing. I wish I knew what to say to her," she thought.

"I'm sorry. I didn't mean to burden you with my problems." She started to sob. "I'm just so very tired! I'm sorry, I..."

"That's okay, Pastor."

Joan cleared her throat and said, "I have to go to the meeting room in a couple of minutes. I'm here in NY at a woman's conference until tomorrow."

"Oh, really? Where is it being held?"

"It's being held in downtown Brooklyn at the Tillary Hotel."

"I know exactly where that is. It's not too far from me. Where are you from?"

"Pennsylvania."

"Maybe before you head back to Pennsylvania tomorrow, we could meet for lunch or something. There are restaurants not far from the hotel."

"Yes, I'd like that. Thank you, Mrs. Boston."

"Call me Trisha."

"Okay, and you call me Joan."

"Joan, I have your number on my caller's ID. When we hang up, I'll text you my cell number."

"I'm looking forward to meeting you."

———

The next day was Monday. Carl remained in bed until noon, which was unusual because he never stayed in bed later than 10 a.m. Trisha fixed Carl a meal and brought it to him.

"Carl, how are you feeling?" Trisha asked.

"I feel wonderful!" he said with excitement and a grin.

Trisha smiled and said, "Oh boy! I'm glad to hear it."

Trisha checked her text messages and there was a text from Joan asking her to give her a call.

"Excuse me, Carl." Trisha stepped outside the bedroom and called Joan.

"Hey, Joan, how are you?"

"I'm blessed and highly favored. And you?"

Chapter Thirty-one

"I'm well."

"Are we going to meet today?"

"Hold on a minute." Trisha stuck her head into the bedroom and said, "Carl? You mind if I go out for a couple of hours?"

"Wow," Carl thought. "This is a prayer answered. I can read more of the diary."

"Sure, babe, go ahead," he said as he stuffed his mouth.

"You sure?"

"Have a good time, Trish."

Trisha put the phone to her ear and said, "What time do you want to meet?"

"What about in a half hour?"

"A half hour it is. How will I know you?" asked Trisha with a giggle.

"Good question. I tell you what, I'll send a photo to your phone."

"And I'll do likewise. I'll meet you at Junior's Restaurant at the corner of Flatbush and DeKalb Avenues."

"Okay, I'll put it in my GPS."

"Good, I'll see you there."

Ten minutes later, Trisha called Carl from downstairs and said, "Babe, I'm leaving!"

"Okay, have a good time."

A few minutes later, Nicholas emerged from his bedroom, peeked his head in the door and said, "Dad, I'm going out with Marsha. Are you okay?"

"Tell her I said hi."

"I will. Bye."

———

When Trisha arrived at the restaurant, she noticed a woman standing by the entrance wearing a two-piece blue sequin suit, with matching hat and pocketbook. She stood a mere five foot six, even with three-inch heels. Her outfit glittered in the sun like a thousand diamonds. Trisha smiled when she saw her. "I would have picked her out even without a photo," she thought.

Trisha felt underdressed wearing a printed casual jumpsuit with brown open-toe shoes. "I hope she's not offended at my relaxed attire."

Trisha approached Joan and said, "Hi, Joan."

"God bless you, Trisha."

Joan hugged her as though they had known each other for years. Trisha opened the door, and they went inside.

Once seated, Trisha said, "You know, I was looking forward to meeting you in person."

"Me too. I felt our spirits connect when I spoke with you on the phone."

"Do you have any other children?" asked Trisha.

"No, just the one. And you?"

"Just one."

Then Joan said, "It's hard to impossible to raise kids nowadays *with* a husband, let alone by yourself. And with the added responsibility of being a pastor..."

"How did you come into the pastorate?" Trisha asked

"Well, at first my husband was the pastor. I was happy as a first lady. I'd preach a little every now and then, but only at our church. How I came to be pastor started with the members coming to me for counseling. I never wanted to be up front. I always pushed my husband, Thomas.

"I started getting invites to preach from other churches, more than Thomas. Most of the congregation supported me. When Thomas went out to preach, however, only a few of our congregants traveled with him.

"It all came to a head one night when Thomas said to me with a nasty attitude, 'Since the people listen to you more than they listen to me, maybe *you* should be their pastor!'"

"What happened after that?" asked Trisha.

"The next week, without warning, he moved out of our apartment and didn't return home or to church."

Joan choked and said, "That was eight years ago and, to this day, he's never returned to the church and explained to them, nor has he apologized to me or his son."

Trisha reached across the table and took Joan's hands in her own.

A tear trickled down Joan's cheek and she said, "Richard was only ten when Thomas left."

"Does he keep in contact with Richard?"

"He does, but not like he should. That's why I didn't bother to tell him about the reefer."

"You said you've been separated for eight years?"

"Yes."

"I hope I'm not being nosey, but why haven't you gotten a divorce and moved on with your life? It's obvious he's not coming back."

"In our denomination they don't believe in divorce. It's a miracle they still let me pastor."

"Your religious tradition doesn't believe in women pastors?"

"The constitution has recently changed, allowing women to pastor. However, some of the old diehards still hold to the prohibition of women pastors. I'm really considering leaving my denominational affiliation."

"Perhaps you should stay and make a difference."

"I would, but some of the traditionalists in our organization treat women unfairly. For example, when they assign pastors to churches the women get the churches that are on life support, while the men get the more desirable assignments."

"Oh, I see"

"Also, some of the male pastors think that just because you're single, it means you're desperate."

"What do you mean?"

Joan's eyes narrowed and she said, "First Lady, you know *exactly* what I mean."

Trisha made a few quick, short nods with her head and said, "Oh, okay. Gotcha."

"One time I was at our church's convention. During the meet and greet session before service, I heard someone call my name, so I turned around. I didn't know him, and I said, 'How are you, brother?'

"He was kinda handsome. I assumed since everyone was wearing a name tag that's how he knew my name. We chatted about church and the challenges of pastoring. Then he had the audacity to ask me, 'How are you making it without your husband?' After which he giggled. I wasn't born yesterday, you know; he was testing to see my reaction. I said,

'Nice talking to you,' and then walked away. Apparently, someone told him I was estranged from my husband.

"That night after service I was in my hotel room getting ready for bed. I heard a knock at the door; it was the pastor that spoke to me at the meet and greet.

"That's just one experience. I spoke with a few of the other women pastors who've had similar experiences."

Joan looked at the menu and mumbled, "Hmm, what am I in the mood for?"

Joan and Trisha said nothing as they looked over their menus. After a couple of minutes, Trisha looked up at Joan and stared. Joan, without lifting her eyes from the menu, said, "Trisha, you want to ask me something don't you?"

"Not really," she said as she unconsciously placed her index finger to her lips.

Joan raised her head from the menu, peered at Trisha and said, "Yes, you do."

"Joan, I don't get into people's personal affairs."

"Uh huh. You're wondering how he knew what room I was in."

"Well...?" said Trisha with a blank stare.

CHAPTER THIRTY-TWO

Joan and Trisha stared at one another until Joan slowly lowered her head. She let out a sigh and said, "Trisha, I was lonely. I haven't had the company of a man since Thomas left."

"How did he know what room you were staying in?"

"I casually mentioned it as we were talking. When he knocked at the door, and I asked who it was, I was shocked that it was him. I let him in, and we talked a little, and one thing led to another—. But it didn't go all the way." she added defensively. "One good thing is that he lives in Florida, so we probably won't meet again."

Trisha sighed deeply and asked, "Joan, is he married?"

Joan bowed her head and did not respond. The server came and took their orders. As they waited for their food, Trisha took Joan's hands and said, "Joan, let's pray."

They bowed their heads, and Trisha whispered a prayer. When their food arrived, they ate but said little else. After they were done, they promised to keep in touch and then departed.

Carl went to his study with the diary, sat at his desk and thought, "Ah, this is good. No one here to interrupt me while I read." He leaned back in his chair and opened the diary to the page where he had left off.

Suddenly he was gripped by a paralyzing fear. For five seconds he stared at the page, unable to look away and too terrified to turn the page. Carl found it hard to breathe, and his heart raced. He was about to dispose of the diary, then decided not knowing what was in the diary would torment him even more than knowing.

He remained still until his breathing and heartbeat became normal. He was about to read when his phone rang. He looked at the caller's ID, saw that it was Peter, and ignored the call. Then he reread a small portion of the diary for continuity:

> *I rushed to the parking lot looking for God knows who. Once outside, I caught a glimpse of the back lights of a car hurtling from the parking lot. I went back into my office and sat at my desk with my head in my hands. Lorraine entered my office and asked if I was okay. I didn't respond. Then she walked over to me, touched me on the shoulder, and asked if there were any unwelcome visitors in church. I shook my finger in her face and said, 'Lorraine, what are you talking about?!'*
>
> *Lorraine curled her lips and said, "Never mind, Morgan."*
>
> *She informed me Reverend Bonds was outside the office waiting for me. I met with Reverend Bonds and invited him to dinner. I asked Lorraine if she wanted to join us, and she said that my executive minister Reverend Michael Samuels and his wife Lilly would drop her home.*

I knew Lorraine wasn't going to come. She was furious with me for pointing my finger in her face. She's mentioned to me how humiliating that was at least a hundred times.

I was in no mood to go out to dinner, however, protocol dictated I entertain the guest preacher. At dinner, he dominated the conversation, bragging about how much he collects in offerings from his congregation on any given Sunday and the new Bentley God gave him.

"You see, Pastor," he said in a condescending tone, "if you teach your members right, you won't have any money issues. My members trip over each other to get into the offering line to give".

I suspect he was alluding to a statement I made during church service that night about a financial need the church had. I guess he thought it was incumbent upon him to teach me how it should be done. Then he stared at me without blinking, as though unsure if I was receptive to his advice.

He continued to boast about how much he paid for his suits and his multi-million-dollar home. After a while, his words amounted to background noise.

After we ate, he said he had an early flight the next morning and should get some sleep. He was silent on the drive to the hotel.

When we arrived, I told him my executive minister would take him to the airport in the morning. He said, "Okay."

Without shaking my hand or saying goodbye, he went into the hotel.

As I drove, I thought of how much of a failure I was as a pastor. I wondered how it would be if I were dead. Lorraine is still young and attractive. She could remarry someone who'd treat her better than I have. Lester would no longer have to deal with the problems that are associated with being a preacher's kid. The church would be better off too. They could hire another pastor, one that is devoted and conscientious, instead of a pastor like myself who doesn't study unless preparing a sermon, doesn't pray unless in front of the congregation, and pays little attention to ministry matters until faced with a crisis.

As I drove, my body ached, and I was gripped by the urge for a fix. I screamed as loud as I could, as though my cries would set me free from the clutches of the monster on my back. I drove, passed my exit, and continued to the fleabag hotel where I would meet Satan's messenger to feed my hellish addiction.

I prayed, "Lord, I'm about to call him. If you hear me, please, please don't let him answer!"

He answered the phone and, mocking me, he said, "Hey, Reverend, do you need to catch the spirit tonight?"

I was furious at myself and ashamed. I answered him in a low voice, "I'll be there in ten minutes."

We met at the hotel. I stared at him and swore this would be my last fix. He looked at me with a sinister grin. The next day I woke up at home alone in my bed with no recollection of how I had arrived there. This is unbearable. There is nothing left in this life for me.

Carl shut the diary, wiped the tears from his eyes, and said, "I need something to calm my nerves."

CHAPTER THIRTY-THREE

Nicholas and Marsha strolled hand in hand as they left the movie theater. Upon reaching Marsha's car, Nicholas glanced at his phone and saw there were numerous missed calls from Richard.

"Richard's been calling. I wonder what he wants," Nicholas said.

"It may be important," Marsha said with a shrug. "Perhaps you should call him back."

"Oh, please," said Nicholas in an apathetic tone. "Knowing him, he probably wants my opinion on a new pair of sneakers he bought or somethin'."

Nicholas checked his voicemail. "Oh, I see he's left a ton of messages too."

"Why don't you at least listen to one of them?"

"Okay, just for you."

"Bro, I just read my mail! Call me right away! We've got a serious problem!"

Nicholas glanced at Marsha as he struggled to remain calm.

"Is everything alright?" Marsha asked.

"Yeah, everything's cool," he said in a dismissive tone. "Marsha, I know I promised we were going out to eat, but I've got to get home."

Marsha didn't try to hide her disappointment. "Nicholas, you're going back to school tomorrow and we've hardly had time together!"

"I promise the next time I come home I will spend *all* of my time with you."

"The next time?!" she shouted.

"Baby, I promise."

Marsha snatched opened the driver's side door and got into the car, slamming the door shut. "Get in!" she snapped.

The couple rode in silence, Marsha fuming as she drove. When they arrived at the house, Nicholas said, "I'll call you later." She didn't respond, but kept her eyes forward and sped off from the curb before he could reach the door.

Once inside the house, Nicholas called Richard. "Hey, man, I got your message!"

"Man, we're screwed!" Richard spat.

"What do you mean?"

Richard read the letter he had received to Nicholas. "What are we going to do?"

"I don't know."

"Did your mail come yet?"

"I'm not sure."

Suddenly Nicholas heard a voice come from his father's study. "Nicholas, is that you?" Carl called.

"Yeah, Dad!"

Carl placed the diary behind the bookshelf and walked into the living room.

"Give me a second, Dad. I'm on the phone."

"It's okay. I didn't want anything."

As Nicholas started upstairs to his room, Richard said, "Ask your dad if the mail came."

Nicholas turned mid-stride. "Dad, has the mail come yet?"

"No, I don't think so."

"My father said he's not sure."

"Okay, good. Make sure you get the mail before your folks see it. And by the way," Richard continued, "my mother asked for your home phone number. She said she's going to call your mother."

"Why?!"

"My mother found some pot in my pocket. At the beginning of the semester, I told her that I was rooming with a PK. Knowing her, she's gonna tell your mother about the pot. Did you say anything to your mother?"

"I told her what you said in case we were caught. That it was only twice and that I was never going to do it again."

"Good! Like I said, as long as we have the same story, and maybe throw in a tear or two, they'll believe us. What are you going to do if they read the letter?"

Nicholas paused for a few seconds and said, "I don't know. You said that we were good. You never said they'd send a letter home!"

"Be cool, Nicholas. I'll think of something."

CHAPTER THIRTY-FOUR

Carl took a plastic cup and a bottle of scotch from behind some books on a shelf in a closet. He looked around, then filled the cup and gulped the whiskey. He had started the habit a couple of years earlier. To justify his excesses, he reasoned, "I don't drink every day and besides, I can take it or leave it. I don't need it." He kept the bottle hidden to keep Trisha from finding out. No one, including Peter and Arthur, knew Carl's secret.

He sat relaxing in his study, drinking his scotch, when he heard the mailman. He went to the door and got the mail. Among the bills and circulars was a letter from Nicholas's college. He opened it, thinking it was a tuition bill. After he read it, his eyes bulged, and he shouted, *"Nicholas, get down here right now!"*

Nicholas ran down the stairs. "Yes, Dad?"

Carl handed him the letter. "What is this?"

Nicholas froze, then glanced at the letter. Before he could read it, Carl shouted, "It says you're expelled for the rest of the semester for possessing contraband!"

"Dad, I was with some other guys that had it. I was just standing there. It wasn't mine."

"So, you're telling me it wasn't yours?!"

"Yes!" Nicholas said defensively.

Carl looked at his son with an incredulous stare. "Do you think that I'm an idiot? Answer me!" Carl didn't wait for his son to respond. "Then why does the letter say you were caught twice with marijuana and that you were placed on probation when they caught you the second time?!"

"No, that's not the way it—."

"You're so dumb you can't even lie right!"

Nicholas lowered his head.

"So, you're smoking reefer now, huh?"

"It was just those two times."

"You mean those were the only times you got caught! Boy, get out of my sight!"

Carl murmured as Nicholas walked up the stairs. "All that money I'm spending to send him to college while he messes around with drugs."

Nicholas went to his room and called Richard. "Hey, man, my father read the letter from school."

"Oh no! What did he say?"

"He's mad as hell."

Richard was incensed. "The dean lied! He said if we went home for a week, we could return to school!"

"What he said was he was going to talk to some people and *try* to get us back into school after a week's suspension!"

"Didn't he say he knew your father and—."

Nicholas's own temper started to flare. "He said he knew *of* my father and would see what he could do!"

"Okay, bro, no need to yell." Richard took a deep, cleansing breathe. "I can hear my mother now. 'Go stay with your father; I can't take this anymore!'"

Carl went back into his study, sat, and gulped the rest of the scotch in the cup. "Trisha is going to be devastated when she finds out her baby smokes reefer. I can't let her find this out."

He refilled the cup and sighed.

———

Trisha returned from her lunch date with Joan an hour later. Carl was in his office, and Nicholas was upstairs in his bedroom on the phone with Lester.

"Hey, Lester! I have some good news!"

"What is it? Do you have the journal?!" Lester said with excitement.

"No, but I know where it is. I didn't get a chance to read it, but I saw it."

"Can you get a hold of it?"

Trisha called to Nicholas from downstairs and, in a panic, he said, "Man, I gotta go!"

Before Lester could finish his sentence, Nicholas ended the call. He sat on his bed and rocked back and forth like a man convicted of first-degree murder awaiting his sentence.

Trisha called again. "She must know something," Nicholas thought.

"I'm upstairs," he said in a tense voice.

Trisha walked upstairs looked in her bedroom before entering Nicholas's room. "Where's your father?" she asked.

Nicholas looked puzzled. "He's not downstairs?" he asked his mother. "He didn't say he was going anywhere."

"Check his study," Trisha ordered.

Nicholas looked in the study where Carl lay motionless on the floor next to the couch, reeking of alcohol. Not far from where he lay was an empty bottle and a plastic cup. At first, Nicholas thought he was asleep. He called his name and shook him by the shoulders, but he was unresponsive.

Nicholas was lightheaded, to the point of nearly passing out. He thought his worst fear had been realized. Gripped by panic he cried, "Oh God, he's dead!"

He hurriedly disposed of the bottle and the cup in the trash next to Carl's desk. Then he shouted, *"Mom call the ambulance! I can't wake Dad!"*

Trisha rushed down the stairs and into the office. She looked at Carl and screamed his name. She rushed to his side and looked at Nicholas, panic and confusion flooding her eyes. By the look on her face, he knew she also smelled the alcohol. Nicholas pretended not to notice and called the ambulance.

Trisha grabbed Carl by his shoulders, shaking him and calling his name. When the ambulance arrived, Carl's pulse was faint, and he was still unconscious.

She tossed the car keys to Nicholas, and he followed the ambulance to the hospital.

In the waiting room, Nicholas said to Trisha. "Mom, this is all my fault."

"Don't blame yourself. You had nothing to do with this."

"Yes, I do—"

Before Nicholas could finish his confession, Trisha sprang to her feet as the doctor approached them.

"Your husband is conscious," the doctor said. "You can see him now."

"Doctor, what happened?" Trisha pleaded.

"We have to run a few tests, so he'll have to remain in the hospital overnight."

"Thank you, Doctor."

Trisha and Nicholas entered the room. Carl feigned a smile and jokingly said, "What are ya'll doing here?"

"How are you feeling?" Trisha asked.

Carl stretched his arms, clinched his hands, and breathed a heavy, relieved sigh. "Ah, I feel wonderful! I'm fine; I just needed some rest."

Trisha's brows furrowed and she said, "Yeah, right! That's what you told me this morning. I ain't falling for that again."

"Trish, I'm fine. I'm ready to go home."

"Carl, you ain't going nowhere! The doctor said you have to stay overnight, so you might as well get comfortable."

Nicholas stared at Carl, shook his head, and whispered, "This is all my fault."

"What did you say Nicholas?" Carl asked.

"Nothing."

"Yes, you did. Speak up, Son. What's on your mind?"

"It was nothing."

The doctor came in and signaled Trisha with his eyes. "I'll be back in a minute," Trisha said as she left the room and went with the doctor.

Chapter Thirty-four

Carl smiled and said to Nicholas, "Come here, Son."

Nicholas walked to Carl's bedside, sobbing, his words caught in his throat as he spoke. "Dad, I'm so sorry. This is all my fault. I messed up in school and…"

Nicholas wiped his eyes with his hands. Carl stretched out his arms, prompting his son to lay his head on his chest as he wept.

"Nicholas, listen to me," Carl said. "This is not your fault. When I get out of the hospital, you and I are going to tell your mother about the incident at school, together. Okay?"

Nicholas stood and nodded his head.

"And we'll work the school suspension issue out together. I just want you to be totally honest with me. Is there anything else I should know?"

"Yes… there is" He said with his head bowed.

Trisha walked in the room, and Carl motioned to Nicholas to stop talking.

"So, what did the doctor have to say?" Carl asked.

"We'll talk about it later. I'm going to need a change of clothes. I'm staying tonight."

"Trish, you ain't gotta—"

"Carl, I'm staying and that's final!"

Trisha turned to her son. "Nicholas, go home, look in my closet and bring my green dress, please."

"Okay, Mom."

"Oh, yeah, I almost forgot; you're supposed to go back to school tomorrow."

"I can't go back to school while Dad is in the hospital."

Trisha didn't have the energy to debate the matter. "Okay, I guess you can make up any work that you'll miss."

———————

As Nicholas drove, he thought about nothing but the empty scotch bottle he found on the floor. When he arrived home, he immediately took the scotch bottle from the trash in the study and put it in the garbage outside.

That bottle symbolized, for him, his father's fall from grace. As a boy, he believed his father was the smartest, most powerful, and God-fearing man in existence. But as he came into his late adolescence, he feared one day he would discover his father was subject to the failings of any other man. To his dismay, that day had arrived.

Chapter Thirty-Five

Arthur sat home, thinking about the diary. Unable to put it out of his mind, he called Peter.

"Hey, Peter. Have you heard from Carl?"

"I called him, but he didn't answer."

"I heard they rushed him to the hospital during church service on Sunday," Arthur said.

Peter was stunned. "Where did you hear that?"

"One of my members whose cousin attends his church told me."

"I guess that's why I haven't heard from him. I have Trisha's cell number. I'll call her later today."

"Yeah, you should. I hope he's okay."

Arthur heard Angela calling from her bedroom. "Arthur, I need to speak to you."

"Angela's calling me. I'll get back to you later, man."

"Okay, Preacher."

Arthur ended the call and sighed. "What is it now?" he said as he entered Angela's room.

"You don't have to answer me so nasty!" Angela griped.

"Look, I'm not in the mood to go through this with you today. What do you want?"

"I just got off the phone with Zelda. Guess what our daughter had to say."

"Get to the point, Angela."

"Our seventeen-year-old daughter is pregnant. I *told* you she was too young to go away to school, but you wouldn't listen!

"Why didn't you let me speak to her?"

"You were on the phone."

"Why didn't you interrupt me?"

"The point is, she's pregnant. Now what, Mr. Know-it-all?!" Her tone dripped with contempt.

"*You're* the one who drove her away!" Arthur shouted.

"What do you mean by that?! I didn't want her to go away to school in the first place!" Angela retorted.

"I mean, waking her at five o'clock every morning to pray, causing her to fall asleep in class, while you went back to sleep after she left for school."

Angela shook her head in disgust and responded sarcastically. "Lord have mercy. God forbid I start the day with prayer."

"You also told her not to date until she was ready to get married!"

"I *knew* you'd bring that up." complained Angela.

Then, out of spite, Arthur said, "Zelda told me she couldn't take it anymore and that's why she wanted to go away to school—to get away from you!"

"No, she didn't!" Angela shouted.

Arthur turned and walked away, a smug grin on his face. Angela followed so close behind him he could feel the warmth of her body.

"Angela, give me some space; I'm warning you!" he said, heatedly.

"I hate you!"

"Stop yelling in my ear, Angela!"

She screamed again, *"I hate you!"*

Arthur turned, pushed her to the floor, and said, "I warned you!"

As Arthur descended the stairs, Angela got up, stood at the top of the steps, and shouted, *"You pushed a woman to the floor. I guess that makes you a big man now, huh?"*

Arthur walked out of the front door, got into his car, and drove to the beach. He parked in a deserted area of the beach, sat in his car, and stared at the water. As he watched the waves, he was pressed by the urge to go to the forbidden cinema. Arthur shook his head and screamed, *"Not today, devil!"*

He called his daughter. When she answered he said, "Zelda, this is Dad."

"Yes, daddy," she said as she wept.

"What's going on, sweetheart?"

"Daddy, I guess Mom told you. I'm so sorry. I messed up. I don't know what I'm going to do."

"What did your mother say to you?"

"She told me that she didn't have sex until she was married, and if God kept her from sinning than I was without excuse. Maybe I should get an abortion or something."

"Not with *my* grandbaby!" Arthur said assertively. "Listen to me, Zelda. Come home ASAP. I'll have a talk with your mother. Call me as soon as you get to the train station."

"Okay, Daddy. I love you."

"I love you too."

Arthur decided to go home and, for the sake of Zelda and their unborn grandchild, apologize to Angela for pushing her down. As he drove, he rehearsed what he was going to say to Angela. When he arrived home, there was a police car in front of his house.

Chapter Thirty-five

Arthur got out of the car and thought, "Now what?"

Angela was in the house with a police officer. When Arthur walked into the house, she pointed at him and said to the officer. "There he is!"

Arthur was confused and asked, "What's going on?"

"Your wife said that you physically abused her."

Arthurs' brows furrowed and he said, "I-I just pushed her a little."

Angela pulled up her sleeve and exposed a bruise on her arm.

"I'm sorry, Mr. Wright, but we have to take you in."

The officer handcuffed Arthur and escorted him to the squad car in view of the neighbors who watched from their doors and windows.

CHAPTER THIRTY-SIX

Even though Clyde and Mae slept in the same bed, he had never felt more estranged from her than he did that night. In the morning, he went into the kitchen and joined his family at the table. Mae was an excellent cook and this morning she had made all his breakfast favorites: grits, salmon cakes, bacon with eggs, and buttermilk biscuits. The grits were smooth, just as he liked them. The salmon cakes were cooked to perfection and seasoned with sautéed onions. Clyde wondered to himself, "Why is she doing this?"

He almost wished she had undercooked the eggs or burned the bacon and biscuits; then he would have an excuse not to eat. But everything was perfect, and he could not justify complaining.

"Mae is using the meal as a way of mocking me," he thought. "She's probably thinking, 'I hope you enjoy the meal because when we divorce, you're really gonna miss this.'"

For fifteen minutes, as they ate, no one said a word. Then Geraldine broke the silence. "Mom, Dad, are you still going to divorce?" There was a tone of cautious hope in her voice.

Mae stared at Geraldine. At the same time, Clyde looked at Mae. "Please, Mae," Clyde thought. "Give me the faintest sign. That's all I'll need to fight to the death to save our marriage."

However, Mae continued eating and did not respond.

With that, Clyde finally accepted his marriage was over. He gave his wife an insincere smile. "Thank you for a delightful meal, Mae. You've outdone yourself this morning."

Mae nodded her head and said, "Thank you, Clyde."

As he rose from the table, he addressed his daughters. "Girls, I have to go to the office. Daddy loves you." The words, barely audible, got caught in his throat as he fought to hold back his tears.

Geraldine and Mary rose from their seats, teary-eyed. They walked over to Clyde, kissed and hugged him and said, "Daddy, we love you too."

Suddenly they burst into tears. Clyde hugged them tight, fighting to remain composed. "C'mon, y'all, everything's gonna be all right."

His statement did little to soothe their hurt. "Daddy ain't going *nowhere*," he said in an assertive voice. Then he smiled and said, "I'll still be around."

They sniffled and said, "Okay, Dad."

Clyde kissed them and left for the office.

Once at the office, Clyde called Nathan Lawrence, an old high school classmate who was also a lawyer.

"Reverend, it's good to hear from you," Nathan said. "How are you, man?"

"Not too good, I'm afraid. Mae is divorcing me, and I need a lawyer."

"I'm so sorry, Clyde. You two seemed so happy. What happened?

"Man, I'm still not sure. I thought we'd be together forever."

"Have you tried counseling?"

"Nathan, I was, and still am, ready to go to counseling. I told her that, but she doesn't want to hear it."

"I guess that's all you can do. If she won't go then..." Nathan took a breath and asked, "Are there any custody or property disputes—?"

Clyde interrupted him. "Nathan, this will be open and shut. I don't want this dragged out in court. She can have whatever she wants—the house, the furniture, the bank account, custody of the kids... whatever."

"Clyde, let's not be too hasty," Nathan cautioned. "Do you know the lawyer she's using?"

"No, I didn't ask," Clyde said as he cursed himself for not having asked her.

"Does Mae still have the same cell number?"

"Yeah."

"I'll call her, get her lawyer's number, find out what she wants, and get back to you."

"Thanks, Nathan."

The hardest thing for Clyde, beside telling his daughters, was announcing the divorce to the church. A myriad of disturbing thoughts ran through Clyde's mind as he agonized over the divorce. He feared that many of the members would leave the church. He was also concerned with what other pastors who knew him were going to say. To add to that, he was worried that Mae had already poisoned the minds of their friends against him. As he sat at his desk, he began to sob. The thought of life without Mae was painful enough, but now he had no close friend with whom to share his feelings.

CHAPTER THIRTY-SEVEN

Trisha was talking to Carl when she heard the text alert.

"Give me a second, Carl," she said as she picked up her phone.

The text was from Joan:

"I'm home safely," it read. *"Thank you for listening to me and providing a safe place for me to unburden myself. You're truly a godsend. I know it was the Lord that paired us together. I thank God for you. I'll call you later in the week."*

"Who's texting you?" Carl asked.

"Nicholas's roommate's mother."

"I didn't know you knew her. How did y'all meet?"

"She called me the other day."

"How did she get your number?"

"Nicholas gave it to her son, and her son gave it to her."

"What did she want?" Carl was suspicious of Trisha's one-sentence answers and wondered what she might be hiding.

Trisha responded carefully, not wanting to reveal the real reason Joan contacted her. "She's a pastor and found out from her son that Nicholas was a PK, and she just wanted to talk. She was in town at a pastor's conference, so we met for lunch today."

Carl, recalling she left that afternoon without telling him where or with whom she was meeting, said, "Oh, so that's where you went. What did she have to say?"

"The usual. How hard it is being a woman pastor—you know—stuff like that. I'm sure you've heard it all before."

"What about her husband?"

"They're separated."

The entire time they spoke, Trisha avoided her husband's eye and kept her hands behind her back. Judging from her body language, Carl surmised she was not being totally honest.

"Well, that's it," she said, eagerly getting off the subject.

Just then, her phone rang. Trisha looked at her phone and said, "It's Peter."

"Don't answer it," Carl said.

"Why not?"

Carl assumed Peter wanted to discuss the diary and said, "Ignore it! If it's important, he'll leave a message."

As Trisha sent the call to voicemail she said, "He's probably calling me because he can't reach you."

"Oh, yeah." he said as he snapped his fingers. "My phone is home. Do me a favor; call Nicholas and ask him to bring my phone when he comes with your clothes. Hurry before he leaves."

"Carl, you don't need your phone—"

"Yes, I do! Stop messing around. Call him."

Trisha took her time, pressed speed dial, then asked, "Where is it, Carl?"

"It's in my study on the desk."

When Nicholas answered she said, "Nicholas, are you still home?"

"Yes, I'm about to get in the car."

"Bring your dad's phone with you when you come, please. It's on his desk."

"Okay."

As Nicholas entered Carl's study he thought about the diary. "It's probably still in the drawer," he thought to himself.

He pulled on the drawer where he had seen the diary, but it was locked. Nicholas went to get the key, then returned to the study. He opened the drawer, but it was empty. Disappointed, he said, "Oh, man, it ain't here!"

He ran upstairs to Trisha and Carl's bedroom and searched the closet and under the bed. After failing to locate the diary, he became furious. "It has to be here somewhere!"

He rushed back downstairs to the study and searched inside the closet that was next to the bookcase where, behind the bookcase, lay the diary. In the closet on a shelf, he found a pack of plastic cups and an unopened bottle of scotch.

"I should flush all this booze down the toilet." he thought. Then he reasoned, "If I do, he'd know I was snooping. I'd be in trouble, and he'd just buy more."

Despondent, he decided to get back to the hospital.

————

When Nicholas arrived at the hospital, the nurses on Carl's floor were frantically rushing around. Loud beeps were blaring throughout the hallway, and the voice on the P.A. was shouting, *"Code blue! Code blue!"* As Nicholas stepped off the elevator, he saw his mother sitting outside his father's room, sobbing. Glancing into the room, he saw several doctors gathered around Carl's bed with the curtains drawn.

Nicholas rushed over to Trisha, fearing the worst. "Mom, what's happening?!"

Trisha, barely able to speak, said, "Your dad coded!"

CHAPTER THIRTY-EIGHT

Peter sat in his bedroom, thinking about Carl and wondering why Trisha hadn't called back. He was about to reach for his phone when Yolanda came in and handed him his mail.

He browsed through the letters with a concerned look. "Arthur told me Carl was rushed to the hospital Sunday morning during service."

"Did you call someone to confirm it? You know how Arthur is with getting the story straight."

"Stop it, Yolanda," he said with a chuckle. "I called Trisha, but she hasn't gotten back to me as of yet."

"Maybe *I* should call her."

Yolanda proceeded to dial Trisha as Peter opened his mail. She left a message when Trisha didn't answer. "She always calls me back," Yolanda said with confidence as she went to the kitchen to get a bottle of water.

Peter's attention was diverted from Carl after he read the letters. There were fifteen letters, typewritten, unsigned, and stating they were from members who were never returning to Resurrection Temple because of his affair with Kimberly.

A few of the letters mentioned that they were praying for him, but the majority were mean-spirited, accusing him of hypocrisy and citing scriptures that referenced hell and damnation. Stunned by what he read, his eyes narrowed, and he grumbled, "When I find out who put these people up to this..."

Yolanda returned from the kitchen. "Peter, did you say something?"

Peter stared at one of the letters and did not respond. He passed the letters to Yolanda. She read a few of them and thought, "I'll bet Deacon Halsey and Tyrone are behind this."

Yolanda knew how much Peter loved and sacrificed for the church. Between grieving for Peter and her anger directed at the church members, she found it difficult to find the words that would encourage him.

"Honey, don't worry," she said in a reassuring voice. "When God is for you, who dare stands against you? God's just purging out those who are not really with you."

From the angry look on his face, it didn't appear her pep talk was having the desired effect. She gave him a loving hug and said, "Everything's gonna be alright."

"Thank you, babe," Peter said as he forced a smile for Yolanda's sake. He took the letters from her. "Well, I'm gonna make this known at the church meeting on Thursday."

"Sweetheart, maybe you should invite Reverend Jeremiah Riley to the meeting. He could testify on your behalf that Kimberly never said you molested her."

"Nah, it's a members only meeting. And besides, he's too busy."

"How do you know that? Did you ask him?"

Peter paused and, with a raised a brow, said, "Maybe you're right, babe." He smiled at her. "I knew I married the right person."

As Yolanda looked on, Peter called Jeremiah. "Hey, Doctor Riley, this is Peter Austin. How are you?"

"I'm good, Preacher. And you?"

"I'm coming along okay. I need a favor."

"Sure, what do you need?"

Peter read one of the anonymous letters he received and informed Jeremiah of the church business meeting he'd called. "I'm asking if you'd come and dispel the rumor that Kimberly told you that I molested her."

"Preacher, I'd be more than happy to, but I'll be out of town from Wednesday to Saturday."

"I understand, Reverend; it's okay. I'll figure something out..."

"Hold on, Doc," Jeremiah said. "I tell you what. I'll make a tape and you can play it at the meeting."

"Sounds like a plan. Thank you."

"I'll call you when the tape is done."

"Thanks again, Preacher."

"Glad to help."

"What did he say?" Yolanda asked as Peter ended the call.

"He's going to be out of town, but he'll make a tape and send it to us."

"Oh, good."

Peter breathed a relieved sigh. "That should straighten out this mess."

———

By 7 p.m. on Thursday, Peter had not heard from his star witness. He checked his voicemail, but there was no message, so he sat in his office, rehearsing his defense.

Seven twenty-five and still no message from Jeremiah. Peter peered into the window of the sanctuary door. The crowd was half the size expected. He turned to his wife as she took his hand and said, "Let's pray."

After they prayed, she placed her hand on his cheek. "Don't worry, Peter. I believe God."

Peter and Yolanda walked in holding hands and sat together on the pulpit. There was some murmuring in the audience when they took their seats, but when Peter stood to speak, the audience became quiet.

"I asked you all here tonight to clear up a rumor, a rumor that I molested a member of this church, and that is the reason she no longer attends here. Some of you were here at our annual business meeting when

Deacon Halsey made the allegation, which was echoed by his niece. Her name escapes me now.

"Let me state emphatically that nothing even resembling this accusation ever happened with the member in question or anyone else!"

Peter scanned the audience and saw one of Deacon Halsey's sons walk in and take a seat. He stared angrily at him, as though he was the only person in the church, and shouted, "Let me make myself perfectly clear, just in case you didn't get it the first time! *Halsey is a liar* and so is his niece—whatever her name is—as is anyone else who says I molested *anyone* in this church! And you can go back and tell them what I said!"

After this statement, he saw Deacon Halsey's son rise from his seat and leave.

"I hope that settles the issue forever," he said calmly. "If you have something you want to say, say it now. Don't duck in the tall grass and whisper. Are there any questions on *this* matter?"

A person raised his hand and asked, "Pastor, what about Reverend Riley, who said on his radio program that Sister Kimberly told him you molested her?"

"I had lunch with him the other day, and he denied ever saying that. As a matter of fact, he wanted to be here tonight and say just that, but he was called out of town."

"Do you think he would come another time?"

"Perhaps so. I'll ask him."

Someone else raised their hand and asked, "Why did Sister Kimberly leave?"

"Why does anyone leave? I have no idea why she left and I..."

Peter stopped in the middle of his sentence, stretched out his arm, pointed to the back of the church and said, "Why don't you ask her yourself?"

The audience turned their heads in the direction Peter was pointing and gasped. It was Kimberly. Yolanda had called Kimberly and asked her to come. She had kept it from Peter, just in case Kimberly did not show.

As Kimberly walked down the aisle, Yolanda beckoned to her to come to the pulpit. The audience stood and applauded as she advanced to the front. Yolanda opened her arms and they hugged as the audience made a rousing applause, every clap louder and faster as the two women embraced each other.

Kimberly left Yolanda's arms, turned to Peter, and fell into his arms sobbing. Peter, teary-eyed, slowly shook his head. The audience continued to applaud until Peter raised his arms, signaling them to stop.

Peter gave Kimberly the mic. "Saints," she said, "I missed you all so much. I can't tell you how much. When I heard the rumors about my father in the gospel, Reverend Peter Austin, I said, 'Nothing is going to stop me from coming back and defending my dad.'

"I've attended this church since I was just a little girl, and Reverend Austin has *never* acted inappropriately with me at *any* time. It's all a lie! I never told anyone that."

She turned to Peter, who stood next to her. "Pastor, I ask you and the church's forgiveness for not coming back sooner and straightening this out."

To everyone's shock, Kimberly got on her knees before Peter and said, "If you and the saints of Resurrection Temple will have me, I want to come back home where I belong."

Peter helped her to her feet and said, "Everybody come up, hug Sister Kimberly, and welcome her back home."

As the people came, Jeremiah walked into the church. Peter waved him up to the front. He walked up onto the pulpit with Peter who whispered, "Doc, I thought you said you would be out of town."

Jeremiah whispered back, "The Lord told me to come back and stand with you. I'm sorry I'm late; my flight was delayed. We were on the tarmac for over an hour waiting to take off."

"I'm glad you're here."

"I see Kimberly's here," said Jeremiah with a grin.

Peter smiled, patted him on the shoulder and said, "Yeah, she's back."

"May I address the audience when they finish hugging her?"

"Please, be my guest."

After everyone hugged Kimberly, Peter approached the mic and said, "Church, I wasn't expecting Reverend Riley to be here but thank God he's here. Let's greet him with an amen."

"Amen," said the audience.

Peter handed him the mic and Jeremiah said, "I greet you all in the precious name of Jesus. Let me start off by saying Reverend Austin is a man of God."

The audience responded with a loud *amen*.

"I flew in from Florida tonight to set the record straight. Sister Kimberly *never* said anything to me about Reverend Austin acting inappropriately, and I've never called his name on my radio broadcast accusing him.

"You all have to understand how the enemy works. James, in the third Chapter of his epistle, tells us that the tongue is an 'unruly evil.' You can kill with the effects of your words. Proverbs 18:21 warns us that 'life and death is in the power of the tongue'. Many think that means you can have the good life by your words. However, that is not the meaning of the text. What it means is that our tongue can build others up or they tear them down.

"That's what has happened to your pastor; he is the victim of vicious lies which were spread by means of wagging tongues, swearing to those lies.

"In closing, I want to encourage you, Resurrection Temple, to pray for your pastor, support him, and don't let *anyone* defame him. If the gossipmongers have negatives things to say, just say, what Jesus said in John 8:7 'He who is without sin cast the first stone.'

"Reverend Austin is my brother, and if you have anything negative to say about him, don't bring it to me because I will rebuke you in Jesus's name!"

Chapter Thirty-eight

Then he turned to Peter, hugged him and said, "I love you, man."

The entire church stood and gave Jeremiah a rousing applause. People called out from all over the sanctuary. "We love you Reverend Austin! Hang in there!" and

"We've got your back, Pastor!"

CHAPTER THIRTY-NINE

As Arthur rode in the police car, he thought about nothing but his daughter. "Zelda is going to call me, expecting me to meet her at the train station. I'll call my brother and see what he can do."

Arthur's brother Drew was a corrections officer and had connections with the police. When they arrived at the station, Arthur called Drew, who came right away and got him released.

"Thanks, Drew," Arthur said once in his brother's car.

"No problem."

"Drew, I need another favor. Would you take me to the train station? Zelda is coming home. I would go home and get my car, but I will be late picking Zelda up."

"Not a problem, Arthur."

"So," Drew said with a smirk, "you finally gave Miss Holier-than-thou the beatdown she's been asking for." He couldn't help but chuckle.

"That's not funny, Drew. All I did was shove her a little. I don't know how she got that bruise on her arm."

"C'mon, Arthur, open your eyes. She did it to herself. She knew the cops weren't going to do anything if she didn't have any marks on her. She wanted you to be arrested."

Arthur was skeptical that Angela would take it that far. He was about to respond when Zelda called. "Hi, sweetheart."

"Dad, I'm at the station."

"I'll be there in a few; I'm not far."

"Okay, Dad."

"Why is Zelda coming home in the middle of a semester?"

"Zelda's pregnant. I told her to come home."

"What did Angela say?"

"You know Angela. She's pitching a fit. I'm not going to let Angela or her relatives, especially her aunt, crucify Zelda like they did other single girls that got pregnant," he said as he rolled his eyes.

Drew chuckled again. "Knowing Angela, she's probably at home right now sewing a scarlet 'A' on all of Zelda's clothes."

Drew's brow furrowed. "That's why I left the church. I'll never forget how they treated me and Cora after she got pregnant. They shunned us and treated us like we were demons or something. It upset her so much that she couldn't function at work. I still believe that's why she had a miscarriage."

When they arrived at the station, Zelda spotted them and rushed to the car, her face beaming. "Hi, Uncle Drew! I didn't know you were coming."

Drew smiled at his niece. "I hope you don't mind. I wanted to see you too."

"Of course not." She gave Arthur a loving squeeze and kissed his cheek. "Hi, Daddy! Where's Mom? She said that she was coming too."

"Did you call her and say you were coming home?"

"No, she called me, and I told her you said for me to come home. She said that I should call her when I got to the Long Island Railroad station. I figured you were going to bring her with you, so I called you instead. I didn't know you were with Uncle Drew."

When they arrived at the house, Arthur turned to his daughter and said, "Go on in Zelda; I'll be there in a little while. I need to talk with Uncle Drew for a few minutes."

After Zelda went into the house, Arthur's brows creased, and he said, "Drew, I don't know what to do. If I go in there and Angela starts some mess..."

"Do you want to stay at my house tonight?"

"No, thank you. I just don't wanna go back to jail. And I don't wanna stay here, because the neighbors saw the cops take me handcuffed into their squad car. I'm embarrassed, and I know my credibility with the neighbors is shot. But I need to stay because of Zelda's situation."

"Arthur, it's dark; nobody can see you. Go in, sleep on it, and decide in the morning."

The men observed Angela open the front door and put the trash out. She took a quick glance at them, looked away, went back inside, and closed the door.

"What are you going to do, Arthur? The offer is still open. You can crash with me tonight."

Arthur took a deep breath. "I guess I'd better head in."

"Okay, man. If you need me, just call."

Arthur got out the car, cleared his throat, and went inside.

CHAPTER FORTY

T risha and Nicholas stood outside Carl's hospital room, holding hands and staring into the room. Trisha said, "Nicholas, let's pray."

Before she uttered the first word, Nicholas bowed his head, sobbed, and collapsed to one knee. Trisha grabbed him by the arm and assisted him to his feet. "Listen, Nicholas," she said as she sniffled. "Your dad is gonna be alright. I believe God." Then she bowed her head and whispered a prayer. Nicholas's hands trembled and his breathing was erratic. The nurse brought a chair to Nicholas and said, "Have a seat, young man."

Nicholas sat down. Trisha stood behind him with her hands on his shoulders. One of the doctors came out the room. Trisha rushed to him and asked, "How is he?!"

"He will be alright. He's resting peacefully now."

"Oh, thank God," she said, breathing a heavy sigh.

"Mrs. Boston, you can go home and get some rest."

"No. I'm going to stay. If I go home, I won't be able to rest."

"Okay."

"Nicholas, are you going home?" asked Trisha.

"Mom, I'm staying."

"Make sure you call the college."

Nicholas looked at her but did not respond. Trisha asked the doctor, "What happened?"

"Your husband had a cardiac episode."

carl"You mean a *heart attack*?"

"No. Did you know he has diabetes?"

"No, I didn't know that and neither does he. Can I go and see him?"

"Yes, but I want to speak to you in private for a minute."

"Can I see him?" asked Nicholas.

"Sure," said the doctor.

Nicholas walked in the room but was unprepared for what he saw. Carl was attached to a monitor with needles in his arms, an oxygen mask on his face, and wires attached to his chest, monitoring his heart. His eyes were partly opened with only a sliver of the white of his eyes visible. Nicholas felt dizzy at the sight of his father. He prayed, "Lord, please don't let my father die. If you spare him, I promise I'll work in the church."

Nicholas held Carl's hand and, teary-eyed, he whispered in his ear. "Dad, I'm so sorry for the way I've acted. You taught me confession is good for the soul. I don't know if you can hear me, but I have something I need to confess. Dad, I not only smoked reefer, but I sold it too." Carl grunted. Nicholas assumed that he heard his confession.

———

Outside the room the doctor said to Trisha, "When your husband was admitted, he reeked of alcohol. He must stop drinking. He could've gone into a diabetic coma."

Trisha bowed her head and lamented, "How could I have not known that Carl had a drinking problem?"

"He needs to get away from the stress too," the doctor continued, "or he could end up with a heart attack."

Trisha responded nervously. "Uh huh. Is there anything else?"

"Yes. When Carl checks out of the hospital, the dietician is going to give you a pamphlet with a strict diet he *must* follow."

"Thank you, Doctor. I'll make sure he does."

Trisha walked into the room, no more prepared than Nicholas had been when he saw Carl attached to those medical instruments. She heaved a deep sigh and said to herself, "Keep yourself together, Trish. Nicholas is watching you. If he sees you losing it, he'll fall apart."

Trisha and Nicholas slept in two reclining leather chairs in Carl's private room. The next day, Carl woke up, blinked his eyes, coughed, and in a raspy voice said, "Trisha, what's going on?"

Trisha's body jolted at the sound of his voice, and she opened her eyes. "Baby, how're you feeling?"

"Other than being a little tired, I feel okay. What happened?"

Trisha spoke softly, not wanting to wake Nicholas. "What is the last thing you remember?"

"I was lying here in the bed; everything else is a blank."

"I spoke with the doctor."

"What did he say?"

She was about to tell him when Nicholas woke up, stretched and yawned, then rushed to his dad's bedside. "Hey, Dad how're you feeling?"

"I'm feeling better."

Just then, the doctor walked in. "Good morning, Mr. Boston. I need to discuss a few things with you and your wife."

Carl looked at his son. "Nicholas, would you wait outside a few minutes, please?"

Nicholas walked out to the hallway.

"Mr. Boston, if you want to be around for a long time, you're going to have to make some lifestyle changes. First of all, what kind of work do you do?"

"I'm a pastor."

"Uh huh," the doctor said with a raised brow. "Your sugar levels were high when they brought you in. You have type two diabetes. I strongly advise that you hold off on the drinking."

Carl glanced at Trisha to see her reaction. Trisha, however, kept her eyes on the doctor.

"I'm not saying you're an alcoholic," the doctor continued, "but if you need help to quit drinking, I can recommend a place that is discreet and can help you.

"Pastors go through a lot of pressure dealing with people, along with the church," the doctor said sympathetically. "You're only human, Reverend, and like anyone else, you need a release. I know a doctor who understands pastors' struggles because he once was a pastor. I'll give you his number. I highly recommend you contact him."

"Thank you, Doctor," said Trisha.

"Pastor, your levels are good. I'm going to release you today. Please think about what I said."

"I will, Doctor," Carl said nonchalantly.

When the doctor left the room, Trisha turned to Carl. "Carl, this is the second time you've been admitted into the hospital in two weeks. The other doctor told you the same thing this doctor did. God is trying to tell you something. You'd better listen!"

"Why did he say that?" Carl asked.

"Why did he say what?"

"I only drink socially, not all the time. I don't need the stuff, you know."

"I didn't know you drank at all," Trisha said, her eyes wide with surprise.

"Actually, I don't drink as in getting drunk, or needing it. I just get a taste every now and then with lunch, that's all. Besides, it ain't no sin. I know how we were taught coming up in church. You know they taught that 'everything's a sin.'"

"Carl, no one said anything about sin."

"And besides, they drank wine in the Bible!"

"Carl, why are you being so defensive?"

Nicholas entered the room and the conversation stopped.

"Nicholas," said Trisha as she smiled, "your dad's being released from the hospital today. The doctor said that he's doing a lot better."

"Good. Thank God," Nicholas said.

"So, you can go back to school today."

Nicholas and Carl glanced at each other.

———

Carl was released from the hospital later that day. When they arrived home, Carl sat in the living room on the couch and, in front of Nicholas, said to Trisha, "Trisha, Nicholas wants to tell you something."

Nicholas cleared his throat and looked sheepishly at his mother. "Mom, I'm not going to go back to school."

"What do you mean you're not going back?!"

"Trish, let him talk."

Trisha's eyes narrowed. "Go on."

In a low voice, Nicholas said, "Mom, I've been suspended for the rest of the semester."

"What for?!"

"I was caught with marijuana."

"You didn't tell me you got caught!"

"I know and I'm sorry."

"And why didn't you tell me you were suspended for the rest of the semester?!"

"I just found this out." Nicholas took the letter from his pocket and handed it to her. Trisha read the letter, her eyes wide, and she felt like she couldn't breathe. Nicholas confessed the entire incident, along with informing her he and Richard also sold marijuana. Trisha flopped in a chair and shook her head.

"Mom? Mom, are you okay?"

Trisha scowled at her son. "What do *you* think?!"

"Trisha, the boy's sorry," Carl said.

"Carl, you need to go upstairs and get into bed. Are you hungry?"

"Yes, I could eat something."

"What about you, Nicholas?"

"Mom, please talk to me," Nicholas pleaded.

Trisha's lip curled into a snarl. "Are you hungry, Nicholas?"

"Yes."

Trisha went into the kitchen, leaving father and son to talk.

"I know your mother," Carl said. "Give her some time to process this. She'll come around. Leave it alone for now."

Trisha was wounded that Nicholas did not confess to her what he had done; they had always had a special bond. At the same time, she was pleased Nicholas was comfortable enough with Carl to reveal it to him; something he'd never done before.

CHAPTER FORTY-ONE

That night Clyde came home to get a few changes of clothes to take with him to a hotel. The thought of sleeping with Mae again made him cringe. He thought, "Last night was like lying in a cold, wet spot in the bed all night."

When Clyde arrived home, he said hello to Mae and she murmured, "Hello."

He heard Mary and Geraldine moving about upstairs and called to them. They ran down the stairs and hugged him. Then Mae said, "Geraldine, Mary, I need to talk with your father. Give us a few minutes, then you can come back downstairs."

"Okay, Mom," they said in unison.

Clyde walked to the bedroom to collect some of his clothes. Mae followed close behind.

"Clyde?"

"Yes, Mae," he said without looking in her direction.

"What are we going to do about Mother Sommers?"

"What do you mean?"

"Is she still going to work here or what?"

"Do you want her to stay?"

"It would be nice."

"Okay, if you want her to." Clyde suddenly wondered if Nathan had called Mae.

"That's all I wanted to say," said Mae.

Clyde put some clothes in a garment bag, slipped on his jacket, and walked to the stairs. "Geraldine, Mary!" he called to his daughters, "come here. I want to say goodnight!"

They came downstairs and saw the garment bag. "Dad, where are you going?!"

Seeing their disenchanted faces, he suddenly changed his mind about staying at a hotel. He took his jacket off and said, "I'm going to the spare bedroom in the basement. I'll talk with you in the morning."

————

Clyde lay in bed that night, staring at his phone. He imagined Nathan calling and saying, "I spoke with Mae's lawyer and straightened everything out. There will be no divorce. Congratulations."

He dialed Nathan's number but hung up after one ring. "Give it up Clyde," he said to himself. "It's hopeless." Suddenly, his phone rang. It was Nathan.

Clyde's stomach rumbled and he said, "I want to know what he's going to say, but I can't bring myself to answer." Clyde's hands shook as he held the phone to his ear. He prayed, "Lord give me strength!"

With trembling hands, he whispered a prayer before answering.

"Nathan?"

"How are you, Rev?"

"As well as can be expected, under the circumstances."

"I spoke with Mae."

"What did she say?"

"To be honest with you, Clyde, I don't think she really wants a divorce. I asked her for her lawyer, and she said it won't be necessary, and that she was waiting on something."

"What does *that* mean?!"

"She didn't say."

"I'm here with her right now, and she's as cold as ice."

"Clyde, I don't want to give you any false hope, but in my years of practice, when one of the parties procrastinates that's usually a good sign. I've seen situations much worse than yours work out. I'll call you when there's an update. Just stay cool and try not to worry."

"Thank you, Nathan. Good night."

"Good night."

Chapter Forty-Two

Arthur entered the house, walked past Angela without speaking, and went upstairs to his bedroom. There was a knock at the door.

"Yes?"

"It's me, Dad."

"Come in, baby."

As Zelda walked in, Arthur patted the bed next to where he was sitting. She sat next to her father and began to lament, "Dad, I know you're disappointed in me—"

"*Zelda! Come here!*" Angela shouted at the door.

"Go see what your mother wants. We'll talk later."

Zelda left the room and closed the door. Arthur heard Angela yelling but could not make out what was being said. He rushed to the door and slung it open. "What's going on?"

"If you lay one hand on me, I'll call the police!" Angela spat.

Arthur stood his ground for the sake of his daughter. "Angela, we don't need your confusion. Zelda needs—"

"What she needs is God!"

"*Angela—!*"

"It's holiness or hell!" Angela shouted.

"Angela, *shut up*! Zelda doesn't need—!

"It's holiness or hell!" Angela cried again. "If it was up to you, she'd—"

"*Ma, stop!*" Zelda pleaded, her eyes flooding with tears.

Angela pointed her finger at Zelda and shouted, "*The blood of Jesus! How dare you go against your mother!*"

Angela hurried into her room and slammed the door. From inside her room, she continued screaming, "Satan, the blood is against you!"

Turning to Arthur, Zelda cried, "*Daddy, I can't stay here!*" She suddenly turned and ran down the stairs.

"*Zelda! Come here!*"

Zelda ran out the front door. Arthur ran after her and chased her down the street, yelling, "Zelda! Come back here!"

He caught up to her when she stopped at a corner, waiting for cars to pass.

Arthur took his child into his arms, calming her in his embrace. "Baby, let's go back home. I promise everything's gonna be alright."

Choking on her tears, Zelda clung to her father as Arthur tightened his embrace. With their arms around each other, they walked back home. As they entered the house, they heard Angela in the kitchen on the phone talking to her aunt.

She became loud and brash when she heard them enter. "I ain't gonna let the devil run my house! No, sir!"

"Zelda, go to bed," Arthur said.

As Zelda headed upstairs to her room, Arthur stood in the kitchen archway and mouthed to Angela, "We need to talk."

Angela turned her back to him, berating him to her aunt. Arthur stepped around her, stood in her face, and said in a measured tone, "Angela, I want to talk to you."

Once again, she turned her back and continued berating him.

"Angela, get off the phone *now*!" Arthur shouted.

With that, he snatched the phone from her and flung it to the floor. It hit the floor with a crash, pieces of the phone hurling in every direction.

"That's it, I'm calling the cops!" Angela raged.

Arthur grabbed the house phone and said, "With what phone?!"

"With the house phone!"

Arthur stood with his arms folded, the house phone in his hand. "No, you ain't!"

"Give me the phone, Arthur!" she demanded.

"No!"

Her voice echoed throughout the house. *"Give me the phone!"*

Arthur pulled up a chair and said, "Angela, sit down and shut up! Zelda needs us right now. What's the *matter* with you?!"

Angela stared at Arthur, then sat with her arms folded and her face contorted.

CHAPTER FORTY-THREE

C arl entered his study and retrieved the diary from its hiding place behind the bookcase. He then retired to his bedroom while Trisha prepared the family's evening meal.

Carl took a deep breath and opened the diary:

> *When I woke this morning, I opened my eyes cursing all of creation. I cursed the sun for shining, the birds for singing, and the children who were playing outside. I looked in the mirror and cursed myself and finally life itself. My life is so devoid of meaning, it's barely worth living.*
>
> *Lorraine came into the bedroom and told me my secretary called and said, Jean, one of the church members, was in the hospital on life support and not expected to live. I put on khaki pants that had a coffee stain on them and a wrinkled denim shirt. Lorraine eyed me disapprovingly. "You can't go to the hospital looking like that!" Changing into proper clothing was too overwhelming for me to be bothered. I left Lorraine there shaking her head and rushed to the hospital. When I arrived, Jean's family gave a sigh of relief and hurried me into her room.*
>
> *I stood at the foot of her bed, looking back and forth between her and the heart monitor. Her family stood at the door of her*

room weeping. Jean lay in the bed, unconscious and dangling from an invisible tether between life and the unknown region we call death. I whispered to her, "Jean, what are you feeling? Please give me a sign. Is there life after this life? Is death more painful than life?"

I watched as the heart monitor flatlined. At first, I envied her transition. Then my envy turned into rage, and I cursed her under my breath for dying and not revealing to me what it was like.

I met with the family and told them, "She's in a better place, where there's no more pain and suffering."

I left the hospital having no idea if I still held that belief.

After reading, Carl put the diary under the bed, laid across the bed, closed his eyes, and thought about his 'heart event' and what the doctors had said to him. He recalled ministers he knew who had died in the pulpit. Carl feared that would happen to him too. As a young minister, he heard some older preachers spout, "They're gonna have to take me out of the church feet first before I quit preaching."

Carl anxiously prayed, "Lord, I don't want to die yet!"

As he grieved over his situation his phone rang. Unbeknownst to Carl, Trisha had come into the bedroom. She grabbed the phone before Carl reached it and said, "Carl, you're not taking any calls."

She answered the phone, paused, then said, "Oh, Bishop Howard. How are you, sir? No, he's not asleep; he can take the call."

Trisha whispered to Carl, "It's Bishop Howard. Don't stay on long. You need your rest."

She handed him the phone, and Carl nodded his head.

"Hello, son," Bishop said. "I was told you had an incident at church the other Sunday and was rushed to the hospital."

"Yeah, but I'm okay now."

"What happened?"

"Well, Bishop, I wasn't myself. I kinda lost my bearings just for a minute."

"What did the doctors say?"

"They said I had a nervous collapse."

"That's doctor talk for nervous breakdown."

Carl didn't mention his second visit to the hospital. He didn't want to volunteer any information because he figured Bishop Howard was going to lecture him as Trisha and the doctor had done.

"You young preachers need to understand that you aren't made of iron!" Bishop Howard said forcefully. "There are some practical things many young preachers ignore. I don't know how your church is set up as far as retirement, but if you haven't started setting up for your retirement by now, you'd better get on it right away or you'll be preaching well into your nineties to make ends meet."

"I own a couple of Brooklyn brownstones and a few fast-food spots. My house is mine! You hear me?! Like I told Morgan, I said, 'Son, get your own house because no matter how the people say they love the first lady, when *you* die, their love dies, and your wife and son will be put out of the house and left in the cold."

As Bishop Howard spoke, Carl responded at the end of each sentence with, "Yes, Bishop."

"Preacher, you need some R and R. I'm going to be the keynote speaker at a ministers' conference in Virginia Beach next month, and my wife and I want to have you and your wife as our guests. You don't have to attend all the sessions. You and the wife can have some alone time in the hotel and on the beach.

"And don't worry about money; as I said, you all are my guests. After the conference my wife and I are going to stay there for a weeks' vacation. I want you and Trisha to stay and vacation with us."

Carl did not interrupt as Bishop Howard spoke to him for a half hour, explaining why he needed to get away. Bishop Howard took a breath and Carl said, "Thank you, sir. I'll check with my wife."

"I don't think you understand." Bishop Howard's tone was firm and commanding. "This was *not* a request; as we used to say in the military, 'This is an order, private!'"

After listening to Bishop Howard, Carl realized what he lacked in his own ministry upbringing—a sage who took a personal interest in him. Carl thought, "So that's why I feel so empty most of the time, even after hanging with my peers. I lack a *spiritual dad*."

"Yes, Bishop," Carl responded. "I'll let Trisha know we're going," he said with a chuckle.

"Now, that's more like it. I'll get back to you with all the details."

Carl concluded that Bishop Howard was *fathering* him. "I guess Bishop misses Morgan, or he senses that I need a spiritual dad," Carl thought.

What continued to puzzle Carl was why Morgan took his own life, seeing as he had a mentor. In any event, Carl was going to take advantage of this mentoring moment.

"One second, Bishop. Before you hang up—I was in the hospital again this week and coded. The doctor said it wasn't a heart attack, but a 'heart event.' Also, I drink too much."

Bishop paused for a few seconds, then said, "Son, you need to know when it's time to quit."

Carl began to weep. "Bishop, I don't know what to do at this point. I feel like I'm lost in a wilderness all alone without a compass."

"Carl, speak with your church board and then your church."

Bishop Howard instructed him what to say to the church body, then they hung up. After the phone call, Carl told Trisha what Bishop Howard said about the trip and what he should do with the church.

"Are you sure you want to do this, Carl?" Trisha asked.

"Yes, Trish."

"I'll back you whatever you decide, honey."

"Thank you, babe."

———————

Carl called the church board to his house that Saturday and told them what he planned to do. None opposed his decision. Sunday came and Carl said to Trisha, "Now comes the hard part; telling the congregation."

As Carl approached the podium, he was greeted with a rousing standing ovation, welcoming him back from the hospital. He raised his arms and smiled. "Thank you! Thank you all so much!"

His arms fell to his sides as he stood smiling and thanking the congregation. After two minutes, the applause stopped and the congregation took their seats.

"God bless you, church," Carl said as he took in their faces. "You sure know how to make a preacher feel appreciated."

Someone in the audience called out, "We love you, Pastor!"

The audience began to applaud again. "Please, listen to me," Carl said. "I have something very important to say, and you're not making it easy."

Many in the church had puzzled looks on their faces, wondering what he was going to say. "Church, please listen up," said Carl as his brow creased.

"The doctor told me I have to make a lifestyle change. One of the changes includes the pastorate..."

"No, Pastor!" yelled several audience members. Others burst out into sobs and others cried, *"Pastor, please don't quit!"*

One of the members became hysterical and the usher, who was a nurse, rushed to her to administer aide. Pandemonium had broken out.

CHAPTER FORTY-FOUR

C arl held up his arms and addressed the congregation. "Hold up, y'all! I didn't say anything about quitting!"

He waited for the audience to quiet down, rested his hands on the podium, and continued. "I need you all to listen and not have a tantrum without knowing all of the facts. I didn't say anything about quitting. However, I do need you to understand where I'm coming from.

"There're some areas in my life that necessitate my *immediate* attention. First of all, my health. As you know, I was rushed to the hospital the other Sunday. The doctor strongly cautioned me to change my habits and slow down, or else. I wish I could say that all I need is a good night's sleep and I'll be alright, but I can't. Saints, I love you all but not enough to die for you. It's imperative that I take a rest, both mentally and physically.

"Secondly, my family. There are some issues that have arisen in my home that also need my immediate attention. Some of you may think just because I'm a pastor, I escape family issues. Well, let me tell you, *because* I am a preacher many of my family issues are magnified.

"And finally, my spiritual strength. I give everything when I minister, leaving a part of myself on this pulpit *every* Sunday..."

Tears welled up in his eyes. "Y'all don't realize the spiritual battles the pastor faces daily. The enemy attacks me even more than he attacks you because I'm the leader. The devil figures if he defeats the leader, then all of you who follow the leader will be defeated as well."

Carl took a deep, cleansing breath. "For the reasons I've stated, I am going to take a three-month sabbatical starting next Sunday. During that time, I will be reacquainting myself with my wife and family, reacquainting myself with life, and—don't let what I'm about to say shock you—reacquainting myself with God.

"While I'm on sabbatical, Bishop Howard will be the interim pastor and oversee the church until I return. The officers of the church will continue to take on the day-to-day operations. There will be a different pastor, chosen by me, who will preach each Sunday. Also, Bishop Howard will stop in every now and then. I've instructed the board to fully cooperate with the Bishop. The weekly Bible classes will continue to be taught by the Bible teachers."

After Carl concluded his statement, he stared at the audience, expecting feedback. However, the church remained still, their countenances frozen as though under the influence of a spell. After a few moments, Carl said, "Well, I guess I'll take my text now."

———

The next day, Carl called Reverend Clyde Jones. "Preacher, this is Carl Boston. How are you?"

"Well, no need to complain, Rev. It doesn't change a thing."

"I hear you. Rev, I'm calling because I need a favor."

"Sure, Doc, if I can."

"I need you to preach for me on a Sunday morning. I know preachers don't like leaving their pulpits on Sunday, but it's an emergency."

"What's happening?"

"I'm going on a three-month sabbatical. If it were only for a couple of Sundays, I'd use my preachers to preach.

"But, Doc, leaving them Negroes alone for three months may give them crazy ideas," Carl quipped. "By the time I return, they'd have built a golden calf and started worshipping it like the children of Israel."

The men chuckled, then Clyde asked, "Which Sunday are you talking about?"

"Well, Bishop Howard is coming next Sunday. What about the Sunday after?"

"I think that can be worked out."

"Good..."

Clyde heard a beep on his phone. It was his lawyer Nathan. "Carl, can I call you back later? I'm getting an important call I must answer."

"No problem. Oh yeah, thanks for consenting to come."

Clyde switched over to Nathan, anticipating some good news. "Hey, Nathan, what's the good word?"

"I received a phone call from Mae's lawyer..."

"And?" Clyde's heart was racing.

"She's going forward with the divorce."

Clyde was stunned. "Why?! I don't get it!"

"Remember I told you she said she was waiting on something?"

"Yeah, what was she waiting on?"

"I called her after speaking with her lawyer, and she told me that she was waiting on you to admit that you were wrong for putting your ministry over her and the girls."

"I've apologized to her a thousand times!"

"She didn't want an apology; she wanted an admission."

"Is that all she wants?! She should've said something."

"You and I know she's not going to accept an admission after she had to tell you what she wanted."

"Okay, Nathan. So, what do I do now?" Clyde said as his voice strained.

"Well, Pastor, if it is a voluntary settlement, it's simple. You and Mae go to the judge and you, Mae, and the judge sign a divorce decree. If it's contested, then that's another story."

"Like I told you before Nathan, she can have whatever. I don't have any fight left in me."

"Okay then. I'll call her lawyer and tell her to proceed."

Clyde spoke in a slow and deliberate tone. "Ain't this something? We got married in the church and joined together by God. And now we're going to the courts before a worldly judge so he or she can rip asunder what *God* has joined together. Nathan, something is wrong with this picture."

With the words caught in his throat, he continued. "How can the world disband what heaven has joined together? I just don't understand it."

"I'm so sorry, Clyde. I wish there were something else I could do," Nathan said sadly.

"Just being there is a great help, Nathan. I appreciate you."

"I'll call you back with the time and date we're going to see the judge and sign the papers."

"Alright."

CHAPTER FORTY-FIVE

Arthur sat in the chair next to Angela and stared at her for three minutes. Angela stared away, refusing to look at him. She folded her arms and made an audible sigh.

"Look at me Angela!" demanded Arthur.

Angela sighed louder with each breath. Arthur kept speaking despite her sighs. "Angela, we need to talk about our daughter. That's what's important now!"

Angela continued sighing. Arthur took a deep breath, threw up his arms and said, "Whatever!"

Then he went to the bottom of the steps and called Zelda. Zelda walked slowly downstairs her eyes red from crying. "Yes, Dad?"

"I want to talk with you." They sat in the dining room. Hearing their voices, Angela entered the dining room, sat, and crossed her legs.

"Who's the father? —" asked Arthur.

"Yeah!" Angela grumbled, interrupting. "Was he the only one you laid with?!"

"Angela, please—" shouted Arthur.

Angela interrupted again. "What about marriage?!"

"Nobody's marrying anyone!" Arthur said, banging the arm of the chair.

Angela's brows furrowed and she pointed her finger at her daughter. "Zelda, I *warned* you! I knew something like this would happen!"

Zelda, unwilling to endure any more of her mother's badgering, screamed and ran upstairs to her room. Arthur called her, but she did not respond. Arthur's eyes narrowed. He stared at Angela and was tempted to express his anger toward her physically, but changed his mind when he thought about being incarcerated again.

Angela paused, stretching out the moment, looked down her nose, lifted her chin, and casually walked back to the kitchen.

Arthur grumbled out loud, "This is it! I can't take this any longer!"

He stepped outside, got into his car, and drove—no place in particular; he just wanted to get away from Angela. As he drove, Rhonda Clark, a childhood friend from the neighborhood where he grew up, called. Without looking at the caller ID Arthur answered the phone in a harsh tone. "This is Pastor! What is it?!"

"Hello, Arthur. Did I call you at a bad time?"

"No, what can I help you with?" he said coolly.

Rhonda, confused by his coldness, asked, "Arthur, are you okay?"

"Yeah..."

"Arthur, we've known each other a long time. I can tell when something is wrong."

"I'd rather not get into it. I don't want to burden you with my problems."

"Arthur, I remember when I was going through my divorce and the many times you came here in the middle of the night, and I cried on your shoulder for hours."

"Yes, I know but..."

"I think it's time I returned the favor. Ever since you helped me, you've been like my surrogate pastor."

"And that's why..."

"And that's why *what*?" asked Rhonda. "Are you saying because you're a preacher, you don't need someone to talk to?"

"No, but..."

"Arthur what are you doing?"

"Just driving around."

"Come over. Let's talk."

Arthur took a deep breath, then said, "I don't know..."

"Why not?"

"Um... I just don't know."

"That's because you don't have a good reason not to."

Arthur knew if he didn't go to Rhonda's house, he'd probably end up at an adult theater, and the mental torment in the aftermath of such a visit was more than he could bear.

"Okay," he said, "I'll be there in about fifteen minutes."

"Good."

————

Angela called her Aunt Dora—the "prophetess"—and made her aware of Zelda's pregnancy.

"Angela, listen to me," Dora said. "You keep a holy standard. Don't compromise, not even for your child. She has to live holy too if she's gonna make it in. God kept you; He would've kept her too if she wanted to be kept! She's without excuse."

"She said that she's sorry, Aunt Dora."

"Sorry she got caught!" Dora snorted. "What's Arthur saying?"

"He's soft-soaping Zelda's sin. Afraid of calling it what it is."

"That's the lust demon that has him afraid to call sin a sin." Dora's voice began to rise. "He's probably guilty of the same sin himself; that's why he won't call it what it is, because he'd be condemning himself!"

Angela now spoke with a smug brashness. "I tell him that all the time! He won't hear me, but he'll hear God!"

CHAPTER FORTY-SIX

Rhonda lived on the second floor of a Brooklyn brownstone tenement. Arthur arrived, parked his car, walked up the front steps to the door, and rang the bell.

"Who is it?"

"It's me. Arthur."

She buzzed him in, and when he reached her apartment, Rhonda was waiting with the door open. When he came into her apartment she smiled and said, "Have a seat, Arthur."

Arthur took a deep breath, sauntered to the couch, and sat. Rhonda sat next to him, peering into his eyes with genuine concern.

"What has you so down, Arthur? I don't like seeing you like this."

Arthur was disgusted beyond endurance with Angela's antics. With tear-filled eyes, he revealed to Rhonda his and Angela's inactive sex life, including what happened the night of their honeymoon. Things he had kept to himself until then.

"Rhonda, I can count on one hand how many times we've had sex in the last five years." Arthur slowly shook his head and lamented, "I guess I got married outside of the will of God."

Rhonda looked at him with an empty stare, searching her mind for the magic words that would at least alleviate his pain in some way, but she came up empty. "I'm sorry, Arthur, I don't know what to say," she said regrettably.

"There's nothing *to* say. Thanks for listening though." Then he sighed as he noticed the time. "I should probably go."

"What's the hurry?"

"I've taken up too much of your time already."

"I'm not going to bed for a while. When you leave, I'm just going to watch TV."

To distract Arthur from his troubles, Rhonda redirected the conversation to their old neighborhood and those they had not heard from in years.

"Whatever happened to your old girlfriend? What's her name?" she said with a sly grin.

"You mean Evelyn?"

"Yeah... I never could figure out what you saw in her."

Arthur just smiled. "She was good people. You just didn't know her." Retaliating, he quipped, "What about that guy you were going with? What did we call him? Little Willie?"

She giggled. "He wasn't *that* little, Arthur."

Arthur chuckled. "He was sixteen years old and just four-feet eleven."

Rhonda inadvertently touched Arthur's hand, which lay on his thigh, and left it there as they roared with laughter. Suddenly, there was the sound of heavy rain. Rhonda squeezed his hand and in a delicate voice said, "I'm curious; how come we never got together?"

Arthur gazed into her eyes and whispered, "I don't know."

They peered into each other's eyes, hypnotized by the soothing, rhythmic pelting of rain against the windows. Arthur caressed Rhonda's hand brought it to his lips, and lightly kissed the tips of her fingers. Rhonda closed her eyes at the tender gesture, breathing deeply, and offering no resistance.

Weary of fighting their shared desire, the friends soon yielded to their rising passions. An hour later the rain subsided, and with their passion sated, they both regretted having taken their relationship to a physical level. Arthur whispered in her ear, "Perhaps I should leave."

Rhonda, too ashamed to look Arthur in his face, stared at the floor and in barely a whisper said, "Perhaps you should."

Arthur stared straight ahead as he walked to the door. The guilt he felt after going to a porn theater paled in comparison to the guilt of adultery. On his way home he lamented not having a close friend with whom he could share this burden and not worry that his indiscretion would be exposed. He also prayed that Rhonda wouldn't tell anyone.

Despite being guilt-ridden, Arthur also felt justified, reasoning that Angela drove him to it. He called Rhonda as he drove. She answered in a soft tone. "Yes?"

His mind went blank when he heard her voice. Stumbling over his words, he sighed and said, "A-are you okay?"

Rhonda paused for a few seconds, too nervous to respond. While she'd known Arthur since they were teens, once they crossed the line of physical intimacy, she felt that their relationship had been irreversibly stained. She swallowed and said, "I don't know."

After three seconds, Arthur said, "Rhonda?"

"Yes?"

"We can't let what happened tonight ever happen again."

"Yes, I know."

They continued talking with dramatic pauses, without mentioning what occurred between them that night, as though by not acknowledging it, it somehow never happened.

———

When Arthur arrived home, Angela was awake, sitting in the living room and waiting for him to come home; something she had not done in years.

"Where were you, Arthur?" she asked suspiciously.

Shocked by her question, he responded heatedly, "I was out!"

Angela stomped her foot, violently shook her head, and shouted, "Arthur are you having an affair with some whore?!"

Chapter Forty-six

Without responding, he walked upstairs to his bedroom and locked the door.

Angela followed him and screamed, "You're going to hell! You hear me?"

Arthur asked himself, "Out of all the nights I've come home late, why did she pick the one night I had an affair to accuse me?"

CHAPTER FORTY-SEVEN

Clyde and his lawyer Nathan met Mae and her lawyer at the courthouse. They appeared before the judge and signed the divorce papers. As they left the courtroom, Mae walked past Clyde. He greeted her, but she continued walking to the exit without acknowledging his presence. Clyde took a deep breath and sucked his teeth.

———

At church on Sunday Clyde summoned the deacons and ministers to his office before the start of the worship service. Brow creased, speaking in a measured tone, he said, "Mae Benton will not be returning to the church."

They stood there, confused, wondering why he had used her maiden name. Before anyone inquired, he said, "The former Sister Mae Jones and I are no more."

There was a collective gasp. Then the deacons and ministers surrounded their pastor, embracing him and patting him on his shoulders. "We're so sorry," Deacon Roberson offered.

"Just keep me in your prayers," said Clyde, "I'll be alright. I wanted you to know before I announce it to the church."

"Do you want one of us to preach this morning, Pastor?" Minister Sloan asked as he placed his hand on Clyde's shoulder. Clyde shook his head but said nothing. Deacon Peterson suggested, "Maybe you should take some time off, Pastor."

Clyde's voice was thick, and his eyes filled with tears. "Thank you all. If I need to, I'll certainly let you know."

———

The choir sang a jubilant song when the worship service commenced. The song stirred the congregation into a euphoric praise. While the people rejoiced, Clyde stood at the podium, frozen in place. He slowly shook his head and stared at the empty chair where Mae once sat dressed in a different church hat every Sunday. Among her favorites were a pillbox hat with faux feather trim and pleated ruffles.

The people calmed down and Clyde continued to stare. As if suddenly aware of his surroundings, he cleared his throat and addressed the congregation. "Saints, many times we pray and still things don't go the way we'd hoped. However, God knows and He's always in control. Nothing catches God by surprise."

The congregation nodded their heads in agreement and responded, "Amen."

"We don't understand it all now, but we will by and by. C'mon, y'all, say amen!" The congregation responded even louder, "Amen!"

"I want you all to know that sometimes even we as pastors don't understand why God allows things that happen." Clyde's brows furrowed and he said, "I'm sick and tired of those preachers that think they have all the answers!

"The apostle Paul admitted to the Corinthians, 'I'm perplexed, but not in despair.' Even Jesus, while on the cross, said to His Father, 'My God, my God why…?!'" The audience, sensing something was drastically wrong, gazed at Clyde without responding. Then speaking in a solemn voice, he said, "Sister Jones will not be returning to church. I'm sorry to announce that we are officially divorced."

The congregation was shocked at his announcement with many responding, "What?" Some cried, "Oh God, no…" while others let out an audible sigh.

"Listen to me, church," said Clyde, "I don't want anyone to look on Sister Jones any differently. If you loved her as your first lady, love her now. Also, I'm asking that you don't call her offering support, advice, or attempting to find out what happened. Please respect our privacy."

Clyde glanced at the minister's section. A few had tears in their eyes, others sat stone-faced.

It did not take long for the news to spread that Clyde and Mae were divorced. Before the day ended, Debra called Mae. She answered the phone coolly. "Yes, Debbie?"

"Mae, what's this I hear that you and Clyde are divorced?"

"Yeah, I couldn't take it anymore."

"Why was I not informed of this?"

"I told you!" Mae said in a harsh tone.

Debra, matching her tone, said, "No, you didn't!"

"I told you that we weren't—"

Debra, interrupting Mae, said, "Mae, stop your nonsense! You never even mentioned the word divorce to me!"

Mae took a breath and said, "Well, maybe I didn't, but—"

"Are you home?"

"Yeah."

"I'm coming over, Mae."

"You don't have to—"

Cutting Mae off in the middle of their exchange, Debra insisted. "I'll be there in about a half hour."

"I ain't going anywhere," Mae said carelessly.

Ten minutes later, the guard announced that Debra was at the gate. When Debra reached the door, Mae let her in. As she entered the house, Debra was shocked by what she saw. The living room was a wreck, with clothes thrown about the floor and chairs.

"Mae, what's going on?!" asked Debra with a raised brow.

"I'm in the middle of cleaning."

"On a Sunday?" she asked skeptically. "Where's Mother Sommers and the girls?"

"Mary and Geraldine are at my mothers, and I guess Mother Sommers is at church. Anyway, she doesn't work on Sundays."

Debra, concerned that Mae had suffered a nervous breakdown, gingerly took her by the arm and led her to a chair that was not cluttered. "You just sit here while we talk. I'll pick up the clothes."

"I'm fine," Mae insisted.

Debra motioned to her to remain still, then began gathering up the clothes. Mae giggled as she watched her friend work. "Girl, put those clothes down. I thought I had enough time to clear them up before you arrived, but you got here before I could finish. I was going through the clothes to give to goodwill. They'll be here early tomorrow morning. I should've just let you pack the clothes up for me," she said with a hardy laugh.

"Girl, I ain't your maid," Debra said with a grin as she dropped the clothes. Pulling up a chair she had cleared, she looked at her friend with sympathetic eyes. "Mae, let's talk."

CHAPTER FORTY-EIGHT

Reverend Michael Samuels, the executive minister of Green Avenue Church, and his wife Lilly dropped in unexpectedly on Lorraine at 8 a.m. Surprised by the early visit, Lorraine answered the door with a dubious look. "To what do I owe this call?" she asked.

"Good morning, First Lady. I hope this isn't a bad time," Lilly said.

"Not at all." Lorraine tried to sound cordial although she wished they had called first. "Come in and have a seat."

Lorraine felt strangely uneasy by the visit. Although she and Morgan had known the Samuels for years, she had heard from them only one time since Morgan's suicide.

They sat down and Michael proceeded. "We feel it's our duty to tell you that there was a trustee board meeting that concerned you last week."

Lorraine was stunned. "Oh, really?"

"Yes. I just wanted to give you a heads up. The meeting was to discuss what they were going to do with the parsonage. Like I told you, right after Reverend Kendal died, they wanted you out."

Lorraine's breathing was suddenly quick and ragged.

"May I use the bathroom?" Lilly asked.

"Sure." Lorraine showed her to the bathroom, then returned to Michael.

When Lilly returned, she did not sit down right away. Instead, she strolled around the living room, looking around, touching the furniture and curtains. She abruptly interrupted her husband. "First Lady, this is my first time in the parsonage..." She stopped and then chuckled. "What am I saying? Of course, I've been here before, but not since you redid the place. It's beautiful. You know, we have the same taste in decorations."

"Thank you," Lorraine said flatly, confused by Lilly's interruption.

Michael sat back in the chair and continued. "I want you to know that I loved your husband. I remember we talked just before he died, and I promised him that if anything were to happen to him, I'd make sure the church looked out for you and Lester."

"Thank you, Michael."

"I probably shouldn't say anything, but the trustees are thinking of consulting with Bishop Howard for suggestions about a candidate for a new pastor. Don't get me wrong; Bishop Howard is a good man, but if he decides to back one of the ministers of his church for the position, I'm afraid they won't look out for you as I would. You see what I mean, First Lady?"

"Yes, I do," she answered anxiously.

Samuels's brow creased. "Like I said to you right after Reverend Kendal died, when they hire a new pastor, you and your son will be put out the house. That would *never* happen if *I* was pastor. I've seen this all before; the wife always gets booted from the parsonage. If I were pastor, I'd make sure they'd either find an apartment or another parsonage for the new pastor."

"What can I do?" Lorraine said fretfully.

Michael sat on the edge of the seat and peered into her face. "When you meet with the trustees, just let them know you want one of *our* ministers to be pastor. As you know, I've worked closely with my good friend Morgan for years, longer than any of the other ministers. You founded the church along with your husband; they'll *have* to listen to you."

Michael stood and took Lorraine by the hand. "First Lady, we've taken up too much of your time. We should go."

"Thank you for letting me know," Lorraine said.

"I just want to keep my promise to your husband and my friend."

They were no sooner out the door when Lorraine called Trisha. "Hey, Trish, I think it's about to happen."

"What do you mean?"

"Reverend Samuels and his wife stopped by this morning."

"This early?!"

"Yeah. I kinda wondered about that too. Anyway, he told me that the board met to discuss putting me out of the house." Lorraine's voice cracked. "See, I told you they were going to do this. What am I gonna do?!"

"Listen to me; I believe they have to give you what they call a thirty-day holdover before they can do anything. And that's thirty days after they serve you a notice. Have you received anything from the courts?"

"Not that I know of."

"Good, then you have time. Do you have a lawyer?"

"Yeah, Morgan had a guy we used. I don't remember his name. I have to find the number. It's somewhere in his papers."

"Get in touch with him right away."

———

Later that day Lorraine received a certified letter from the church's trustee board. The letter requested a meeting with her at an attorney's office five days from the date of the letter. Lorraine promptly began searching the house for the lawyer's number but could not find it, nor could she remember his name.

After three days of searching in vain for the number, she called the board chairman, Edward Boone, to get a postponement for the meeting. The chairman told her it was too late for a postponement and that she should've called earlier in the week if she wanted to put it off.

In a panic, Lorraine called Trisha, sobbing. "Trish, I have a meeting with the board and their lawyer tomorrow, and I can't find Morgan's lawyer's number!"

"Lorraine, we have a lawyer we use that's a member of our church. I'll call him and get right back to you."

"Thank you, Trish."

Trisha called back right away. "Lorraine, I'm so sorry he's out of town. What time is the meeting tomorrow?"

"Nine in the morning."

"Where at? I'm going with you."

"It's located in downtown Brooklyn."

————

The next morning, Lorraine drove to Trisha's house.

"Are you okay?" Trisha asked after seeing Lorraine's swollen nose and red-rimmed eyes.

"Would you drive, Trish? Please?" Lorraine pleaded.

They arrived at the office and drove around looking for parking. Lorraine's hands shook when she recognized the board chairman's car.

Trisha stopped the car and turned to her friend. "It's 8:45; you'd better get going."

"You ain't coming with me?" Lorraine asked nervously.

"Give me the room number. I'll get there as soon as I find a parking spot."

Lorraine gave her the room number and went into the building. She found the room and knocked on the door. She heard someone say, "Come in."

When she walked in, her hands trembled. Seated at a conference table was the chairman of the trustee board, along with three other men. They greeted her, then one of the men said, "For the record, Mr. Boone, you are the board chairman and are here representing the church?"

"Yes, sir."

He then looked at Lorraine. "For the record, you are Mrs. Lorraine Kendal?"

Her voice trembled. "Yes, I am."

"I'm David Patrick, attorney. If all parties are present, let's get started."

Lorraine was terrified at the thought of being evicted with nowhere to go. Her lips trembled, and she did all she could to quell the tears that were about to burst like a dam.

CHAPTER FORTY-NINE

Lorraine scanned the faces of the men around the table a second time and noticed that Mr. Patrick looked familiar but could not place his face.

"First of all, Mrs. Kendal, I want to give you my condolences at the loss of your husband."

"Thank you," she said, still trying to place his face.

"Reverend Kendal was a good man and a good client. I hope that you keep me on as your council. If you need any advice, all you have to do is call me."

Lorraine's thoughts screamed, "Thank you, Jesus! Now I recognize him! That's Morgan's lawyer!" Lorraine breathed a sigh of relief for the first time since she received the certified letter from the church. "Thank you," she said as she smiled.

Mr. Patrick then turned to the board chairman. "Mr. Boone, I need you to sign these papers where I made an 'X.'" He gave Lorraine a different set of papers and pointed to an area on the paper. "Mrs. Kendal, you sign here."

Papers were shuffled around the table from person to person in an organized chaos. Lorraine read only part of what she had signed, blindly trusting Mr. Patrick. She recalled Morgan saying to her, "Lorraine, I'd trust David Patrick with my life." After the signing they all smiled at her and the attorney said, "All debts are settled. Congratulations, Mrs. Kendal. The house is yours, free and clear."

Mr. Patrick gave her the folder that contained the papers she had signed. He then looked at Lorraine, his tone grave as he spoke. "Mrs. Kendal, it's urgent you give me a call *today*. I have a pressing matter I *must* discuss with you."

Lorraine offered her thanks and left his office. Tears filled her eyes as she boarded the crowded elevator. Unashamedly, she raised her hands, lifted her head, and whispered, "Thank you, Jesus." Those in the elevator gawked at her, but Lorraine did not lower her hands or her head until she exited the elevator at the ground floor.

As she walked out of the building, a breathless Trisha rushed toward her.

"I'm so sorry, girl! I just found a parking space!"

"You ain't gonna believe what just happened," Lorraine said, staring at her friend in disbelief.

"What?!"

Lorraine had just begun recounting all that had happened in the office, when Brother Boone walked up behind them. "Sister Kendal, I know you're glad it's over."

"Yes, I guess I am," Lorraine said with a puzzled look. "Um... Brother Boone, what just happened in there?"

Stunned at her question, he said, "Are you serious?"

"Yes, I am."

"May I speak freely in front of Sister Boston?"

"Sure."

"Let's sit in my car."

They all sat in his car and Brother Boone asked, "Sister Kendal, did Reverend Kendal tell you about the issue with the house and the monies the church owed him?"

"No, he didn't. He rarely shared church business with me."

"Did you receive any correspondence from your lawyer?"

Lorraine knew she had been neglectful with respect to the business, going weeks without opening the mail.

"Well..." She remarked as she cleared her throat, "I haven't been keeping up on things as I should've been."

Brother Boone felt sorry for her and to save her anymore embarrassment, he said, "That's okay, I'll just start from the beginning. Years ago, Pastor Kendal took out a personal loan for the church. With the church mortgage looming overhead and other expenses, the church had trouble paying the loan. Because of constant late payments, the interest on the loan amounts was astronomical.

"Although the church began doing better financially, we were unable to pay back the loan and keep the payments up on the parsonage. So, Pastor Kendal, his lawyer Mr. Patrick, and the church board brokered a deal. The parsonage would stay in the church's name for tax purposes, however, Pastor Kendall would pay the mortgage. Upon his death, the insurance would pay off the house and his heirs would take possession."

Lorraine was practically speechless. "I was told that the board was going to evict me from the house."

Brother Boone lips curled, his eyes narrowed, and he said, "Who told you that?!"

"I'd rather not say."

"It was Michael Samuels, wasn't it?!"

Lorraine stared but did not confirm or deny.

"Let me share something with you," he said, as his brow furrowed. "For years, Samuels has wanted to take over Greene Avenue Church and live in the parsonage. The board warned Reverend Kendal many times about Samuels. Pastor refused to accept what we said because, as you know, he'd known him for years and he was a charter member."

Brother Boone took a deep breath and said emphatically. "Look, do not listen to a word Samuels says! First Lady, you and your son enjoy your house; ain't *nobody* gonna put you out!"

"Yes, sir. Thank you," Lorraine said with a full-toothed smile. And with that, they said goodbye. Lorraine and Trisha left his car, got in Lorraine's car, and drove off.

CHAPTER FIFTY

B ishop Howard called Carl early Tuesday morning. "Hey, son. How did things work out at church on Sunday?"

"I told them what you told me to say, and it worked out better than expected. Thank you, Bishop."

"You're welcome, son. By the way, what are you doing today?"

"I have no plans."

"Why don't you stop by my house for lunch, let's say about noon. I want to talk to you about a few things."

"Sure, Bishop. I'll see you then. Oh, should I bring the diary?"

Bishop paused then said, "Yeah, bring it."

Knowing how time conscious Bishop Howard was, Carl arrived at Bishop Howard's house at exactly noon. Bishop invited him in, pointed at a chair in the living room and said, "Have a seat, son."

As Carl walked to the chair, Bishop Howard sat wearily in his recliner, his feet propped on the footrest, and sighed heavily. "I invited you here today to share some things with you."

Carl stared at Bishop Howard and, showing no emotion, nodded his head.

"My heart goes out to you young preachers," Bishop Howard began. "When I first started pastoring, my mentors told me to avoid strong drink, women, and greed, but they never said *how* to avoid them. My pastor, Bishop Charles Larrimore, mentored us young preachers by scaring the hell out of us, with threats of damnation and eternal fire if we took part in any of the practices they warned us to avoid.

"So, we spent much of our waking hours horrified of going to the bottomless pit. We lived for God because we were terrified of hell."

Carl sat stoned-faced, eager to absorb the wisdom he anticipated would flow from Bishop Howard's lips. It was what he'd prayed for his entire ministerial life.

Bishop Howard continued, "You young ministers today have it extra hard. Nowadays, sexual indiscretions are more acceptable, resulting in promiscuous behavior running rampant. To add to that, greed is no longer the sin, *not* being rich is. The monies being made by those prostituting the gospel make it even harder not to become a gospel pimp. As they say, everyone has their price. To make matters worse, along with strong drink there is a drug epidemic among preachers."

The Bishop paused, put his hand to his chin, then stared as though in deep thought. Carl seized the opportunity to ask a question. "Bishop, if you could speak with your younger self, what advice would you give that young man?"

Bishop Howard responded instantly, as though anticipating the question. "I'd tell my younger self to make sure to spend quality time with his family."

He dabbed a tear from his eyes, his voice strained with regret. "Sister Howard and I had a biological son. Joel Isaiah Howard, the 2nd."

"What happened to him?"

"He joined a gang and was shot and killed by a rival gang. He was only fifteen years old."

Carl slowly shook his head. "I'm so sorry."

"If he had lived, he would've been about your age. The day he was killed, I was out of town. I remember that whole day. I had an uneasiness that something terrible was about to happen. I didn't know what, but I felt that whatever it was would be devastating.

"After Joel was killed, every waking hour I agonized over his death. I dreaded going to sleep because I was tormented by my dreams. I felt partially responsible for his death because I was so busy saving the world, that I wasn't as responsive to my son's needs as I should've been. The guilt I felt was unbearable, so I started drinking. Many times, I preached while under the influence. Other times I was so intoxicated I couldn't stand up, let alone preach. There was a small circle of preachers whom I trusted and shared my troubles with, but instead of reaching out and offering me help, they made me and my drinking problem the subject of their sermons. It hurt me deeply when my so-called friends betrayed me. So instead of reaching out for help, I mostly kept to myself."

Bishop Howard grimaced. "That was the worst mistake I could've *ever* made. The last thing I needed was to be alone." He looked pointedly at Carl and raised his voice. "You hear me, Preacher?"

"Yes, Bishop," Carl said as he anxiously cleared his throat.

Bishop Howard abruptly changed the subject. "Did you bring the diary?"

Carl wanted to ask other questions but was too nervous to speak unless asked a question. He thought it better to let Bishop control the direction of the conversation.

Carl took the diary from his attaché case and began where he'd left off the last time he read to Bishop Wallace.

> *Lorraine and I got home from church late tonight. She went to bed first and was asleep by the time I got to bed. For no particular reason, I shook her and told her to wake up. She stirred but kept her eyes closed. "Are you sleep?" I asked her. "I'm talking to you, Lorraine!" I found myself almost shouting. "Are you ignoring me?!" She continued to lay still without so much as a grunt.*

> *My chest heaved with fury. "Okay, keep ignoring me. I know you're a part of the conspiracy. I should've left you where I found you in the ghetto, poor and living hand to mouth. I'm the best thing that ever happened to you! I could've had anyone I wanted! I married you because I felt sorry for you!"*

> *There was banging at our bedroom door. It was Lester. He shouted, "Mom, are you okay?!" Lorraine finally spoke and told him to go back to bed and that she was alright. Lester made a desperate plea to Lorraine to open the door. She got up and walked to the door. She cracked it opened and said she was fine and to go back to bed.*

Lorraine stared into my eyes and asked if there was an unwelcome visitor in church tonight. I pushed past her, ran to the door, and bolted down the stairs. I rushed to the garage got into my car and thought, "Something has got to give!" I opened the glove compartment and fixed my eyes on the loaded revolver I kept in the car. I picked it up, stared at it, and declared, "This is the answer to all of my ills."

Then I took a deep breath and placed the revolver back into the glove compartment and closed it. I screamed, "Demon of suicide, I rebuke you!" After which I returned to the house, laid on the couch in the living room and fell asleep. I was awakened the next morning by the gentle touch of Lorraine's hand rubbing my forehead. Her eyes overflowed with tears, accompanied by deep sighs and whispered prayers.

CHAPTER FIFTY-ONE

Angela continued ranting. Zelda was in her room, sobbing into her pillow. Arthur, concerned for his daughter, unlocked his door and walked past Angela. He knocked on Zelda's door. "Zelda, are you all right?"

She did not respond but could be heard sobbing. "I'm coming in," he called to her.

Angela was still shouting as he went into Zelda's room. "Y'all deserve each other!" She then stormed to her bedroom and slammed the door.

Zelda lay under the covers. Arthur sat on the bed beside her. Still whimpering, she looked at her father with wet, swollen eyes. "Dad, why is Mom this way? I mean, why is she so angry all the time? She praises God in church but she's so mean to us at home. I don't understand."

Arthur shrugged and slowly shook his head. "I came in to see if you're okay. I'm going out for a bit. Will you be alright?"

"I'll be okay."

"If anything happens before I return, call me right away."

"I will, Dad."

———

Arthur drove around for about a half hour before he decided to call his brother Drew. "Hey, man, I think I'm going to take you up on your offer to stay the night. I have to get away from Angela."

"No problem. Come on over."

Having secured his lodging for the night, he proceeded to call his daughter.

"Yes, Dad," she answered, her tone low and sad.

"Why are you whispering?"

"Hold on, Dad." Zelda paused for a few moments, then still whispering, said, "Mom thinks I'm sleep. I don't want her to know I'm up."

"What's going on?"

"Mom is on the phone, talking with her sister and sobbing."

"Who? I didn't hear you."

"Her sister, Aunt Ruthie."

"Oh. What is she crying about?"

"Hold on, Dad." Zelda paused again, then said, "Okay, she hung up."

"What's happening?"

Zelda was whispering more nervously. "I think you should get here right away."

When Arthur returned home, he tip-toed up the stairs to Zelda's room. "Zelda, what's going on?" he whispered.

"Mom was crying to Aunt Ruthie."

"About what?"

"She said Aunt Dora told her that you were probably out messing around with another woman. Mom told Aunt Ruthie that you went out to meet with her again."

Arthur slowly nodded his head and thought, "So that's why she thought I was with someone tonight."

"Then Mom said that she wanted her husband back."

"Are you *sure* that's what your mother said?" a disbelieving Arthur asked.

"I heard her clearly."

"Okay."

Arthur slowly walked to Angela's room, mumbling to himself as he went. He took a deep breath and knocked on the door. "Angela."

"What?" she answered in a raspy voice.

"What's wrong?"

"Nothing." Her voice barely audible.

"May I come in?"

Angela opened the door without looking at her husband. They talked for twenty minutes, then came out of the room. Arthur went to Zelda's room and knocked on her door.

"Zelda. Your mother and I are going out. We won't be out long."

Zelda opened her door. "Okay, Dad."

———

Arthur and Angela took a leisurely walk around the neighborhood. While walking, Angela, sobbing profusely, confessed, "Arthur, when I thought you were with another woman, it drove me crazy... I need you and I love you. And I want us to stay together." Then she pleaded, "Please, let's give us another try. I promise things are going to change." Arthur dried her tears with his handkerchief and smiled. Then, as they stood under a streetlight staring into each other's eyes, they embraced and passionately kissed. At that point, they were oblivious to anyone who might have happened by.

They returned an hour later, holding hands. Once upstairs, Angela went directly to her bedroom and closed the door. Arthur knocked on Zelda's door to inform her they were back, but she had fallen asleep and did not respond. Arthur went into the bathroom to get ready for bed. He called Drew and told him he wouldn't be staying the night. He then proceeded to his bedroom, opened the door, looked inside, and gasped. Lying on his bed and wearing the sheer negligee he had not seen since he purchased it for her ten years earlier, was Angela. Arthur gazed at her for a moment, then said as he smiled, "Are you lost, Miss?"

Angela responding with a giggle. "Do you know the way to Lovers' Lane?"

"Why, yes. As a matter of fact, I *believe* I'm headed there now. You need a ride?"

Angela smiled and slowly nodded her head.

CHAPTER FIFTY-TWO

On Sunday, Emma Richards walked into Resurrection Temple and took a seat near the front row. She was aware of rumors that had spread throughout Resurrection Temple that she tried to seduce Pastor Austin and Reverend Jeremiah Riley. She greeted those she knew but received a less than cordial response. She eyed Kimberly in the choir stand, waved and smiled. Kimberly reciprocated with a casual nod, then turned her face away.

After the service, Peter stood by the front door shaking hands with visitors as they exited the church. Emma approached him with a sinister smile. "I'm back."

Peter gave her an icy stare. "God bless you," he said flatly.

Emma left the church, unaffected by the snub she had received from the congregation. The next Sunday, she walked into church and sat as close to the front as possible. For three weeks she attended Resurrection Temple and received the same halfhearted reaction.

Emma complained to a co-worker about how the people of Resurrection Temple avoided her. "Emma, why do you continue to go to that church?" the co-worker asked. "It's obvious from what you've told me that you are not welcomed."

"The pastor knows what he tried to do to me," Emma said scowling. "I'm going to sit there every Sunday, as close to the front as I can, and make him uncomfortable!"

Her co-worker looked at her wide-eyed. "What did he do?"

Emma's lip curled into a snarl. "He knows what he did and now he's denying it!" But what he *doesn't* know is that I have audio tape of a phone conversation we had which will expose him and prove that I wasn't lying. And I'm going to play it before the whole church."

————

The next day, Emma called the church and told an office worker to inform the board she had proof that Reverend Austin had tried to molest her. She claimed she knew of other former members that were willing to testify that he attacked them too. She left her phone number and asked if someone would contact her.

That night, Emma received a call from Bradley Hartwell, chairman of the Resurrection Temple Board of Trustees.

"Sister Richards, this is Brother Hartwell. I was told you have some rather damaging information about Reverend Austin."

"I sure do!" she said boastfully.

"What is it pertaining to?"

"I would like to play a tape in front of the whole congregation, so they would know what kind of man Reverend Austin is!"

"Well sister, the board would have to hear it before you present it to the congregation. Can you meet me and the board, let's say, 7 p.m. this Thursday at the church office?"

"We'll be there."

"We?"

"Five other former members he's sexually harassed and who now want to tell their stories will be joining me."

As he ended the call, Hartwell decided not to inform Pastor Austin of the meeting until the board heard the tapes and the accusations from former members.

CHAPTER FIFTY-THREE

On Thursday night, Resurrection Temple's trustee board waited at the church's office for Emma and company to arrive. When she did not show up by 8:30, they called her, but there was no answer. They waited until 9:30 and when she did not show, they left.

Bradley Hartwell decided to call Peter and let him know of Emma's claim that she had damaging information about him, just in case she had spread it to others in the church.

"I'm not surprised," Peter told Hartwell. "I received a call from Reverend Riley a couple of weeks ago, warning me to be on the lookout for Emma. It seems her sister had visited him at church and told him that Emma's husband had left her. We won't be hearing from her anymore."

"How do you know that?" Hartwell asked.

"I spoke with Reverend Riley again last night, and he said that Emma was killed in a freak car accident. An eighteen-wheeler jumped the divide and ran headlong into the car she was driving. There were three other people in the car, and she was the only one killed. The others walked away without a scratch."

"Well," the board chair said indignantly, "the Bible does say *not* to touch God's anointed!"

Trisha debated if she should call and inform Joan her son sold pot. Knowing how she would feel were she in Joan's shoes, she decided to be the one to break the bad news.

"Hey, Trisha," Joan said, happy to hear from her new friend. "I was just thinking about calling you. What have you been up to?"

"You know, doing the first lady thing. How's the church?"

"A few of the young people have left."

"Oh, really? Why?"

Joan sighed wearily. "The kids say I play favorites and let some, especially my son, get away with stuff that no one else gets away with. I don't know what they're talking about. I treat them all like they're my children."

The women continued chatting about church matters until Trisha abruptly changed the subject. "Have you heard from the pastor from Florida who visited you in your hotel room?"

"I saw an advertisement that he was preaching at a church in Philly not far from me. I may as well be honest; I probably would've gone if I didn't have a revival at my church that week. My sister, let me tell you," she added firmly, "God *is* good! You hear me?"

Trisha wanted to gently broach the subject of Joan's son with her but decided that a direct approach might be best. "So," she said changing the subject again, "how is Richard doing?"

"He's has some night job somewhere, and he helps me around the church more too. So, I don't complain."

"Joan," Trisha said with heavy sigh, "I don't know how to say this."

"What's wrong, Trisha?"

"My husband and I had a long talk with Nicholas, and he told us that he and Richard were not just using marijuana; they were selling it too."

The phone went silent for five seconds. Then Joan cleared her throat and asked, "How do you know Nicholas is telling the truth?"

"Joan, I know my son, and I know when he's lying. Trust me, he's telling the truth."

"Well," said Joan defensively, "I know my son too, and he ain't no drug pusher! You think just because my husband ain't in the picture that my son's pushing drugs?!"

"Joan, what are you talking about...?!" Trisha was puzzled by Joan's strange accusation.

"Um... Trisha, I have something to do." Joan said dismissively and without saying another word, she ended the call.

CHAPTER FIFTY-FOUR

Arthur woke the next morning with Angela lying next to him, fast asleep and with her arm across his chest. He gazed at her, savoring the moment, being careful not to disturb her. Ten minutes later, Angela stretched, smiled, and whispered, "Good morning."

"Good morning," he said, returning her smile. She gazed into his eyes and in her most sensual tone she asked, "What do you want for breakfast?"

Arthur had not heard that phrase pass from her lips in two years. He was so shocked he was stuck for a response.

"Um..."

"What about pancakes?" she suggested.

"Sure," he said as he grinned.

Angela rose from the bed, washed up, woke Zelda, and went to the kitchen to start breakfast. For the rest of the week, Angela and Arthur slept in the same bed. It appeared their marriage was making a positive course correction until one morning, as they lay in bed, Arthur made an unwelcome suggestion.

"If we're going to have a successful marriage, I read in a book that we have to make sure we don't push each other's buttons."

"Good idea," Angela said. "What is it I say that, as you say, 'pushes your buttons'?"

"I hate it when you call me carnal."

"I *never* said that!"

"Are you serious?!"

"Yes, I am! I never said you were carnal!"

Arthur's brow furrowed, and he sat up in the bed. "You not only called me carnal, but you also said that I have a lust demon!"

Angela pursed her lips into an angry pout, lifted her head, and looked down her nose at her husband. "I've *never* said any of those things to you! But since you want to go there, let's talk about *you*, out there running with that woman!"

"There you go!" he shouted. "Listening to your aunt again!"

Angela's eyes narrowed. She then sucked her teeth and stormed out of the bedroom.

Arthur fell back onto the mattress, his fingertips pressed against his throbbing temples. He knew if she wasn't willing to admit how she'd treated him, she would only repeat it, and he refused to go through that again. He conceded that his marriage to Angela was hopeless. He sprang from the bed and started pacing and mumbling to himself. "I'm tired of praying! I've suffered enough! This marriage hasn't worked for twenty-five years and there is no reason for me to believe it will in the future."

Weary of pacing, he flopped on the side of the bed, rubbing his head with his hands. He knew when it became public that his marriage was ending, people were going to talk. But he'd just have to grin and bear it. Besides, they hadn't walked in his shoes. Tears welled up in his eyes as he thought, "They have no idea what I've endured over the years."

Arthur rose from the bed, showered, dressed, and said good morning to Zelda. He made a phone call, then left for his appointment with the lawyer he's just spoken to.

On his way to the lawyer's office, he called his brother Drew and informed him of the decision he'd made. Drew was pleased and relieved that Arthur finally made a move toward terminating his marriage.

"It's certainly about time, little brother."

"Drew, I was wondering if I could stay with you until I find myself another place."

"Stay as long as you need to Arthur, I have plenty of room."

"Thanks."

"What do you think the church is going to say when they find out that you left your wife?" Drew asked.

"I don't know. What I do know is that I will *not* remain in this hell any longer! Drew, I have something to do. I'll call you when I'm on my way."

"Sounds good."

———

When Arthur returned home, Angela was in the kitchen cooking breakfast. She looked at Arthur with an icy stare.

"You want some of this?" she asked carelessly.

Arthur went straight to his bedroom without bothering to answer or look her way. Twenty minutes later, he exited his room with a suitcase filled with clothes. He went to Zelda's room, knocked on the door.

"Yes?"

"It's Dad, sweetheart."

Arthur explained that he was leaving her mother. To his surprise, she simply said, "I understand, Dad."

"I'll be at Uncle Drew's. If you need me for *anything,* just call."

"You don't have to worry about me, Dad. I'll be okay."

They hugged and Arthur went downstairs with his suitcase. As he opened the front door Angela stood in the kitchen archway, her lips poked out and her hands on her hips.

"So, you're going to leave me for your girlfriend!" she shouted.

Arthur looked at her and in a calm voice said, "If you need me, I'll be—"

"God don't like ugly!" she spat, cutting him off. "You *and* your whore are going straight to *hell!* God sees you, Arthur!" She smirked and added, "And you call yourself a preacher!"

Without responding, he continued to walk out the door. Angela followed him, stood at the door, and shouted, *"Go live with your whore!"* Then she slammed the door behind him.

CHAPTER FIFTY-FIVE

Trisha sat on the sofa, regretting her decision to tell Joan her son was selling pot. Her phone rang. It was Joan.

"Hello, Sister Boston," she said sheepishly.

"How are you, Pastor?" Trisha asked coolly.

"I'm not doing so well."

"Oh?"

"First of all, I want to apologize for the way I acted the other day when you told me that my son was selling pot. I realize now you were just trying to be a friend."

"I understand. I'm close to my son too and—"

"Let me get this out, please." Joan said, interrupting her. She paused for a moment, and Trisha thought she heard sniffling. "I just got back from paying bail to get Richard out of jail. He was trying to sell pot to an undercover cop."

"Oh no. I'm so sorry, Joan," Trisha said earnestly.

"Come to find out, when he said he was working, he was actually pushing pot."

"Did you tell Thomas?"

"Yes."

"What did he say?"

"For the first time since leaving me eight years ago, he apologized to me and Richard." Joan snorted sarcastically. "It took Richard getting arrested for Thomas to recognize that he needs to pay attention to his son." She sighed deeply. "Thomas is going to take Richard to stay with him."

"How do you feel about that?"

"I feel that it's about time. Richard needs his father. I'm going to miss him but I could use a break. I've prayed for years that Thomas would pay more attention to Richard. I didn't expect my prayers to be answered this way, though. Like the Bible says, 'All things work together for the good.'"

————

Lorraine arrived home from the closing and immediately called Mr. Patrick. "Hello, Mrs. Kendal. I'm so glad you called."

"You said that it was urgent."

"Yes, I have something for you that Reverend Kendal left in my hands just in case something happened to him."

Lorraine wondered what it could be.

"It's an insurance policy for you and Lester," Mr. Patrick continued. "For some reason, he thought it would be safer leaving it with me. I tried contacting you when I heard of his death. Believe me, I sent you mail and even tried calling but…"

"It's okay, Mr. Patrick. Thank you for letting me know. When can I come by and pick it up?"

"I'll be here all day tomorrow until four."

"Good. I'll be there before four, and thanks again."

Lorraine called Trisha and told her what the lawyer said. "Trish, I don't know why, but I'm kinda nervous. Would you come with me to the lawyer's tomorrow?"

"That shouldn't be a problem," Trisha assured her friend.

"Thanks, Trisha, for supporting me through all this stuff. I don't know what I'd do without my bestie."

————

The next morning, Lorraine and Trisha drove to the lawyer's office to pick up the policy that Morgan had kept secret from her for fifteen years. When Mr. Patrick informed Lorraine of the amount of the policy, she dropped to her knees in the lawyer's office and sobbed.

CHAPTER FIFTY-SIX

Arthur was at Drew's house, discussing his decision to divorce Angela.

"Drew, I don't know if I should inform the church after I get the divorce or tell them now so they can get used to it."

"Arthur, are you *definitely* going to do it this time?" Drew asked skeptically.

"Yup," he said casually.

"Remember the last time you said you were leaving but changed your mind because you were worried what the members of the church would say, because you've preached against it for years?"

"Yes, I know. But this time it's different."

"How so?"

"I've about had it—"

Drew interrupted him. "You can't '*about* had it.' You have to be certain and persuaded, then willing to suffer the consequences of your decision, whatever those might be."

Arthur's eyes narrowed. "I'm divorcing Angela and *nothing's* gonna make me change my mind!"

"Then I don't see any reason you should put off telling the church."

Arthur leaned back in his chair and gazed into the distance, attempting to anticipate every possible scenario and question that would arise from the congregation, along with his response.

Drew looked at him and asked, "What's wrong, man?"

Arthur slowly turned his face toward Drew and sighed. "I ain't changing my mind," he snapped.

"I didn't say you were. Don't be so defensive."

"I'm not! It's just that this is a serious move. My whole life's about to change. I want to make sure that I anticipate every eventuality..."

"Arthur, it's next to impossible to anticipate everything."

"True." Arthur took a deep breath and frowned. "I'm gonna call a meeting with the church leaders."

Arthur took his phone from his pocket, called his secretary, and instructed her to call the church leaders for an emergency meeting. After he hung up, Drew said, "Don't beat around the bush when you meet with them. Be right up front."

———

The next day, Arthur met with the trustees and auxiliary heads at the church's office. He expressed to them how unhappy he was in his marriage and that he was leaving. After he spoke, the group sat stone-faced and silent.

Mother English, one of the church's most senior members, slowly rose to her feet, wincing and grunting with every movement. "Well," she said, "I've never believed in divorce, but in this case, I have to say, it's about time."

The other church leaders nodded their heads in agreement. "Pastor," she continued, "I've always believed 'til death do you part, and that one should remain with their spouse no matter what, until someone I knew was killed by her abusive husband. Ever since then, I don't judge anyone because I don't know what they're going through."

Arthur, shocked by her response, said, "Mother English, why did you say that it's about time?"

"I think I can speak for most of us when I say that Sister Wright doesn't get along with any of us. If it wasn't for you, we would've left this church long ago."

A collective "that's right" echoed around the room.

Sister Baines, one of the other auxiliary heads, called out, "She even talks about your private life to some of the members, telling them you're too carnal."

After the revelations by the church leaders, Arthur was wounded and felt betrayed by Angela. He had no idea she was backstabbing him and sharing their private life with others in the congregation.

Shame and despair gripped Arthur's heart. While he'd been preaching to the church, they had been thinking of all his family ills. He couldn't face them again, knowing they knew Lord knows what about his private life. With his credibility shot, Arthur knew he would have to resign.

CHAPTER FIFTY-SEVEN

A s Carl sat reading a part of the diary, Bishop Howard breathed a heavy sigh.

"Boy, Morgan was in a conundrum," Bishop said sadly.

"Yes, I'd say so," Carl concurred. "Should I continue?"

Bishop brow furrowed. "You might as well."

Carl continued reading:

> *Another Wednesday night prayer service and the Dark Lady was present, sitting on the first row, legs crossed and her arm on the back of the pew. No matter how hard I tried to concentrate on the lesson I was teaching, it was all for nothing. I finally gave up and said to the congregation, "Church, I'm going to continue this lesson next week." Everyone looked confused. That night, I taught for only ten minutes—typically, I teach for at least a half hour. Although puzzled by my curious behavior, no one questioned if I was sick or if something else was wrong. After I gave the benediction, those gathered, including the Dark Lady, somberly left the sanctuary and departed. When I arrived home, Lorraine looked into my eyes and asked, 'Were there any unwelcome guests in church tonight?' I sucked my teeth, walked out of the*

house, and got back into my car. To my shock, when I entered the car, I realized I was not there alone.

Bishop Howard remained still as Carl read the rest of the diary. When Carl got to the end, Bishop Howard gasped, then shook his head.

"Son, we can't keep this to ourselves. We *must* tell Lorraine."

Carl could neither breathe nor speak as his heart raced.

"Son, let me hold the diary for a few days or so. I want to read it some more."

"Sure, Bishop," Carl said, handing him the diary.

Bishop's cook came into the room and announced that lunch was ready.

"Good," Bishop said. "Let's eat."

As they ate, they spoke briefly about the conference where Bishop Howard would be presenting. Other than that, little was said.

———

Trisha and Carl decided to drive to Virginia for the conference. When they arrived, they met with Bishop Howard and his wife and drove together to the college where the conference would be held. The pastors met in a classroom with stadium seating and capacity for a hundred people. The podium was set in the front of the classroom. There were eighty men present with fifteen women pastors spread about the room. The pastor's wives convened in another classroom.

Those in the room were speaking in soft tones with each other. When Bishop Howard entered, a hush came upon the room. Carl walked in with Bishop Howard and sat in the front row near the podium.

The MC presented Bishop Howard. Bishop Howard greeted everyone then said,

"Everyone hurts!" he declared, his voice echoing throughout the room. "No matter how much you pray and fast, or positively confess the Word, from Genesis to Revelation, something or someone, one time or another, will cause you hurt."

As Bishop Howard spoke, Carl looked around the room, and to his amazement, seated together near the rear of the class were Peter and Arthur. He wondered how they knew about the conference.

Bishop continued. "These distractions come to hinder us from doing the will of God. The enemy knows when to attack and when to stay his hand. Sometimes we slack off in our prayer life. We continue to work for God, but no longer worship the God we work for. Work should never replace worship.

"How many of you have decided or were tempted, after a hurt or disappointment, to dismiss everyone and keep to yourself? The enemy wants to get you alone.

"Pastors, many times we work too hard without a break. You think your members can't live without you?" He snorted sarcastically. "Oh yeah? Die and see what happens.

"There are a few things we should do when we get distracted. First, *refocus*. Remember when God first called you to ministry and His instructions to you. Sometimes we get thrown off track by others' success. God has given you a grace for *your* assignment, not for someone else's assignment.

"Whatever you do, don't believe your press. You're never as good or as bad as people say you are.

"*Repent.* Yes, you heard me—I said repent. Not just for slacking off in our worship, but for not taking care of yourselves, and many times, ignoring your families.

"Then *return* to *your* calling, no matter how far you've drifted."

The distinct sound of light sniffling was heard from some in the audience. Bishop asked the pastors to stand, then turned the service over into the hands of the song leader, who led the audience in the hymn, *Come Thou Fount of Every Blessing*. Everyone joined in, and they came to the verse that says,

"Prone to wander, Lord, I feel it

Prone to leave the God I love.

Here's my heart, Lord,

Take and seal it,

Seal it for thy courts above."

The sound of weeping was heard, competing with the few voices that were still able to sing without tears.

Bishop Howard suddenly chimed in. "Now, before you sing the last verse again, remember if His Spirit does not seal us, none of us will be saved.

"I want the song leader to sing that verse again. Only now, take your time." Bishop Howard gave the signal, and the song leader repeated the last verse but changed the tempo, slowing the pace, and drawing out the words. The cries of the audience were now louder than the singing.

Though it was getting late the pastors continued weeping aloud, some on their knees at their seats. The pastor's wives, who had just walked in from their session, started weeping and joined their husbands in prayer. Many apologized to their wives for the insensitivity to their needs they'd shown by putting ministry above their families.

With tears gushing, Arthur promised God he would continue as pastor and get help for his porn addiction.

CHAPTER FIFTY-EIGHT

As the audience disbursed, Carl rushed to his car to avoid confronting Arthur and Peter. After Bishop Howard, his wife, and Trisha joined him in the car, they drove to the hotel. On the way, they complimented Bishop Howard on his timely message and how great the service was.

When they arrived at the hotel, Bishop said, "Why don't you all come up to my suite in about an hour and have lunch with me and the wife?"

"Thank you, Bishop, we'd love to," Carl said.

———

An hour later, Carl and Trisha went to Bishop Howard's suite. There, sitting in the living room along with Bishop Howard, were Peter, Arthur, and Lorraine. Carl gasped as he walked into the room.

"Have a seat, Carl," Bishop Howard said.

Carl looked sheepishly at Arthur and Peter. "Hello, Reverends."

"How have you been, Doc?" Peter asked cordially. "We were beginning to think that you were avoiding us."

"No, brothers. I was just busy. You know how it is sometimes."

"Yeah, we know," Peter said with an amused smirk.

Carl turned his attention to Lorraine. "Fancy meeting you here, Lorraine."

"Yeah, I needed to get out of town for a few days."

Bishop Howard chimed in. "I invited Lorraine to come down and keep Sister Howard company while I'm in my sessions. I invited Reverend Austin and Reverend Wright too. Reverend Wright don't mind me telling it. He's going through a divorce, plus there is another issue he's dealing with. I'll let him tell you. I asked Reverend Riley to come too. By the way, why isn't he here?"

"Um… Bishop, he was asked to perform Clyde Jones's wedding," Peter said.

There was a collective gulp as they glanced at each other.

"Oh my," Bishop Howard said. "The ink ain't dry on his divorce papers yet, and he done found another mate."

"Well, actually… he's getting reacquainted and remarried."

"You mean to tell me he and Mae are getting back together?"

"That's what Riley told me," Peter said with a broad smile.

Everyone clapped and declared, "Glad to hear it!"

"What changed their minds?" Carl asked.

"Mae had a long talk with Debbie Porter. I'm not sure what she said, but they are getting married this Saturday."

"He preached for me this past Sunday, and when I spoke with him, he didn't say a word about getting remarried," Carl said

Bishop Howard smiled. "Let's get to why I invited you all down here. I have a passion for you brothers. Especially since my son in the gospel, The Reverend Doctor Morgan Kendall, took his life. I can't bring him back, but I can help you all not to make the same mistakes I've made as a novice pastor.

"I invited Lorraine because she has insight into Morgan's life that I believe will be of help."

Bishop Howard opened the drawer of the end table next to where he sat and removed Morgan's diary. He turned his attention to Carl. "Son, I want you to show Lorraine where you left off reading with Reverends Austin and Wright. Then she'll take it from there."

Carl obediently turned to the page where he had left off, and handed the diary to Lorraine. Lorraine took a deep breath and began to read.

> *When I arrived home, Lorraine looked into my eyes and asked. "Were there any unwelcome guests in church tonight?" I sucked my teeth, walked out of the house, and got back into my car. To my shock, when I entered the car, I realized that I was not there alone. There, sitting in the front passenger seat, was the Dark Lady. She had been following me all week. When I went to the store, she was there. When at a restaurant, she was there. Even at church, she sat on the front pew, gawking. Now here she was again. She wanted to finally*

consummate our 'relationship'. I didn't have to hear her say it. I felt it. I'd rather die than succumb to her. Before I gave her the satisfaction of conquering me, I'd choose to never see the sunrise again.

"I looked into my glove compartment and there lay my revolver, loaded and ready to be fired.

"Lorraine, sweetheart, it's impossible for me to express why, but I can no longer trust myself not to harm you and Lester... I must leave here tonight! You will never hear or see me again. Try and understand and please forgive me. I love you. Goodbye."

Lorraine wiped away the tears that were streaming down her face. "That's it," she said, her voice soft and raspy.

Everyone in the room stared at Lorraine and was at a loss for words. Lorraine turned to Bishop Howard. "Thank you, Bishop, for inviting me here to say what Morgan would've wanted me to say." She then turned to the other men present in the room, friends and colleagues of her dearly departed husband.

"Pastors," she said softly, "there's a serious issue in the church that's kept hidden. If the church doesn't begin to address it, there are going to be more incidences of suicide among pastors. How can I put it?" She stopped and took a deep breathe. "There is a mental illness crisis among the clergy. Morgan was diagnosed as being bipolar years ago."

"Why didn't he get treatment?" a stunned Peter asked.

"He didn't go back to the doctor because he said that he was believing God for his healing. I believe he didn't go because of the stigma that is attached to mental illnesses. He tried dealing with it by himself. That's how he ended up addicted to drugs."

Lorraine turned to Carl. "Carl, I planted the diary among the books I gave you, hoping you'd find it. Morgan loved you like a brother. He told me that if anything were to happen to him, I should give the diary to you."

Carl was now fighting back his own tears. "Why? Why me?"

"Morgan knew you'd read it and warn others about this crisis."

"And what if I hadn't looked through the boxes and saw the diary?"

"Then Trisha would've led you to it."

Carl turned to Trisha. "You knew about the diary and didn't tell me?"

"Yes, I knew about it." Trisha said sheepishly. "Actually, one time you caught me with the diary."

"When?"

"Do you remember coming into your office, and I had the diary in my hand but pretended to be looking for a receipt on your desk?"

"What about the part in the diary that mentioned Morgan being sued, and the assistant pastor leaving with the members?" Peter asked.

"The choir director yelled at one of the members in the choir," Lorraine responded. "The mother of the choir member complained to Morgan, but there was no lawsuit."

"Morgan also suffered from paranoia," she added. "The assistant pastor's job moved to South Carolina, so he moved with his job. And as far as him taking members with him, nobody moved to South Carolina with the assistant pastor. Those that left, left because Morgan accused them of betrayal. Oh, and by the way, he said in the diary that Lester and I hardly came to church. We were out *one* Sunday because I had to go out of town for a family funeral."

Arthur took a deep breath and spoke in a measured tone, "Please... tell us who the Dark Lady is."

"Morgan personified his depression, calling it 'The Dark Lady'. When he became depressed, his eyes would become glossy, accompanied with a far-away stare. I'd ask him if there were any unwelcome visitors in church. If he felt her 'presence', he'd get angry."

"If you knew that, why would you ask him that?" Arthur said.

"I wanted to know for sure what I would be in for that night. If he responded with a smile, I knew things would be peaceful. But if he got angry, I knew I had to be on my guard. Morgan fought hard not to—what he called—'consummate their relationship.'"

"What did he mean by that?" Peter asked.

"Morgan told me that sometimes a strong urge came upon him to inflict pain upon perfect strangers. Yielding to those urges amounted to consummating the relationship."

Bishop Howard chimed in, "See what I mean, brothers? We as men of God need each other and must not be so quick to judge each other so harshly without knowing the facts. Stand by your brother."

"Lorraine," Peter said, "have you considered making the diary public?"

"No, I haven't thought about it."

"I mean turning it into a book."

"I don't know..."

"You can title it, 'The Preacher and the Dark Lady,'" Carl said.

"What about, 'The Chronicles of a 21st Century Pastor?'" Arthur suggested.

In a commanding voice, Bishop Howard said, "Hold on, y'all, I got it. The book should be titled *Diary of a Burned-Out Pastor.*"

About the Author

J ames Blocker is founder and pastor of the Maranatha Tabernacle in Queens, New York. As an itinerate evangelist he has traveled extensively across the United States and overseas. He is also founder and president of the *Jesus Loves Jamaica Crusades* in Jamaica N.Y. He did his undergraduate studies at the College of New Rochelle in NY, where he received his BA degree.

He has taught in Bible institutes and is the president of Clergy United for Community Empowerment, an ecumenical organization that provides housing for those living with AIDS, along with other services, in the Queens community and surrounding areas.

Pastor Blocker is the husband of Wandra. They have three children and three grandchildren, all of whom work in the ministry.

This is his fourth book. His first book, *The War Against the Church,* is about how the church can contend with the forces of evil. His second book, *Yours Because of Calvary: The Life and Times of Apostle Arturo Skinner,* is about the life and ministry of the inimitable Arturo Skinner. And his fourth book, *Space Brothers,* is a Christian sci-fi novel that exposes occultic practices within the Christian church.